GETTING IT
RIGHT

GETTING IT RIGHT

A NOVEL

KAREN E. OSBORNE

OPEN
LENS

Published by Akashic Books
©2017 Karen Osborne

ISBN: 978-1-61775-538-5
Library of Congress Control Number: 2016915367

First printing

Open Lens
c/o Akashic Books
Brooklyn, New York
Twitter: @AkashicBooks
Facebook: AkashicBooks
E-mail: info@akashicbooks.com
Website: www.akashicbooks.com

To Bob, my friend, partner, and love of my life

And to Marci Korwin for helping me save my life

CHAPTER ONE

Jim Smyth died young but not soon enough.

The coffin hovered over the grave. In front, a protective canopy snapped in the wind, which smelled like newly turned earth and fading roses. Short rows of collapsible chairs held fifteen mourners underneath the covering and a few others clustered around the edges. From her vantage point on a hill several yards away, Kara watched the hat- and scarf-covered heads and tried to imagine who they might be. Why would anyone mourn Big Jim?

Flyer wrapped his right arm around her. Slushy rain hit their shared umbrella, making a soothing white noise. She leaned in and rested her head on his shoulder.

"I wish they'd hurry and cover him up," Flyer said.

Tuesday stood a few steps away, her thin arms hugging her body. "They'll wait till everyone is gone." The rain made her face glisten.

Flyer dug his left hand into his pocket. "Let's scare 'em off." He gestured with his chin toward the gravesite. "Run down there, yell and holler."

"We should go." Tuesday stepped half under the umbrella, some almost-snow slipping down the side of her jacket. "It's over."

Kara agreed it was time to go. She prayed Tuesday was right about it being over. The three of them were huddled under a leafless sugar maple in Woodlawn, the Bronx's largest cemetery. March had barreled in announcing the death of their childhood torturer, and they couldn't stay away. Kara had thought if she saw Big Jim Smyth in a deep, dank, and lonely hole, it would bring her peace, and she could move on. They all could.

To the south, the 4 train rattled by; the threesome headed in its direction. Discrete signs along pathways named to hide their true destination marked the way: *Alpine Lane, Laurel Road*. Bare trees cast stark, shifting shadows. Woodlawn Cemetery stood as an unlikely oasis in the urban borough. Multifamily brick houses edged the northern border; to the west, cars droned along the congested Major Deegan; to the east, the Bronx River Parkway curved around the four hundred acres of the cemetery. Whenever a train banged its way uptown or down, the mourners received a jolt of life.

Kara slowed. The feeling was back—someone or something was watching her. She looked around and saw only rows of headstones jutting up behind the stand of evergreens, icy bits of frozen rain coating the grass.

Tuesday said, "Can you believe it? He's really dead."

"Well, I'm not buying it." Flyer tilted the umbrella toward Kara.

Tuesday rocked from side to side. "When I heard he was sick, I began to hope."

"We should have gone to the wake," Flyer nodded his head vigorously, "walked right up to the coffin, and pulled out a mirror—checking for breath like they do in old-time mobster movies."

"After praying for it night after night . . ." Tuesday trailed off.

The hairs on the nape of Kara's neck rose. She twisted around quickly and Flyer stumbled. "Sorry." Twigs cracked under the feet of scrambling squirrels. The heavier sound, more deliberate, had disappeared. Was she imagining things?

"Is something going on with you?" Tuesday asked Kara in the same angry tone she always used, no matter the subject. "You've been jumpy all day."

"We're all wrecked," Flyer said. "This has been a hell of a day."

But that wasn't all of it for Kara. How could she explain what had no substance? "Just the jitters." That barely covered it. She felt stalked.

"I keep expecting him to leap up and say he was only kidding," Flyer said.

"Come on, you two." Kara slipped her right arm through Flyer's left and her left arm through Tuesday's right. "He's dead," she said, as much for her own benefit as for theirs. "He can't terrorize us anymore."

Besides, there were other things to worry about now. She glanced sideways as they walked; Flyer looked even worse than the last time they had been together. Always thin, now his brown skin was sallow, and it hung from his prominent cheekbones as if he had contracted some killer disease. *Could he have . . .* She stopped the thought in its tracks. Worrying was a time-waster. Zach always admonished her for seeing trouble when there was none.

"Why the grin?" Tuesday sounded accusatory.

"Am I grinning?"

"Yeah." Even her affirmatives sounded like challenges.

"The guy I'm dating just popped into my mind." Kara's smile reappeared; she couldn't help it. "Did I tell you about him?"

"No."

Flyer asked, "Serious?"

"Pretty much." Better leave it at that. Tuesday was sure to say something scornful.

Several people approached from the opposite direction. A sobbing woman dressed in sneakers, a black skirt, and rain jacket. Close behind two men followed, their collars up, heads ducked down. A child ran to keep up, her hood flopping around on her back. As the three friends stepped aside to let the strangers pass, one of the men stared at them—not just a quick glance, a full once-over.

This happened often enough. They had been together since Kara was six, Tuesday five, and Flyer four; first in the Smyths' home in foster care, and then in a group home until Kara aged out at eighteen. They probably wouldn't be friends if they met each other today. Twenty-eight-year-old Flyer played drums in various bands in obscure clubs. Music plus odd jobs paid the rent for his shared apartment in a dodgy neighborhood. He was dressed in baggy cargo pants, his oversized jacket dwarfed his frame, and dark smudges lined his eyes. Up close, his spiked dreads smelled unwashed. Drumsticks lodged in his back pocket tented his jacket. Tuesday, on the other hand, seemed as healthy as ever. Her dyed-blond Afro, buzzed close, gleamed with pomade. She barely came to Flyer's chest but sported an ever-present scowl that kept most people at bay.

In many ways, Kara was the oddest one. She was thirty, with honey-beige skin so fair that when people asked where she was from and she told them the Bronx, they acted disappointed, as if she should be from somewhere exotic. Almond-shaped, amber eyes and long legs often brought unwanted comments. In fact, her looks brought her more pain than happiness, and had often been the reason for Big Jim's violence.

"Don't go silent on me, Kara," Tuesday said. "Who is this guy you're dating?"

Flyer pulled out his drumsticks, waved them both in the air like the double-fisted conductor of a grand overture, and pronounced in his rapper voice, "What difference does it make? She's happy. We should all be happy."

"Humph." Tuesday kept eyeing Kara.

"Shit, this is a day of celebration! He's dead and we're free. We'll mark this one as a high holiday."

"Don't be an ass," Tuesday said. "The Lord won't like you talking like that." She caught Kara's eye. "And I hope you're not being one either. Is this one single?"

Kara flushed. Tuesday rolled her eyes. She wasn't wrong. But this time things were different: Zach's wife had cheated on him and broken his heart, but with young children to consider, it was going to take some time to work things out.

"Let's hurry, I'm freezing my buns off here," Flyer said.

The three began a slow jog, holding and bumping into each other under the oversized umbrella. Kara tried to assess her feelings: an evil chapter of her life had closed. She had a great teaching job, she was in love with a good person this time—a catch, as her landlady Mrs. E. would say. Although she still worried about Flyer and Tuesday, they were doing okay. Best of all, Jim Smyth was dead. So why the constant dread?

They reached the gated exit of the cemetery. Goose bumps dotted Kara's flesh. Dare she spin around?

"You're twitching again," Tuesday said.

"I'm fine." But she wasn't. Who was out there?

CHAPTER TWO

Alex Lawrence couldn't get a word in edgewise. Still wet from the shower, her strawberry-blond curls dripping, a towel wrapped around her, and her cell phone mashed against her right ear, she tried to understand her mother's shouts.

"Mom, where are you? What's wrong?"

"I'm on my way to the hospital. Get yourself over there."

"What's going on?"

"Your father is dying."

"Dying?"

"You heard me."

"Was he in an accident? What?"

Alex could picture her mother's face, eyebrows drawn on carefully in spite of having rushed out of the house, droplets of spittle at the corners of her mouth.

"Call your sisters."

"I need details." Years of practice had taught Alex to question everything her mother said. *Dying* could mean anything, from, *He didn't come home last night so he must be dead*, to, *He's gone in for a checkup so he must have Ebola*. "Tell me what happened."

"I did."

"Mom—"

"He had a heart attack."

That couldn't be true. Her father was as healthy as their horses, galloping at full tilt. "When?"

"How fast can you get to Northern Westchester?"

Before Alex could respond, her mother yelled, "Oh no you don't! Idiots. Who gives these people licenses? They probably don't even speak English."

Alex suppressed a scream. Her mother constantly uttered disparaging remarks about almost every ethnic group, and nothing Alex did or said seemed to quell it.

"I heard that."

It was eerie how intuitive her mother was about some things, and how dense she was about others. Still naked, Alex pushed *Speaker* on her phone and put it on her nightstand so she could towel dry. "How bad is it?"

"How would I know? That Ms. Don't-Tell-the-Wife-Anything assistant of his called. What are you doing? You sound like you're in a tunnel."

"Did you contact the hospital?" Alex took the phone off speaker, pressed it to her left ear, and used her right hand to rip through her closet in search of a clean pair of jeans. "What did they say?"

"Find your sisters."

"Mom, what did they tell you?"

"I'm here. Hurry." She clicked off.

Oh dear God. Poor Daddy. The muscle under Alex's left eye pulsed. She massaged her temples and tried to think. Water seeped from her scalp. She plugged in the blow-dryer and waved it around her head.

It would take her at least thirty minutes to get to the hospital in Mount Kisco. Did her mother remember to bring their insurance information and her father's toiletries? Better swing by the house just in case. What else would he need?

A futile search for clothes left Alex with yesterday's jeans and a wrinkled cobalt T-shirt pulled from the hamper. She sniffed the armpits and tugged it on. In spite of her mother's hysterics, this sounded like the real thing. The eye muscle jumped again.

Alex stepped into her cowboy boots. The toes were scraped raw and the heels worn to crooked angles so they felt as good as a pair of slippers, a level of comfort the day might require. Inside her front pocket, she discovered a frayed cigarette. With care, she rolled it between her thumb and forefinger. *He couldn't be dying.*

Full grocery bags from last night's 7-Eleven run made navigating the short distance between her bedroom and kitchenette tricky. *Where was he when it happened? Not at home . . . again.* The assistant who called Alex's mother was a woman in her late sixties and probably not his evening companion.

Alex snatched up her jacket and backpack from the chair where she'd dumped them, stuffed her still-damp curls under a Mets baseball cap, grabbed her keys, and left the apartment. The elevator creaked to the lobby. Alex strode quickly past the red and blue upholstered chairs and fake potted plants speckled with dust as she glanced at her watch. If she stopped in Bedford before going to the hospital the detour would only add an extra ten minutes. She could be with him in forty-five minutes at the most. She picked up the pace.

It was silent except for the crunch of her boots on the tar-and-gravel pavement and the rhythm of the icy March drizzle. The sky was dawn-dark as the moon held on. Streaks of gray barely colored the horizon, and the air smelled like impending snow. She clambered into her Jeep Cherokee.

Light traffic allowed Alex to drive faster than the forty-five-mile-per-hour speed limit on Route 133 East. The thought of her all-powerful father lying vulnerable in a hospital was hard to accept. She decided to wait to call her sisters until she knew more—no sense alarming them without all the facts. Vanessa would be okay, but Pigeon was twenty-five going on thirteen. Sean—she needed to call him too. She'd promised her business partner she'd finish an overdue project today, no matter what. Well, that wasn't going to happen.

Alex reached Bedford in record time. It was 7:25 a.m. The pale sun edged over the horizon. She drummed her fingers on the steering wheel waiting for a light to turn green. To calm herself, she placed two fingers against her lips, closed her eyes, and inhaled. She could almost smell and feel the phantom smoke going deep into her lungs. A horn honked behind her.

"Asshole."

She accelerated, made a right onto Green Lane, and then followed the twisting, narrow Bedford roads to the Lawrence's driveway. Alex took another drag on her imaginary cigarette. She'd thought about e-cigarettes but no, she had quit. Done. She gripped the steering wheel with both hands.

The house, with its wraparound veranda, emerged on the crest of the hill. Memories zipped through her mind: her dad giving her a thumbs-up at her high school debut as Annie Oakley; horseback riding on the purposely unpaved Guard Hill Road; her parents yelling at each other in the kitchen while Pigeon and Vanessa hid in Alex's bed.

She climbed the stairs to the veranda. Her key turned easily in the lock. She stepped into the entranceway, took the stairs two at a time, and hurried down the hallway to her father's home office. Bookshelves lined the walls. His executive chair stood in a lonely vigil in front of the oak desk, one of the few pieces of furniture he'd chosen himself. She took a moment to enjoy the view from the picture window. Fog hugged the rolling hills like fallen clouds, and the barely-there sun backlit the scene. He'd be at his desk again soon.

Feeling like a little girl doing something wrong, Alex opened the top desk drawer in search of insurance cards. It was a jumble of papers, pens, a stapler, different types of eye-glass covers. She sifted through the debris until she found them in an envelope marked *Healthcare*—two insurance cards and copies of his Social Security card and passport. After extracting the insurance information, she shoved the envelope back in its spot. She was about to close the drawer when a picture she'd disturbed caught her attention, and she picked it up.

Her father was young, his curls cut short. Sun freckles dotted his arms, and a stripe of sunburned skin crossed the bridge of his nose. Next to him was a petite black woman, as small as Alex's mother, her caramel skin glowing. Her dad held a young Alex in one arm, but in the other was an unfamiliar child with amber eyes, suntanned skin, and three braids tied with ribbons—one in the front and two in the back. *Who are these people? Why don't I remember this?* She flipped the photo over but there was no date or notation. For several seconds she pondered the picture. A glance at her watch, however, told her she needed to hurry, so she slid the photograph back into its spot and went in search of toiletries.

Parking at the hospital was as easy as following the signs to the receptionist, who directed Alex to her father's floor. When she reached the critical care unit, she found her mother sobbing on Aunt Peggy's well-padded shoulder.

Peggy waved her over. "He's asking for you."

Alex leaned in and kissed Peggy's forehead.

"Go on in, honey." She waved a plump hand toward

Worth Lawrence's room. Her two-carat diamond ring flashed in the fluorescent light. "I'll take care of your mom."

Her father was propped up by the slant of the bed, plastic tubing through his nostrils. He looked old, his complexion mottled and pale, his violet eyes cloudy. For the first time Alex noticed how thin his blond hair had become, its characteristic curls lying flat against his scalp. Although only fifty-eight, he suddenly seemed mortal. An IV drip snaked out of a bag filled with a clear liquid and hung from a stand down to his taped wrist. Monitors hummed.

Alex cleared her throat.

"Hey, kitten." His voice croaked. "Seems your old man did himself in this time." He shifted in his bed, trying to get comfortable. "Warning sign to Dorian Gray." He touched his cracked lips. "Maybe more than a warning."

She didn't know what to say. Tears crept into the corners of her eyes.

A dry cough jerked his chest. Alex winced and waited, her left eye muscle throbbing.

"I guess I'd better pay attention."

She reached for his hand and tried for a teasing tone: "Mom had you dead and buried, but you seem great to me."

"Wishful thinking on both your parts."

"Daddy, you know she loves you." It came out more forcefully than she had intended. "She's Auntie Mame with a sharper edge is all." Alex pulled off her baseball cap and tugged her fingers through the still-damp curls. "How *do* you feel?"

"Tired." Another raspy cough. "This time, she had a right to be upset. It scared the shit out of me. I was visiting a . . ." He paused, a slight flush coming to his stubble-covered cheeks. "I was visiting a friend when it happened." His face scrunched.

"*Wham*, a wrenching pain. My left arm went numb and my chest tightened."

Alex covered her mouth.

"I couldn't catch my breath. We . . . I was able to get my service to send a car around in just a few minutes."

Ignoring the *we*, Alex asked, "What did the doctor say?"

"That I'm lucky to be alive." His laugh sounded strained. "I've always been lucky. But this time, if I make it, I'd better make some changes."

"I've heard this before."

"No, I gotta quit smoking like you did—slow down, simplify." He licked his lips. "Make my peace with God."

A chain-smoker since he was a teenager, her father worked seventy- to eighty-hour weeks—or at least he was gone that long. Often, after a dinner meeting, he stayed overnight in her parents' New York City apartment, unable to make it back to Bedford, an hour away by train. His law practice, focused on hedge fund managers, took him to Europe and Asia several times a year. Even when the economy struggled, his firm and confidence seemed untouchable.

"We'll all help you." Alex smoothed his sheet. "Don't worry, Daddy. Besides, it would be good if you spent more time at home."

He gave a sardonic snort.

"You always wanted to take up cooking as a hobby, now's your chance—low-fat gourmet."

His chuckle turned into a body-wracking cough. Alex waited, more afraid than she could ever remember. She handed him a tissue.

"Kitten, I need you to do me an important favor." His tone had become parental. In fact, she knew the words that would follow: *I know I can count on you.* How she dreaded that phrase. *I'm counting on you to take care of Pigeon and Vanessa until Aunt Peggy can get here, until I can work things out.*

It wasn't just her father—her mother used those words with equal weight and frequency: *I'm counting on you Alexandra. Lord knows, I can't count on your worthless father. Worthless Worth, that's what my mother called him. She warned me, but did I listen? No, I was too headstrong back then. At least I know I can depend on you.*

Alex felt ten again.

"I don't know if I'm going to recover from this," her father said.

"You will, don't say that."

"They're worried about the extent of the damage."

"Is it reversible?"

He shrugged. "I know I haven't been the best dad to you girls."

Alex made sounds of protest.

"You're kind to your old man. We both know I've let my girls down, your mother included." He glanced away. "That's why I need this favor before it's too late. I need you to find someone."

"Find?"

"I have to make things right." He refocused on her. "People make mistakes." His voice dropped down to almost a whisper. "I've made more than my share." As if bewildered by this state of affairs, his mouth pulled itself down and his brow furrowed.

Alex felt a powerful need to ease his pain.

CHAPTER THREE

Eight p.m.—Zach was late. Kara tried to appear at ease in the crowded Midtown bar. In spite of being jammed between an electronics store and a rundown café, Joey's still managed to look upscale. It was decorated in a retro-eighties style: cloth-covered love seats, faux Tiffany lamps, and a bookcase with battered paperbacks made a nook in one corner; toward the middle of the room, small tables lit by votive candles lined the edge of the dance floor where a vintage jukebox supplied the music.

At one end of the bar, Kara sipped a glass of the house Merlot, her unopened paperback, purchased from a street vendor, on the counter beside her. For the umpteenth time, she glanced at her cell. No text or missed call from Zach.

"This seat taken?" A short, bald man with nicotine-stained teeth grinned at her.

"I'm waiting for someone." She turned her back, making her bushy curls swing, and the man sidled a few barstools away.

This was why she didn't go to places like Joey's alone— Zach needed to show up, *now*. The music from the jukebox drifted into her consciousness, a ballad she recognized but couldn't name. Had something happened to Zach, an accident, trouble at the office, his children, his wife? She tried to push thoughts of his family away.

Somebody laughed just to Kara's left; she shifted her gaze toward the sound. A tall woman with strawberry-blond curls stepped up to the bar. Kara willed the woman to turn toward her, and she must have felt Kara's psychic pull because their eyes met; Kara lowered hers. She always expected every head of red-gold curls to be Alex. It never was.

Kara dug into her Macy's-on-sale tote, her back to the crowd, and pulled out the picture of her missing family. In a once-a-day ritual, she examined the slightly faded photograph, safely encased in its plastic sheath.

First, she smiled back at her mom. Full, glossy lips, hazel eyes, just as Kara remembered her. Then she reread the words on the back: *Rock Creek Park, Kara, Alex, Worth, and me.* Kara turned the photo over again, examining the slim white man with violet eyes and bow-shaped lips. He towered over her mother, holding a little girl in each sun-freckled arm. At three years old, Kara had already been tall for her age. Kara studied her creamy beige skin, her amber eyes flecked with gold, her thick lashes. Three fat braids bound by green ribbons hung to her shoulders. Alex was just as tall and about the same age. Her legs dangled along Worth's right one. Blond tangles streaked with red hung down her back and framed her heart-shaped face. A crusty bruise on her right knee looked fresh.

What were they doing that day, and why were they all together? Who took the picture? Did her dad and Alex ever wonder about her?

"You doing okay, honey?" The bartender, her muscled arms decorated with several heart tattoos, lifted Kara's empty wineglass. "Can I get you anything else?" She wiped the bar down in front of Kara.

"Sure." Kara eased the photo back into her bag. "I'm waiting for someone."

"Uh-huh." The woman produced a bowl of popcorn from under the counter and placed it in front of Kara. "Merlot, right?"

Kara nodded. Zach had said he'd be there no later than seven thirty, and a check of her watch confirmed he was now forty-five minutes late. She swiveled in her chair and surveyed the bar again.

The bartender shouted to another customer, "Be right with you, handsome." She poured wine into a clean glass, slapped a cocktail napkin down, and placed the glass on top. Purple splashes stained the paper.

"Thanks." Kara stretched her neck to see the entrance. Instead of Zach, her eyes met the hard stare of a man standing just to the left of the door. She caught her breath; dark hair, average height.

"I'm so sorry I'm late."

Kara jumped.

"It's just me, sweetheart." Zach shrugged out of his London Fog, swung his overflowing Tumi briefcase up onto the bar, leaned forward, and kissed her neck. His hands traced her cheek and chin. "Were you expecting someone else? Should I be worried?" His laugh was a deep rumble.

She glanced back at the entranceway, but no one was there. Kara slipped off her eyeglasses. "I was getting worried."

He took her hands and pressed them against his cheeks. "You are beautiful." He sniffed her hair, nipped her ear, and nuzzled her neck. "You smell and taste luscious."

Kara couldn't help but grin. "Well thank you, kind sir. You're looking rather handsome yourself."

At forty, Zach's creases around his mouth made his face interesting; his clear blue eyes reflected his intelligence. He was wearing the maroon tie she had given him for his birthday, and her favorite Armani suit, tailored to accent his broad shoulders.

They'd met at the gym. She was the guest of a friend who

had a nodding acquaintance with Zach. Well, Paul was sort of a friend—he taught music at the Jesuit day school at which Kara taught fourth and fifth grade reading. Ignoring Paul, Zach had helped Kara use the Universal and balance on the Bosu ball as they discussed cardio exercises and strength training. She was intrigued. He seemed interested in her answers to his questions, laughed easily. She'd checked for a wedding ring or tan line where one might have been. To her delight, they both loved old movies, especially Hitchcock, devoured mystery novels, and preferred jazz to most other music.

Later, after Paul had left, Zach asked her out for coffee and she'd said yes without thinking or asking questions about his life. Not that she had regrets. Well, maybe a few. Besides being the most successful and handsome man Kara had ever dated, he was also the oldest. Unfortunately, he was not her first married man, as Tuesday had been quick to remind her.

Zach ordered a Stella Artois, grabbed a handful of popcorn, and shoveled it in his mouth, bits falling onto the bar and his lap. He brushed them aside as he chewed.

"You could have texted me and let me know you were running late." Kara tried not to sound as upset as she felt.

His beer arrived. "Don't be mad." He gulped, wiped his mouth with the cocktail napkin, and took Kara's arm. "Come dance with me." They weaved between the tables onto the miniature dance floor.

It was a love song. He held her at the small of her back with his left arm, her right hand in his, pressed against his heart. As they swayed to the music, she could feel him getting hard against her groin. One song ended and another began. Little tugs pulsed deep inside of her. His thighs trembled.

"I do miss you, sweetheart." He breathed into her hair, his

voice heavy, his breath hot against her scalp and face. "You're the best thing that ever happened to me—do you know how much I love you?"

Although he said it often, Kara didn't really *know*.

He pulled back. "You do know I love you?"

Kara burrowed her face into his shoulder.

The song wasn't finished but Zach stopped dancing. "That's why it kills me that I have to leave in a few minutes."

Kara stared at him; her face stiffened into her fake *I'm fine* expression.

"Don't look at me like that."

Although they had been dating for less than five months, he'd already figured out a lot about her.

"You know I wouldn't do this unless I absolutely had to—it's a work thing."

"But it's almost eight thirty."

He guided her back to their spot at the bar. "Remember the favor you did for me last month? This deal is even bigger." He stroked her cheek with the back of his hand. "I can't go into the details here, but I'll explain everything in a few days."

"We planned this; it's been over a week since we've been together."

"I know, baby. I'll make it up to you." He tapped her chin. "Please don't be sad."

"I'm disappointed, that's all." The lie slid off her tongue. "Of course I understand."

Zach reached into his briefcase and brought out a large manila envelope, holding it low. "Put this in your bag. I need you to drop it off at the same address as last time—Sam Westin's office. You remember, right?"

She slid it deep into her bag. The last time had made her feel uneasy, as if she were doing something wrong.

"I wouldn't ask you, baby, but there's drama at the office—backstabbing stuff."

"Isn't there someone on your staff who could do this confidentially?"

"You're the only person I trust." He slid both hands along her thighs. "We'll celebrate when it comes through—maybe go away for a weekend, just you and me."

They'd never had a whole weekend together. What a magnificent thought: waking up next to Zach, smelling his sleep scent, having a leisurely breakfast, spending a whole day as a couple.

"Where would you like to go? We'll find a bed-and-breakfast somewhere upstate, or maybe go south, catch some sun."

"Sun sounds good."

"So you'll do this for me? I wouldn't ask if it wasn't crucial."

"Okay. And you'll explain everything soon?"

"Excellent."

"Can you give me a hint?"

Zach leaned in. "You have to keep this between us." He scanned the crowd. "Sam and I are going to be ahead of the curve *again*. This could be a homerun for me, baby." He cupped her face in his hands, brushed her lips with his, and kissed the tip of her nose.

It felt so good being with him—warm and safe, but exciting at the same time. She closed her eyes and kissed him, her tongue circling his lips and then slipping into his mouth. He kissed her back.

Eventually they broke their embrace. Zach grabbed his beer and finished it in a quick pull. He swept up his raincoat. "You make it mighty hard to leave you, but I gotta go."

"Don't worry about it," she said, this time meaning it. "I'll stay and finish my wine." She patted her tote. "I'll deliver this first thing in the morning."

Zach dragged on his coat, pulled her close, and kissed her again. "You're so beautiful. I'd better stop or I'll never get out of here." He picked up his briefcase and placed a handful of bills from his wallet on the bar. Then he offered her a twenty. "Take a cab home."

"No thank you, I'm fine."

"Okay, my stubborn princess. But promise me you'll take a taxi."

She didn't.

CHAPTER FOUR

Alex was trying to understand. A love child, like in some sleazy romance novel? "Tell me."

Her father shifted, the bedsheets caught between his legs. "It was years ago. Your mother didn't like to travel and traveling was all I did. I mean, there were no kids, she wasn't working."

He sounded accusatory, the way he often did when he spoke about her mother.

"Anyway, in those days DC was one of my regular stops."

His cough came back full force. Alex searched for something to help him, locating a cup of water with a straw and placing the tip against his lower lip. Several sips later, the coughing subsided, but a sour smell took its place.

He mopped his eyes. "The long and short of it is, I met someone and we fell in love."

With his peripheral vision, he peered at Alex, who was trying hard to keep her expression neutral. This was not the sort of thing a child, even a grown one, should hear.

"I didn't go looking, kitten. It just kinda happened."

She gave him an understanding smile—it was fake, but it did the job.

"She was young and not sophisticated, not well-traveled, I guess I mean. But she was also smart, funny, the kind of pretty that grew on you. We laughed all the time . . ." He trailed off. "Not that I didn't love your mother. I did. I do."

Alex squirmed and plucked the corners of the sheet.

"She got pregnant, and she wouldn't have an abortion."

Again, he peered at Alex out of the corner of his eye, but she lowered hers.

"I begged her, but she was adamant—a church-going woman." A mini shrug. "Adoption seemed like the next best choice."

The silence felt awkward.

"Find her for me, Alex."

She finally looked up. "Who, exactly?" The woman? Both of them?

"The girl." His voice dropped an octave. "My other daughter."

An unintended groan escaped.

"I know this is a lot to ask." He made it sound as if it weren't, as if he were waiting for her to deny the craziness of the request. "The last address I have is her grandmother's in the Bronx."

Find some kid he conceived while cheating on her mother? A childhood rage welled up. What she couldn't understand then, and still couldn't, was *why* her parents did this to her. What about *her* needs? What about Vanessa and Pigeon? How was he going to make it right for them? She pushed these thoughts down, swallowing an all-too-familiar bitter brew. New thought: her mother would go apeshit if she knew. If Alex helped him, she would have to keep it under her mother's exceptional radar.

Her father sank back and closed his eyes. Alex contemplated what she'd just heard. Her mother had accused him of cheating with the regularity of the seasons, and apparently she was right.

* * *

Alex vividly remembered the first time her mother had threatened to kill herself. How old was Alex then, ten? Vanessa
must have been six and Monica—known as Pigeon—would
have been three.

A trip to France had stretched into weeks, and her mother
was sure there was another woman . . . again. Wrapped in an
old terry-cloth robe, her small hands peeked out of oversized
sleeves.

Screaming into the phone, she held a serrated knife to
her wrist. "I'll do it right in front of your precious daughters—
don't think I won't." Blood oozed from beneath the knife's
teeth. "I know you're with some whore. You think your girls
don't know? You think Alexandra is too young to understand
your mongrel ways? Tell him, Alex." She thrust the phone in
her daughter's face. "Tell him you're with me and that I've cut
myself."

With shaking hands, Alex had taken the phone. "Mommy's
hurt," she whispered tearfully. "Please come home, Daddy."

"Don't cry, kitten." His voice sounded tired and sad. "I'm
on my way. Mommy's going to be fine."

"She's bleeding."

"Call Aunt Peggy, and take care of the girls until she gets
there. Okay, kitten? Can you be a brave girl for Daddy?"

Alex said yes and gave the phone back to her mother.

With a dish towel, her mother staunched the blood flow.
Tears creased her makeup. She slipped to the floor, stringy
hair damp with perspiration falling into her eyes, the knife
and phone clattering on the tiles. That's when Pigeon walked
in.

"Why's Mommy crying?" Her teddy bear tucked under
her arm, she pulled a frayed blanket behind her.

"Everything's okay, baby girl," ten-year-old Alex had said.

She gave Pigeon a hug, picked up the phone, and dialed Aunt Peggy.

Aunty Peggy and Alex were a tag team.

Almost a year later, Vanessa, who even back then seemed weary of the family dramas, had interrupted Alex studying in her room: "Mommy's using bad words and littering."

Alex composed her calmest expression and strode into her parents' bedroom. The scene was comical today, but not at the time. Her mother stood in her silk nightgown with Pigeon by her side, frosty air rippling the curtains. Mouth agape, Alex watched her mother tear through her husband's suits with a butcher knife, cutting off the arms of the jackets, slicing the legs and crotches of the pants, and then launching them out the window. Between each thrust, her mother lifted her thumb-sucking youngest daughter, and together they watched the garments sail down to the lawn below.

After her mother hand flung the last shreds, Alex grabbed Pigeon, hustled her sisters out of the room, put them to bed, and once again called Aunt Peggy. By the time Peggy arrived, dressed in a mink coat over a size-sixteen nightgown, Alex and her mother were sitting at the kitchen table pretending to eat canned tomato soup gone cold. Peggy nodded her head toward Alex and joined them—she neither asked a question nor offered a remedy.

Worth's cough brought Alex out of her memories. She wasn't ten or eleven anymore; she was thirty, with her own almost-successful marketing company. Saying no *was* an option.

"What's this person's name?" she asked.

"Kara Lawrence." He lifted his body up on his elbows. "I don't know her adopted name."

He gave her *our* name?

"It shouldn't be too hard to find her."

Why should she do this?

"I told Martin Dawes to expect your call." Mr. Dawes was the very proper family lawyer: hooded eyes, tight-collared shirts, subdued ties, sparse dark hair clipped short. "He can give you her grandmother's name and address."

"Why can't *he* find her?"

"I need *you* to. I want her to be receptive, to know that I'm sincere. That I care."

"I have to think about this, Daddy."

Another coughing spasm wracked his chest. "Better not take too long."

Alex walked out of the CCU, her head down and shoulders slumped.

"Well?" Her mother approached her. "What did he want?" She was already suspicious.

"To see you." In truth, he had drifted into a fitful sleep, but Alex needed to speak with Aunt Peggy alone.

The moment her mother was out of earshot, Alex asked, "Did you know he had another child?"

Aunt Peggy's lower lip quivered. "I knew." She tugged at her suit jacket. "What did he tell you?"

"That he has an illegitimate child out there somewhere. He sounded sad and ashamed—well, maybe ashamed. In a way, I think he blames Mom." Alex heaved her shoulders. "I think he was more embarrassed to tell me than about what he did." She looked at Peggy for confirmation but she said nothing. "She was adopted and now," her voice rose, "he wants *me* to find her."

"I never heard any of this from your father. You'd think he would have told me something so important."

"He was probably trying to protect you."

Peggy snorted in disbelief.

"He made a mistake and did what he thought best. It's not like he could bring her home to Mom." As a kid, Alex envied her friends whose fathers were home every evening, who did what her dad did on those rare times he was around: kissed their children goodnight, read them stories, listened to their prayers.

"Wait, if Daddy never told you, how did you find out?"

"From your mother, of course."

"Mom knows?" Alex was incredulous. She had thought her mother had no boundaries when it came to complaining to Alex about her father, but obviously she had kept something hidden.

"She said he paid child support for years. That's how she discovered his grand deception." Peggy pulled out a hankie and patted her throat. Specks of linen caught in the creases. "Evidently, she found e-mails between your father and that lawyer, Dawes somebody, trying to find evidence of some new misdeed, no doubt."

"She never said anything to me."

"Remember when she took a whole bottle of vitamin pills and ended up in the hospital with acute diarrhea?"

Alex closed her eyes for a second.

"You remember, you were maybe six. She had run out of Valium and tried to kill herself on One A Days."

Alex sat down next to Peggy. She chuckled, but soon it blossomed into a full-throated, hysterical roar. She didn't remember the vitamin suicide, but it sounded just like something her mother would do. "Oh, Aunt Peggy, what a mess we are."

"Not so much."

"A hot mess. Why can't we be a normal family?"

"I'm not sure there is such a thing."

"He wants me to find her, this other daughter, before he dies." She quickly added, "Of course, he's not going to die."

"Absolutely not."

"I don't want to search for her."

The two women sat in silence for several minutes. Every few seconds, Peggy patted Alex's leg or rubbed her back. Then something else occurred to Alex. She peered at her father's only sibling. "Did you say he paid child support for years?"

"A good deal of money."

"I thought they put her up for adoption."

"Oh, that was much later. No, he did the responsible thing and sent the woman money for the child's education and up-keep. Your mother found the e-mails and called that lawyer."

"Martin Dawes. He's supposed to help me find her."

"He was the one who explained everything."

"But why adoption after . . . how many years?"

"The woman died."

"Her mother died and Daddy thought adoption was best?"

"When you say it like that . . ."

"How else could I say it? Jeez, Aunt Peggy." Alex stood up and paced. "What do you know about her, the kid?" From the expression on her aunt's face, Alex knew she sounded angry again. "Sorry, I didn't mean to yell at you. This is just so upsetting."

"Of course it is. Shameful. Anyway, I don't know anything more."

"All he told me is that her name is Kara and she was born in DC. You have to know something else about her."

"Your mother never gave me any details." Peggy pushed her glasses up the bridge of her nose. "It's not like he didn't have tons of affairs from the day they were married."

"Tons?"

"I'm sorry, Alex."

Other women from day one? Alex sat down. Did he ever even love her mother?

"I do know that the child was born the same year you were, and that infuriated your mother even more than the affair."

How much worse could this story get?

Peggy pursed her lips and continued: "She's black— African American, I guess I'm supposed to say, you know, to be politically correct." She made air-quotes around the words.

Alex cringed. Both Aunt Peggy and her mother had a list of people they didn't like. When Alex brought home friends from school who were Asian, Latina, or black, she lived in dread that either would say something stupid, and they usually did. After a while, Alex stopped inviting friends over.

The photograph in the desk drawer flashed into Alex's mind; the one of the black woman and the little girl with honeyed skin and long braids. "Did Daddy visit them? Did he ever take me?"

"I wouldn't know."

That woman seemed happy in the picture, and her father was laughing. There was something familiar about the girl: her wide-set eyes, shaped like Alex's, just a different color—Alex's were violet like her father's, Kara's were brownish-gold. Even her eyebrows arched like Alex's, and the high cheekbones were definitely a Lawrence trait, as if someone had snuck into a Native American's bed back in the day.

Peggy cocked her head to one side. "What are you going to do?"

"Find her, I guess," Alex replied, surprising herself. Then she realized her response was no surprise at all. "He's counting on me."

CHAPTER FIVE

Kara watched Zach push his way through the crowd and go out the door. Damn. She drank the last of her wine, shrugged into her coat, settled her eyeglasses in place, and left the bar. Taxi drivers didn't like fares to Harlem. All too often, she'd end up in an argument with drivers who refused for no good reason other than their ignorance, even though Harlem was as safe as any other place in the city. Moot point. A taxi home would cost the same as three lunches, but there was no sense in sharing that with Zach, especially if she wouldn't let him help her. He offered often, but she always said no—even when her bills piled up on her nightstand and her bank account held less than a hundred dollars. Kara headed for the subway.

The icy drizzle had stopped but now a stiff wind had picked up and the street was empty. Perhaps that was why she noticed the man. Or was it because he seemed familiar? He was walking in the opposite direction from her, about Flyer's height—two inches taller than Kara—with ruddy cheeks from the weather or genes. He wore a wrinkled raincoat and a baseball cap pulled low over his eyes. Just as quickly as he registered, she put him of her mind and continued walking fast toward the station.

The night air felt heavy with moisture as if it were going to rain again, or even snow. Kara fastened the top button of her coat. Damn it. She snapped her fingers in recollection, realizing she had forgotten her novel at the bar. Turning around, she found herself staring at the man in the baseball cap. Although she couldn't quite make out his face, he appeared startled by the encounter. She sidestepped so that they wouldn't collide and hurried back toward the bar.

After about two blocks in her high heels, Kara decided the book wasn't worth it. The mystery was just so-so and she'd already guessed the ending. Plus it was late, and she had a long way to go before she'd reach the Times Square station. She stopped and pivoted. Once again, she walked directly into the path of the man with the baseball cap.

Her heart rate quickened as she peered into his face.

The man mumbled something, tugged on his cap, and moved away.

He had to be following her. Why else would they have had three encounters within five minutes? In spite of the cold, she began to perspire; her breath came in short bursts as if she'd been running. Could he be a stalker? Was he the person she'd felt watching her for the last few days? Was he at the cemetery this morning? Was he the same man she had seen in the bar staring at her from the entranceway? She pulled her coat tight against her throat and tried to calm down. Why would anyone be following her?

Kara walked as fast as she could, and as close to the streetlights as possible, until she reached Times Square. Finally she made her way down to the subway platform.

By the time her train came, she decided she was just on edge. Big Jim's death and all the memories it brought back had unnerved her, plus the two glasses of wine had clouded her judgment. Now, she checked the platform before stepping into the subway car—no sign of him. She squeezed into an empty seat between a rotund man and a teenager listening to his iPhone; no one seemed to notice her. When the train stopped at 135th Street, she stepped onto the platform, glancing at the people around her. A man just to her right got off the train as well. Not that white men and women were unusual in her neighborhood, but he still seemed out of place in a dark business suit; an inside-out raincoat hung from his arm. He was hatless with a short, graying military haircut. Kara didn't think it was the same man, but she couldn't be sure.

Taking the stairs two at a time in spite of her heels and pencil skirt, Kara reached street level and looked around. The Schomburg Center and Harlem Hospital anchored Lenox Avenue and 135th Street. The museum had long since closed for the night, but there were still lots of people going in and out of the hospital. The stranger was nowhere in sight. As a precaution, Kara stepped into a convenience store and studied the rack of magazines, peeking over her shoulder. People moved past the shop, almost all black and brown. No white man with a crew cut or baseball cap in view. She stepped back onto the sidewalk.

Kara walked fast, her tote tucked securely under her arm. Both too exhausted and revved up to stop for a chat, she acknowledged her neighbors with a friendly but not inviting nod. Finally she reached the weathered brownstone where she rented two rooms and a bath. She loved this old, tall, narrow house with bay windows on each of the four floors. The brownstone stood in a stately row of similar buildings, but this one had terraced flower boxes—empty now, waiting for spring planting—edging the steep steps that led to the front door.

Kara surveyed the block. In spite of the damp night, many people moved along the tree-lined street. The hooded boys and flirting girls gathered in clumps as they listened to music, laughed, and teased. With another quick look around, seeing nothing suspicious, Kara unlocked the carved wooden door. She pushed it open and glanced over her shoulder for one last check. Out of the corner of her eye, she saw a man in an open raincoat rounding the corner of Lenox, moving fast.

She stepped into her entranceway and peered back up the block, but he was gone, so she closed the door and locked it; the clunk of the bolt provided a measure of solace. An adrenaline crash followed as the full impact of the events of the day hit. Her head ached, and she could feel the pain in her teeth and jaw.

A light from the kitchen welcomed her inside as she bent down and took off her pumps. Steam hissed from the radiators; the grandfather clock chimed ten times. Mrs. Edgecombe, the seventy-something owner of the house, was usually up until midnight, but maybe she'd gone to bed early. In case she was asleep, Kara tried to walk softly on the wooden floors. A part of her, however, wanted to make noise so Mrs. E. would come out of her bedroom and ask Kara about her day, offer her some sweet she'd baked and a hot cup of tea.

When Kara arrived on Mrs. E.'s doorstep almost a year before, fresh from a painful breakup, eyes bloodshot from non-stop crying, a crumpled introductory note from Kara's principal in hand, the older woman had welcomed her. Mrs. E. invited Kara in, brewed a pot of chamomile tea, and made her laugh with funny stories about her days as a math and science teacher in the public school system. It turned out they had a fair amount in common. Although Kara didn't share her past, she learned Mrs. E. had taken in many other young people, who, like Kara, Tuesday, and Flyer, had aged out of the foster care system with no money, no family, no prospects, and nowhere to live.

Now, still walking on tiptoes, Kara moved past the shrouded

living room, the largest of the three rooms on the first floor. The home was a classic brownstone, with ten-foot ceilings, parquet floors, and plaster walls. To her left, she could see the outlines of Mrs. E.'s lace- and photograph-covered piano, the rocking chair, overstuffed sofa, wing chairs, and the huge fireplace mantle against the wall. Graceful, if a little world-weary, the house exuded the comfort of one hundred Christmases and thousands of family meals. Just breathing in its smell made Kara feel better.

She let the day's events replay in her mind. There had to be a relationship between the feeling she had at the cemetery, the man she thought she saw in the bar, and the stranger in the raincoat. But what? Could it have something to do with Big Jim? Could the state finally be investigating? Did one of his foster children file a complaint? Flyer, Tuesday, and Kara never talked about going to the authorities. In fact, they never talked at all about what had happened to the girls. Just thinking about it now sent sharp pains to her temples. Kara had almost brought it up when the Catholic priest scandals surfaced; all those men came forward and spoke of the sexual abuse they'd experienced.

The three of them had met for breakfast, the front-page headlines staring up at them from the *New York Post*. Their shared truth sat on the tip of Kara's tongue, but Tuesday's gaze bore into Kara, her eyes screaming as loudly as the headlines, and Kara had swallowed her words. *If you say it aloud, it makes it real.*

With a wave of her hand, Kara banished the memories. She climbed the stairs to her apartment, one floor below Officer Danny Waters's rooms. There weren't any physical demarcations between the different apartments. Mrs. E. lived on the first and second floors. Until a bad fall last winter, her bedroom was up one flight. Since then, she made the first-floor sunroom, with its jutting bay window, her bedroom. A friend had added a prefab roll-in shower stall to the small powder room. Guests now had to use the less lovely powder room off the kitchen.

Danny lived on the fourth floor and Kara on the third. The open staircase, with no doors or other indications it was a multifamily dwelling, allowed Kara and Danny to have the run of the house. This was home, her sanctuary. She suspected that Danny felt the same.

Maybe he was home . . . not that Kara would confide in him. Sharing troubles brought complications. It would be good, though, just to have a normal conversation about a whole lot of nothing. That's what she thought she'd be doing with Zach. Well, that and other things. But there was no sense in dwelling on it. Sad thoughts just led to more headaches and sleepless nights. Once again, she waved her hand in front of her face to wipe away her negative thoughts and dragged herself up the last flight of stairs to her room. She dropped her keys on the whatnot table and put her shoes and tote down. Marty, her rescued three-legged feral cat, came out of the hall closet to say hello. How pitiful that he was her only confidant.

Every night before going to bed Kara pulled out the picture of her family. Often, she imagined playing with Alex as a child in a house they shared. Sometimes the house was on Long Island near the water, sometimes it was a tucked-away refuge with a garden lush with irises, roses, and chrysanthemums— her mother's favorites. Saved from the devastating cancer by a miracle cure, her mother called them to dinner just as their father came home from work. In most of her fantasies, she had Flyer and Tuesday with her, adopted by her mother and father.

Reveries with her and Alex as adults were less frequent but equally compelling: a knock on the door, Kara's dad standing there, his eyes filled with remorse, Alex shyly waiting for an introduction. Kara never mentioned her fantasies to anyone, but they comforted her. Tonight her fantasy was dinner with her father, Alex, and Zach. Zach had left his wife and gotten custody of the children. Her dear landlady Mrs. E. was babysitting.

The intrusion of Zach into her imagination left her edgy instead of calm, and she placed the photograph next to her tote. The envelope Zach had asked her to deliver in the morning poked out. There was nothing written on the outside, and it was sealed and taped closed. Why not deliver it himself? He made it sound like people were watching him. The same people watching her? This wasn't productive. Kara rose and walked to the bathroom. It was time to get ready for bed—she'd think about the envelope tomorrow. Marty trailed her, his thunder-rumble purrs making their own music.

The bathroom had a shower stall barely wide enough to turn in, a sink, and a toilet. On the open shelves over the toilet, Kara kept lavender potpourri and purple towels. Rows of plastic pockets hung on the back of the door like a shoe caddy. Each pocket held a different necessity—shampoo, makeup, tampons, lotion, comb, brush. She shed her clothes.

"Maybe I should search for them . . . What do you think, Marty?"

The cat's ears perked up.

"A quick Google search might be all it would take." She turned the shower knobs on. "Wouldn't that be better than playing all these silly reunion games in my head?"

Marty stretched and walked away. Obviously, he was tired of this particular conversation; they had it often.

She let the water run until it was hot and stepped into the stall. How hard would it be to find these people, Worth and Alex Lawrence? They would be stunned. Would they even recognize her?

She poured body wash onto her washcloth, her mind returning to her counterargument. How hard would it have been for them to find her? They didn't want to. They didn't want her then, and they don't want her now. She needed to let her fantasy go. It was time to grow up.

CHAPTER SIX

lex exhaled, scanning the hospital corridor. No sign of Vanessa and Pigeon, even though she'd called both of them before her cell phone battery died. That had to be over an hour ago. She reached for one of the pay phones facing the CCU elevator bank and dialed the office number.

"McCormick and Lawrence Graphic Designs." Sean sounded muffled. Alex pictured him scrolling through his e-mail messages, coffee mug in one hand, muffin crumbs sprinkled across his chest, phone pressed between his shoulder and ear, tufts of disheveled hair standing on end, his handlebar mustache waxed and curled.

"Hi."

"Alex, where've you been?"

"Family emergency." With her left thumb and index finger, she manipulated the frayed cigarette in her jean pocket. A *No Smoking* sign stared down at her. "I won't be in today."

"Okay." He dragged out the vowels, making it clear that it wasn't. He sounded like her mother and often acted as if he were—an upsetting thought.

"My dad's sick. I'm at the hospital." She heard him swallow. "It's serious."

Whenever Alex spoke with Sean on the phone, she was reminded why she hated it—long silences followed by unexpected or unwelcome responses. She drummed her fingers on the top of the pay phone and waited.

"I'm sorry. What's wrong?" he finally asked.

She told him everything she knew. "I'll be here all day." She kept her tone professional. "Is there anything I need to know, anything urgent?"

"As a matter of fact, yes. Jonas Frankel is on the warpath again."

Alex groaned.

"He called three times asking for you."

"About what?" she replied, although she knew the answer.

"The first call came at eight thirty this morning, just so you know, and the last one was a few minutes ago."

"What did he say?"

"I'm getting to that."

Alex closed her eyes.

"You promised to complete his designs today. Designs that—and correct me if I am wrong—you told me you would have finished by last Friday."

The cigarette crumbled in her hand. "Sarcasm is not helpful." Dried bits of tobacco stuck to her fingertips.

"I told him you had a meeting this morning but would be in any minute."

Whenever Alex complained about Sean to Vanessa, her sister asked why she partnered with him. What Vanessa didn't know was how creative he was, how he could be insightful and sometimes kind. He was a bit rough around the edges, but also loyal and hardworking.

"You'd better call him now," Sean continued. "We can't afford to lose this account. I don't mean to sound unsympathetic, but things are lean around here, in case you haven't noticed."

She'd noticed. Over the last several months, they had pitched two significant companies, competing with firms

much larger than their boutique operation of three employ-
ees. Sean had been reluctant to invest the time and money
needed for their sales presentations, but Alex knew they were
talented enough. She believed they had a real shot at one of
the two clients, or maybe both. Unfortunately, neither had
chosen them in the end, although they were now on the radar
of some major corporations. And yet Sean was right—they
had no money coming in.

Thinking about that disappointment, Alex softened her
tone: "I'll call him right away to smooth things over." She balanced the phone against her ear and pulled out a pen, scrib-
bling his number on the palm of her hand. "I'll come in early
tomorrow and stay until the Frankel job is done." She waited
for Sean to respond, but when he didn't, she added, "I promise. If anything else comes up, just leave me a message on my
cell phone." Then she remembered her dead battery and the
charger in some unknown place in her apartment. "Actually,
I'll check in," she amended.

"Okay."

She waited in case there was more he wanted to say.

"Should I come over? I don't mind. That is, if you need me
. . . if you want me to."

That's what she had wanted to hear at the beginning of
the conversation. "Thanks, but no. Although I appreciate the
offer." In the space of one conversation, Sean would go from
critical mother to would-be protector to senior partner and
back to friend. "Don't worry about me, Sean. I'm fine."

"I always worry about you."

The emotion in his voice startled her. "What?"

"Just call Frankel."

Then Sean hung up before Alex could reply.

What was that about? She was pretty sure he'd said he

always worried about her. Argh. She didn't need unwanted complications. It was better to focus. As much as she hated to admit it, she knew he was right. With only a couple of small projects under contract and almost nothing lined up, Frankel's marketing package was their only bill-paying project. She dropped the last of her change in the pay phone slot and dialed Frankel's office.

"Hi, big sister."

Alex spun around. Pigeon stood in front of the elevator doors. Her dark hair was streaked with purple, and she was dressed in a leather miniskirt, coral blouse, and a man's bomber jacket.

"Frankel and Hobson," Alex heard on the other end of the line.

She hung up and hurried over to Pigeon. "I am so glad you're here." She hugged and kissed her. "You okay?"

"I can only stay a few minutes."

"Daddy's sleeping now, and Mom and Aunt Peggy are in the cafeteria."

"Just tell him I came."

"You *have* to go in." It pained Alex when Pigeon missed family gatherings with excuses like colds, tyrant bosses, and last-minute mishaps. Pigeon eluded eye contact. "Mom's going to be disappointed too," Alex said, forcing Pigeon to look her in the eye.

"Okay."

"Are you hungry?"

"I need to talk to you about something."

"Sure, what's wrong?" There was always something: lost apartments with nowhere to go, lost wallets and no way to pay her bills, and lost boyfriends as well. Although Alex sometimes grew tired of the endless list of troubles and plans gone awry, she was never too weary to help.

A janitor pushed a bucket ahead of his mop, leaving the strong smell of disinfectant in his wake. Alex waited to hear Pigeon's latest crisis. Maybe this was how Sean felt about her. Not that she ever let the business suffer, but she had to admit there was always something going on with her—a lost portfolio, late for an appointment, computer trouble . . . something.

"Cool Breeze and I are moving to LA. We're leaving tonight."

"Who the hell is Cool Breeze?"

On cue, a linebacker-sized man with a white, shaven pate and scraggly flaxen beard stepped off the elevator and walked over to them. He had to be at least forty—fifteen years older than Pigeon.

He scooped Pigeon up off her feet. "Miss me?" Then he turned to Alex. "You're Alex, right? Nice to meet ya."

Alex tried not to stare at his manicured fingernails, painted black, or the multicolored tattoos climbing up his forearm. "Same here." She hoped she sounded friendly, and not scandalized.

"He's got this gig, and I'm going with him."

Cool Breeze grinned. "Monica makes a great road manager —lining up good places to crash, finding all-you-can-eat diners that are open late-night."

Trying to process what she'd just heard, Alex missed her mother's swoop-in arrival, all 105 pounds of coiled indignation advancing on them.

"So there you are—*finally*. Your father laying on his deathbed, and where were you? Is your hair purple? The orange streaks weren't enough to put me in my grave? And pull down that skirt; I can see all your secrets and so can everyone else. If you needed money for decent clothes, all you had to do was ask."

Pigeon shrunk against Cool Breeze. Alex opened her mouth to defend her little sister, but the large man jumped in.

"You must be Mrs. Lawrence."

Peggy trundled behind Alex's mother, glasses askew, her hands full of sodas and chips.

"And you must be the famous Aunt Peggy. Monica told me so much about you both."

Peggy giggled and bobbed her head as her glasses slipped further down her nose.

Alex's mother asked, "Does your mother know you have those tattoos, or do you hide them when you visit?"

"She has a few of her own."

Judy looked startled, but stayed quiet only for a beat. "Monica, introduce us."

"Thomas Cole, but my friends call me Cool Breeze."

"Why on earth would anyone want to call you such a ridiculous name?"

"It's my stage name. But you can call me Tom or Breeze—whatever you like." He pulled over a couple of chairs and helped Aunt Peggy with her bounty, bestowing a killer smile on each of the women in turn.

"How did you come up with *Cool Breeze?*" Aunt Peggy inquired.

"I wanted to be memorable."

Alex watched in amazement as Cool Breeze asked about Worth's health, followed by a discussion of the music scene in LA. From there they went into the cultural differences between the Northeast and California. When Judy inquired about gang violence, once again eyeing his tattoos, Breeze managed a conversational pivot with an ease Alex envied. He seemed comfortable and knowledgeable discussing almost any topic. Pigeon listened with rapt, quiet attention, holding his hand.

Her mother finally pulled herself together and got her razor's edge back. "What exactly do you do, Thomas?"

"I play lead guitar with a band, The Bombers. We have a contract with Warner Bros., and our new album is moving up the charts."

"What kind of music do you play?"

He laughed. "You wouldn't like it at first, but I bet you'd come to appreciate it. Monica told me you sang professionally back in the day."

"Not really." Judy beamed. She liked to tell her daughters about her piano-playing, nightclub-singing days. When they pressed her, Judy admitted it was only a summer job in a small town upstate.

"Your daughter must have gotten it from you. She always knows if we have something good going. I find her perceptions to be spot on."

"A contract with Warner Bros. is impressive."

Alex couldn't believe it—her mother had been taken in by this child seducer. "Would I have heard of your band?" she asked, trying to get "call me Tom, or Breeze, or whatever" back into the role of the villain.

"Do you like hardcore?"

"Some." She wasn't sure what hardcore music was, or if she'd ever heard it.

"Check out our videos on YouTube and let me know which cuts you like."

In spite of herself, Alex couldn't stay annoyed with him. His earnestness seemed real. "Where are you guys going to live?"

Before he could answer, Pigeon jumped up. "We have to go. I'd better go peek in on Daddy, and then we gotta hit the road." She bent over and kissed her mother, aunt, and Alex on their cheeks, tugged on the hem of her skirt, grabbed her boyfriend's hand, and pulled him down the hall.

"Monica Lawrence, where do you think you are going?" Hands on her narrow hips, her mother yelled at the retreating pair: "You just stop right there, young lady."

Cool Breeze slowed but Pigeon pulled on his arm.

"Wait," Alex said as she ran after them. "How will I get in touch with you?"

"I'll call you the minute we get settled."

"But there's something important I need to talk to you about."

"Just call my cell or text me." Pigeon wrapped her arms around her sister. "He loves me, Alex. Be happy for me."

Then, without entering their father's hospital room once, Pigeon disappeared with Cool Breeze behind the closing elevator doors.

CHAPTER SEVEN

Kara's eyes flew open. The dream was now occurring nightly, whereas before, she'd only have it maybe once a week. Blood, crashing waves, her mother's extended hand reaching for her. The ocean water became mud, sucking Kara under. Now, she dreaded closing her eyes. The nightmare left her fatigued but unable to actually rest, much less sleep.

Now fully awake, covered in a clammy layer of sweat, Kara pulled back the covers. Marty jumped.

"Sorry, kitty, I'm going crazy." She got up. "I am crazy."

Of course, the dream was about Big Jim. But why, now, was it haunting her every single night? Kara donned her robe, eyeglasses, and flip-flop slippers. She needed to shake off the feeling left by the dream.

"You deserve some cream and I need a cup of tea." Kara often found that after a cup of chamomile tea she could fall back asleep and the nightmare wouldn't return. With Marty at her heels, she eased down the stairs and into the warm light of Mrs. E.'s kitchen.

Wheelchair bound from last winter's fall, Mrs. E. sat tall in her chair. An intricate pile of mostly white braids framed her dark, round face.

"I thought I heard you come in."

"I didn't mean to wake you."

"I napped too long. I could use some tea and company." Mrs. E. rolled her chair over to the stove. "So how was your day and your date?" The kettle was a permanent fixture. A whoosh of flame followed the *click, click, click* of the burner. "Hungry?"

"I'm starving." The last meal Kara had eaten was popcorn at the bar; before that, a cheese sandwich at noon.

The gathering of cups, saucers, spoons, and napkins filled the silence.

"So?"

"Oh, the date. It went okay." Kara tried to sound untroubled by the events of the evening. "He had urgent business so we only had time for a drink and a dance."

Mrs. E. made a sucking sound between her teeth.

"He's involved in some big deal and had to go back to work."

"Most men would love a chance to spend the evening with a beautiful, smart woman like you."

"We're going away for a vacation when his deal is closed."

"They wouldn't be dashing off, leaving you alone." She shook her head as if to underscore the stupidity of Zachary Lowe.

"He's a good man."

The face Mrs. E. made belied her words. "I'm sure he is."

The two women finished setting the table in silence.

Kara was tired of defending Zach to others—that's why she didn't want to mention him to Tuesday. It was harder to hide at home, of course. Mrs. E., Danny, and Kara knew a lot about each other's comings and goings.

The kettle screeched.

"Chamomile?"

"Perfect."

Mrs. E. poured the boiling water into a porcelain teapot that was topped with a strainer holding loose tea. "How come you don't date a nice boy like Danny?" She uncovered a pyramid of brownies and placed the plate on the table.

"You don't know Zach." Again, Kara thought about the night he had told her about his wife's betrayal, his eyes watering, his voice thick with humiliation. It had been a turning point for them, a moment of rare intimacy for Kara. "Danny and I are friends. Anyway, isn't he seeing that Willa person?"

Right then, Danny walked into the kitchen still in his uniform: his Glock angled from his right hip, a belt holding his cuffs and other gear circled his waist. "Her name is Willow." Tall, cocoa brown, slender, with long arms and feet, Danny grinned at the two women. "And no, he's not still seeing her."

How much of the conversation had he heard? Kara flushed.

Mrs. E. hummed under her breath in that *I'm not involved in this* kind of way she had.

Without turning Kara remarked, "You're home late."

"Came to catch a few winks, then I gotta get back."

"Trouble?"

"Overtime."

His voice was deep and smooth, the kind you hear late at night on the radio, a voice to trust. Maybe she should mention to him what happened today.

Kara sat down at the table and Mrs. E. pushed her wheelchair into place.

Danny unholstered his gun and slid it on top of one of the kitchen cabinets. He lowered himself into a chair, leaned back, balanced it on its two back legs, and grabbed a brownie. Kara only nibbled on hers in spite of her earlier hunger. She tried to analyze her hesitation in telling Danny about her stalker. Was it that she'd have to explain too much, about where she had been when she saw him? They both knew she'd aged out of foster care, but neither Mrs. E. nor Danny knew about the abuse. Unfortunately, they did know about Winston, last year's unfaithful boyfriend, and definitely disapproved of Zach.

"What have you two lovely ladies been up to?"

"Kara had a date. Ended quite early," Mrs. E. answered.

"With that old man?"

"You don't know anything about him," Kara said.

"Do you?"

What was that supposed to mean? So far, the tea and the conversation hadn't calmed her. She wanted to change the topic. "Did both of you buy your lottery tickets? Mega Millions is up to $110,000,000."

Danny licked crumbs from his fingers.

Mrs. E. said, "I bought one for each of us. Maybe this is our time."

Kara felt Danny's scrutiny but she didn't look at him.

"What would you do with that much money, Danny?" Mrs. E. asked.

"Give it all to you, every penny."

Mrs. E. made a clucking sound but she appeared pleased. "And some to the church?"

"No doubt."

Kara stirred broken brownie pieces on her plate with her right index finger. If she had millions of dollars, first she would help Flyer and Tuesday—pay their bills and hers. But her dream would be to start a fund for foster kids living in group homes. How many times had she gone to school hungry, or without a notebook or pen, in hand-me-down clothes? If she had money, she'd take all the kids shopping every spring and fall so they had new clothes and school supplies like everyone else. No one would know where the kids lived, or how they lived. She'd buy them laptops and tablets. They'd fit in—belong. "Me too," she said. "I'd give it all to you, Mrs. E." It would take too long to explain her dream and its genesis. Besides, no one wanted to hear other people's sad stories. "How about you?"

"A nice chunk to the church. Fix this place up. Maybe take a trip to see my granddaughter."

Mrs. E. had never mentioned she had children, much less grandchildren. Kara had inquired about the photos in the living room, and Mrs. E. said they were her parents and grandparents, aunts and uncles, cousins. She had never mentioned a husband or any children. "Where does she live?"

"In South Africa. Can't imagine how long it would take to get there."

"You'd have to get on an airplane." Danny laughed, his even, white teeth flashing. "And we know how you feel about that."

Mrs. E. shushed him.

"What does she do?"

"She's a volunteer, and she's studying to be a doctor." Mrs. E. smiled. "I haven't seen her in two years. She used to live here, in your rooms, Kara."

"What happened to her parents?"

"My Lucy is an orphan. She's my sister's granddaughter, but ever since her parents died, she's been mine." Mrs. E. shook her head as if disagreeing with her inner dialogue. "Enough about that. Can I get anyone else some more tea?"

This time the silence was more comfortable. In one corner, Marty cleaned himself, the bowl of cream now empty. Mrs. E. hummed under her breath. From a distance, despite the late hour, Kara could hear muffled street sounds of cars, teens, and rap music. She finally began to feel better. Her head barely hurt; she didn't think about the nightmares, or Zach's sudden departure, or the man in the raincoat.

After several minutes, Kara felt Danny's gaze on her again. She looked up as if to ask, *What?*

"How *are* things going with that old white dude you're seeing? Isn't he married?"

His tone was kinder than his words, but it was still a mean way to ask.

Zach and Danny had met a few months earlier, when Zach had come to pick her up and Kara hadn't gotten to the door fast enough. She found the two of them in the narrow hallway. Danny, dressed in his civilian clothes, his arms crossed, his full lips curled under, stared Zach down. For his part, Zach seemed more amused than intimidated, if that was what Danny wanted to achieve. She introduced them, but that was it. How did Danny know Zach was married?

"Great." She squared her shoulders. "Why are you both so down on him? Do I comment on your girlfriends? Speaking of which—"

"Yes, you do comment, as a matter of fact."

"What happened between you and Willa—I mean Willow?"

Danny's laugh was low and warm. "Didn't work out." He arched one eyebrow into a steep V shape. "It happens. Some things are just meant to be," he shrugged, "some aren't."

Kara wasn't sure whether he was referring to her relationship or his.

"Anyway, I gotta get some sleep." He rose, kissed Mrs. E. on the cheek, grabbed another brownie, and with a back-handed wave strode toward the hardwood steps. He had the practiced gait of an urban black man, smooth and gliding with a hint of attitude.

"What's the matter with him?" Kara asked.

"You need to tend to your own garden and not peek into the neighbor's, much less scramble over her fence."

Kara rolled her eyes in a classic Tuesday move. Suds sloshed in the sink as she began washing their dishes.

Mrs. E. wouldn't let it go. "You know, honey, sometimes we want something so bad, we fool ourselves into thinking we already have it."

It was time to say good night. From experience, Kara knew there was no end to Mrs. E.'s aphorisms. Besides—she wasn't fooling herself. She knew the likelihood of Zach leaving his wife and marrying her was slim, though maybe marriage wasn't what she wanted anyway. Who did she know who was happily married? No one. And Zach loved his young children, as he should. Kara finished wiping the table and placed the daffodil-filled vase at its center. The grandfather clock chimed midnight.

"I just want you to be happy. Danny's a nice boy, single, and your own kind."

What *kind* would that be? "Thanks for the tea, Mrs. E., but I'm pooped."

"Don't you know he's crazy about you? I'm not so old I can't tell when a man has that spark."

This conversation was going in the wrong direction. "Like I said before, Danny and I are just friends."

"Humph."

Kara leaned over and kissed the top of Mrs. E.'s head. "Good night."

"He's got nobody, you know, just like you."

Kara let that sink in, and then said, "See you in the morning." She walked to the stairs and, mimicking Danny's move, gave Mrs. E. a final backhanded wave. Was Danny like her? He never spoke about his people. When she asked an occasional question, he abruptly changed the subject. That sounded like Kara. Marty hobble-hurried past her, his missing leg only slowing him down a bit. "At least we've got each other, fella."

Her three rooms were just as she had left them, keys on the whatnot, front room dark, and bedroom lamp still on. Kara appreciated her part of the house. Her bedroom had a queen-sized bed, nightstand, small desk, bookshelves, and Marty's litter box—the bathroom was too small for it. Her exercise bike took up a corner. The room had a window overlooking Mrs. E.'s backyard, which was lying in wait for spring. An air conditioner rested under the window, topped with a cushion, creating an unattractive but useful winter seat and Marty's sleeping space of choice. The hall, its polished parquet floors softened with scattered rugs, had two closets, one for clothes and one for linens. She always kept one closet door cracked open for Marty. The best part was the little sitting room at the front of the house, with a nonworking fireplace crowned with a cherrywood mantle. A bay window, framed with a gauzy curtain and decorated with a plush pillow, faced the street, bringing in light and the sounds of neighborhood activity. Marty spent most days sitting there.

The day Kara had moved in, she came with nothing—having left her furniture, stereo, and most of her clothes in the apartment she and Winston had shared for six months. She was too embarrassed and miserable to go back and claim them. Necessity, however, overcame pride. Danny had helped her retrieve her items and move them into her new rooms. Now a beloved ottoman, love seat, and stereo helped make the front room her favorite.

That's where she went now. She lowered one hip onto the pillow, pulled up the blinds, and peered out the window. All was quiet, no man in a raincoat. Relieved, she brushed her teeth again and got into bed. She desperately needed sleep. The alarm clock was set for 6:30 a.m. and it was already after midnight.

Marty circled several times on her coverlet, then curled into a ball, tucked his head, and closed his eyes.

Starting at one hundred, Kara counted backward, willing herself to sleep. Eventually, she drifted off. But after only an hour or so of calm sleep, the nightmare began again.

The wave of mud grew bigger, closer, and once again crashed down on her, burying her alive.

CHAPTER EIGHT

Vanessa finally arrived. Dressed in a navy-blue and white–striped power suit, she glided into the waiting room on polished black pumps. With a sharp look, she took in Alex's unkempt appearance and demanded a "concise status report." Vanessa had an amazing aptitude for making others do her bidding, and Alex was no exception. Alex dragged her fingers through her tangles, straightened her back, and tucked her scuffed boot–clad feet under her chair before providing Vanessa with the requested information.

"The next twenty-four hours are critical," Alex concluded.

Vanessa knitted her brow and drummed her fingers in a familiar Lawrence-family gesture. For the next hour, Vanessa went into action. She spoke with all the nurses and aides, who listened respectfully. The conversations resulted in a cot for their mother in the hospital room—something Alex had asked for hours before—and an overdue sponge bath for their father—another thing Alex had requested several times. Within less than thirty minutes of receiving the cot and the bath, their parents both fell asleep.

For a few minutes the two sisters stood at the doorway of their father's room and watched: their mother was curled in a tight ball, hugging her pillow the way Pigeon used to snuggle her teddy bear; their father, mouth agape, hair disheveled, looked deathly pale. Alex thought about how much she loved them. She knew firsthand how difficult her mother made her father's life—so many histrionics and so little warmth. In fairness, it must have been hard for her mother to be last in her husband's affections. In her heart, Alex knew she was first, followed by her sisters, and then who—his other women? Alex studied her sleeping father. No, he loved her mother more than he loved those other women, more than his dead mistress and Kara. Did Vanessa know he loved Alex best?

She draped her arm around her sister's shoulders and squeezed. "Thanks for all of your help. It's been a hell of a day."

"I can see that," Vanessa said, pushing Alex's hair out of her face.

The sisters returned to the lounge to pack up an exhausted Aunt Peggy. After many reassurances that they would call if anything changed, they took her to the lobby, wrapped her ancient mink over her shoulders, and bundled her into a taxi.

On the elevator back up to the CCU, Alex filled Vanessa in on Pigeon's escape to LA. "I'm worried she'll do something stupid and get married before she even knows him. Or worse, he'll dump her in LA, and she'll be too proud to come home."

"Maybe she needs to grow up." Vanessa pointed to a string of empty chairs in the waiting room. "Maybe you need to let her."

The sisters sat side by side. Vanessa picked up an old copy of *Vogue*.

Alex tried to figure out how best to tell Vanessa about Kara—she needed her sister's moral support but had no idea how she would react.

"Stop jiggling your foot."

Alex stopped. She tugged on her lower lip.

Vanessa thumbed through the magazine, one of her high-heeled pumps loose and hanging from her toes.

A male physician walked by the glass-encased waiting room, hungrily taking in Vanessa, who didn't appear to notice. This always happened, at least whenever Alex was around. It wasn't that her sister had movie-star looks. Vanessa was the same height as Alex and had Aunt Peggy's honey-blond hair, smallish gray-green eyes, a pug nose like their mother's, and her best feature—full, pouty lips. What Vanessa also had, at least according to Sean, was movie-star attitude: great legs, short skirts, high heels, and an I-couldn't-care-less-about-you demeanor. When Alex declared Vanessa skinny, Sean had smirked and said, *Skinny with great boobs.*

"What are you sighing about?"

"There's one other thing I need to tell you."

"Shoot."

Alex explained about their father's illegitimate daughter and his sickbed request for Alex to find her.

"How's Judy taking all this?" Vanessa had started calling their parents by their first names on her sixteenth birthday. *I'm too old to have a mommy and daddy,* she'd declared.

"I don't know. She must have made peace with it."

"Ha." Vanessa laid her magazine down on the chair next to her. "More like stored it away for future torture."

"How did she not tell us?"

"You mean how come she didn't tell you, her Miss Fix-it confidante."

Alex let that pass. "Dad's heart attack has thrown her off."

"How can you tell?" Vanessa rose and faced Alex. "Everything is a firestorm and nothing is ever in proportion to the situation." She took a deep breath. "Who cares?" She sat back down.

"I don't know if he told her, you know, about asking me to find his . . ." Alex couldn't call her *his daughter* or by her name.

"You know he didn't; thus the covert operation."

"I'm thinking I'll Google her, go on Facebook."

"Do you know her adopted name, date of birth, Social Security number?"

"Right." Alex bit her lip. "Dad said to call Martin Dawes; he had the grandmother's address, but the information is about twenty years old."

"Maybe the national adoption registry?"

"What's that?"

"I read about it in some article. Adoptees register and hope the parents who deserted them might find them."

Alex ripped the corner off the back page of a magazine and made a quick note.

"If he'd asked me, which of course he never would, I'd hire a private detective."

It was true: her parents never asked Vanessa to help them. In many ways she was smarter and more successful than Alex and the more logical choice. The difference, however, was that Alex always said yes.

"He wants her to be receptive to being found, and he thinks I can smooth the way."

"Tell him you tried and couldn't find her."

"I can't do that."

"Why on earth do we want to find another—probably neurotic—sister? Really, Alex, you don't have to do everything he asks."

Of course, they both knew that wasn't true.

They settled on Alex calling Mr. Dawes in the morning and the two of them making a trip to the last known address of Kara's grandmother in the Bronx on Saturday.

CHAPTER NINE

Kara came downstairs Friday morning to see Danny ripping open a packet of instant oatmeal with his teeth and dumping the flakes into a bowl.

"Want some? I make a mean breakfast." He added milk and placed the bowl in the microwave.

"I'm not hungry, but thanks."

The microwave beeped. He pulled out the bowl, straddled the chair, and sat. "You okay?"

"Sure, how about you?"

He laughed. "Well enough, for a man who gave you such a hard time last night."

She gave him a no-teeth smile. "I guess I gave as good as I got," she said and grabbed a banana.

He had returned from his night detail just as Kara had come down to feed Marty. At first it was a bit awkward, but Danny had a way of making her feel comfortable and putting her on edge at the same time.

They ate in silence and once again Kara considered telling Danny about the man who'd followed her. Danny watched, leaning on his elbows over his now-empty bowl, as if he could tell she was debating with herself. Her private self won, and it was time to get going. Kara rose from the table at the exact same moment as Danny. She reached for his bowl to put it in the sink and their hands touched.

"I'll wash." He took the bowl and spoon from her, his eyes still on her face.

They stood close; she could smell brown sugar on his breath. The thought that he might kiss her sped through her mind, and she scrambled for a conversation topic. "How's your studying going?"

"The sergeant's exam?"

"Are you studying for something else?"

He watched her for a few beats. "Fine."

Kara decided she'd imagined the almost kiss.

In a decidedly casual tone, Danny said, "If you're leaving now, I'll walk you to the subway. I need to grab some decent coffee."

She had definitely imagined it.

Icy rain stung their faces, and Kara lowered her umbrella. Her breath fogged her glasses as they passed Asian grocers, coffee shops, and a dimly lit laundromat. Her temples throbbed. Last night, after the horrific dream woke her up in a cold sweat, she'd sat in bed and watched movies. This morning she felt hungover.

Danny's voice cut into her thoughts: "Something's wrong, isn't it?"

"Just tired, or maybe it's the weather."

He nodded. "It's supposed to get better this weekend. Maybe you and . . ." He trailed off without finishing his sentence.

"I just remembered I have to run an errand before work." She quickened her pace. "Thanks for asking how I'm doing." She moved ahead of him. "See you."

Kara ran down the littered steps of the 135th Street station, jostled by people closing wet umbrellas, her own leaving a trail of drops behind her. An approaching train clanged into the station, so she quickly swiped her MetroCard, pushed through, and made it just as the doors began to close. She should have said something nice to Danny, but he flustered her. Why was that? She made a sound in her throat. Mrs. E. had an answer, something about sparks. Well, Kara's life was complicated enough.

The train rattled into another station and more people squeezed on. Kara tucked her tote in close and pressed her back into a corner, protecting as much of her body as possible. She hated having strangers so close to her. Danny popped back into her mind. Maybe tonight she'd make a point to thank him again for his concern.

After taking the shuttle from Times Square to Grand Central, she emerged at 42nd Street and Lexington Avenue and walked east. The slushy rain had turned into wet snow and the wind sliced through her. Try as she might, Kara couldn't shake her heavy mood. She steadied the umbrella. Just as she reached her destination, she saw him in the doorway. Workers were pushing through the adjacent revolving doors, but in spite of the hat pulled low, there was no mistaking him.

Kara didn't know what to do or where to hide. She took two steps back, spun around, and ran across the street just as the yellow light counted down to zero. A coffee shop on the corner appeared crowded and safe. She ducked inside, looking over her shoulder, but tilted umbrellas and the avenue packed with cars, trucks, and yellow cabs obscured her view of the building's entrance across the street. A man pushed past her in the doorway she blocked. "Do you mind, lady?"

Undeterred, Kara watched the street scene steadily. There he was. He crossed against the light and darted around the slow-moving traffic.

She moved farther into the doorway. The umbrella was wet against her side as she made her way to the back of the café. This was as terrifying as her nightmares, except it was real, here and now, while the dreams were about things from long ago. A yellowed paper sign told her she was near the women's bathroom—a place to hide where he couldn't follow. As she tried to decide what to do, an elderly woman in a plastic raincoat slipped around her and went inside the one-person lavatory. The door clicked shut.

Kara dug her cell phone out of her bag; she needed help. She punched in Zach's number, her dull headache becoming a sharp pain.

"Mr. Lowe's office," a no-nonsense voice answered.

"May I please speak with him? It's an emergency." She tried to steady her breathing.

"May I ask who's calling?"

"Kara Lawrence. Please, I must speak with him right now."

Kara searched the faces in the café but she didn't see the man. At six feet tall, she knew she stood out, towering over the women and most of the men. With the same self-consciousness she'd had as a teenager, she folded her frame from the middle, rounded her shoulders, and ducked her head. She felt her breakfast—or lack thereof—churn in her stomach.

The woman put her on hold, and soft music played.

"I'm sorry, Mr. Lowe is not available. Would you like to leave a message with me or on his voice mail?"

Kara pushed the red hang-up button, her eyes filling up with tears. Why wouldn't he take her call? His assistant must not have conveyed the urgency. Kara thought about calling back and demanding that the woman get him on the phone. Instead, she dialed the number of the 17th Precinct.

"Officer Waters, please." Her legs sagged and she felt light-headed, so she leaned against a wall that was covered in questionable substances. Zach was probably in a meeting, and had asked the secretary not to interrupt him, so she didn't tell him. The desk sergeant on the phone asked her to hold on.

"Officer Waters."

"It's Kara. Some man is following me, and I'm scared, and I'm sorry to bother you."

"Where are you? I'm on my way."

"I think I'm going to be sick."

She could hear him shout rapid-fire instructions: "Patch this to my cell, sarge." Then to Kara: "Are you someplace where there are other people?"

"Yes."

"Stay put. Give me the address."

"On the east side." She scanned the shop again—the man was nowhere in sight. Now the coffee shop, filled with the sounds of friendly conversation, didn't seem sinister. People laughed, newspapers crackled, and voices ordered coffee and bagels to go.

"Do you know what street?"

Over the phone, she could hear the door slam, the engine of his patrol car turn over, and the seriousness of his tone. "I'm sorry, I shouldn't have called. I just got scared." She started to cry.

"Kara, ask someone there for the address."

Getting back on the train felt impossible. She had to steady herself just to remain upright, and she could still feel her intestines cramping. She got the address from a man with a strong Russian accent and gave it to Danny.

The old woman flushed and opened the bathroom door. The smell, however, changed Kara's mind about going inside. Instead, she found an empty stool and ordered a cup of tea. Most stalkers were actually harmless, weren't they?

CHAPTER TEN

Alex drove under the speed limit. Patches of ice covered the road. She and Sean took turns opening the office at eight a.m., and today was hers. Unfortunately, she and Vanessa had stayed up until three in the morning before the night nurse convinced them to go home. Now Alex was way late, again.

It took forty minutes to get from home to their White Plains office during the morning rush. At nine thirty, however, traffic was light and she made it in thirty. The parking lot was full so she pulled into a *Visitors Only* spot. A quick glance in the rearview mirror confirmed she looked as poorly as she felt: dark smudges outlined bloodshot eyes; their violet irises faded. She grabbed her tangled hair and, using a rubber band she found in the cup holder, pulled it into a ponytail. It would have to do.

McCormick and Lawrence Graphic Designs shared space with thirty other small businesses in a multitenant office building just off the Hutchinson River Parkway at the intersection of the Cross Westchester Expressway. The rent was a little pricey, but it was a good address that gave the business legitimacy. Alex took the stairs, hurried down the hall, and pushed open the front door.

Sean was sitting at Gracie's desk—she was their half-time receptionist, customer-service rep, and office manager. He glanced up from the computer screen. "Nice of you to drop by."

"Good morning," Alex said, ignoring his sarcasm.

A former college basketball player, Sean still appeared fit at fifty years old. He was handsome in an unkempt sort of way, the 1800s swirl of his mustache adding panache. They had met when Alex was a graduate student at NYU's Wagner Business School. She interned for the firm where Sean worked, and they had hit it off even though he criticized her more than he complimented her. He had a good eye and strong technical skills, and he said that Alex had a lot of "creative promise." He became her mentor. It was only natural that when Alex decided to hang her shingle, she sought out Sean for advice. This led to a revelation that Sean had always wanted to work for himself, and thus the birth of their little company.

Whenever Alex complained about Sean to Vanessa, which was often, her sister pronounced him dull, untalented, and a drag on the business. "You're the franchise; you don't need him." None of that was true. Alex was good at marketing and graphic design, and Sean provided most of the technical expertise and made sure the invoices got out on time. He dealt with all things financial and unpleasant. He balanced her out.

He could also be her knight, coming to her rescue more than once over the years. Alex recalled an incident from just a few months ago. She had been sitting at her desk trying to solve a complex design problem. Deep in thought, she was toying with a crystal bear Gracie had given her for her birthday. On the umpteenth toss, just as a solution came to mind, the bear slipped from her hand, hit the edge of the desk, and shattered. Alex bent to the floor to retrieve the pieces, and as she lifted one of the larger shards, she noticed droplets of blood pulsing from her wrist. Perhaps it was the amount of blood, or the childhood memory of her mother's cut wrists, that made her knees buckle. The glass slivers and chunks she'd just picked up slipped from her fingers. She must have cried out as she hit the floor because the next thing she remembered was Sean lifting her and racing down the stairs as she drifted in and out of consciousness.

"Stay awake, kiddo, don't pass out on me." He'd kicked open the outer door with his foot.

Once in his car, they zigzagged through traffic to the hospital. Sean had one hand on the steering wheel and the other on her throbbing wrist, staunching the blood flow.

"Did you hear the one about the guy who asked why golf is called golf? Because *oh shit* was taken . . . Did you watch *Jimmy Fallon* last night? Let me see if I can remember how it went."

They laughed a lot that night. Sean didn't even know how hilarious he was. In the past, he'd made her laugh so hard her stomach ached, but not because the stories he told were funny. He botched most jokes—rushed them, forgot the punch lines. It was just that he tried so hard. Sometimes he acted out all of the parts, jumped around in uncoordinated abandon. That night he stayed with her, convinced the doctors she hadn't tried to kill herself, drove her home, and spent the night on the couch, just in case.

Other times, he did just the right thing in his own peculiar way. After a difficult fight with her mother last week, Sean offered an imitation of Judy that was spot on. By the end of it, Alex had forgotten how upset she'd been.

Sean now cleared his throat loud enough to bring Alex back to the present.

"I know you're worried. I'll call Jonas."

"You mean you didn't call him yesterday?"

"Damn it, Sean, ease up."

"He's practically our only client."

"I've got a lot going on."

Sean curled his lips under so that all she could see was the oversized mustache.

"I'm sorry, okay? I need a little sympathy. I'll call him."

"Fine," he said, drawing out the vowel sound. "So how is your father?"

Alex sat down at her desk and swiveled her chair so she partially faced Sean. "They're running tests." She powered up her computer. "I better read my e-mail and get to this Frankel job." His silence made her turn back to him. He looked hurt. "We can talk at lunchtime, okay?"

Without a word, Sean left her office. It was quite confusing. Most of the time, Alex wasn't sure what she had said or did to make him upset.

She picked up her phone and called her father's private number at the hospital.

"When are you coming back?" her mother demanded.

"After work, around—"

"I can't manage these disrespectful people. You need to be here now."

"Mom, who's being disrespectful?"

"The helper people, I just told you."

Alex knew this conversation would not advance in a productive manner, so she promised to speak with the head nurse when she visited later that day. Then she hung up. No way was she going to call the nurse with her mother's complaint. "*Helper people*, jeez," she muttered to herself.

Next, Alex read and responded to all of her urgent e-mails. It was eleven a.m. before she had a chance to call Jonas Frankel. But she called Martin Dawes instead.

"Well, Alexandra, to what do I owe this pleasant surprise?"

Martin Dawes and her father had been friends since law school, so he knew Alex before she was "a fully formed thought," as he was fond of saying nearly every time he saw her.

"I need your help, and my dad suggested I call you."

"I'll do my best."

"He asked me to find my half-sister, the one he put up for adoption." There was a long pause on the other end. "Mr. Dawes, are you still there?"

She could imagine his shocked expression. Formal in his manner, Martin Dawes reminded Alex of a prep school head-master on an ivy-covered New England campus.

He harrumphed a couple of times before he responded: "Why would your father make such a request?"

He clearly thought she was making this up. She explained about his heart attack, that this was a sickbed wish, and her plan to start with the house in the Bronx. "It's important to him," she concluded. "Please help us, my dad said he could always count on you." She couldn't believe she'd used the *count on you* phrase. She hoped it didn't irritate Mr. Dawes as much as it did her.

"Heart attack? How is he doing?"

"Touch and go; I'm sure he'll be okay." Her voice caught.

Papers shuffled. She could almost hear him weighing her news. Finally, he cleared his throat again. "Of course, let me get you the particulars and I'll e-mail you this afternoon. Would that be satisfactory?"

"I really appreciate it, thank you." Alex drew a deep breath.

"Is there something else?"

"As a matter of fact." She hadn't intended to quiz him; confidentiality was his middle name, but she needed to understand. "Do you know how all of this came about? The girl, I mean?"

"You should ask your father."

"He's not able to tell me much." This was almost true. "Lots of painkillers."

The persistant silence on the other end of the phone reminded Alex of her conversations with Sean. She waited Martin Dawes out.

"They met at a Washington event, as I recall."

Alex remembered her dad saying he'd made frequent trips to the capital.

"Your father had powerful political connections through old family ties in the beginning, but later through his own cult of personality."

"He charms everyone."

"Indeed. Anyway, he attended numerous events; the party affiliation did not matter. I believe the young woman in question worked for a New York congressman, but I don't recall who." Mr. Dawes made a nervous coughing sound before continuing, "There was never a question of him leaving your mother. Your father was, and continues to be, committed to her."

Alex had always believed that but now she was less sure— an illegitimate child was pretty damning evidence to the contrary. "Is that what he told you at the time?"

"Not in so many words."

"Why do you think he betrayed her?"

"Your father cares deeply about his family. Surely you agree, Alexandra."

Alex did not respond.

"You see, the child was African American, and that had to be a factor."

He said this as if it explained everything, but it didn't. So what? She was his blood, his daughter, just like Alex.

"And yes, your father made it clear to me, in word and deed, that your mother, your sisters, and you were his first priority."

Alex remained quiet. She leaned back in the chair, pulled out a cigarette from an old pack stashed in her desk, and rolled it between her fingers. Were there other children? Was Kara the only one he'd left behind? Was her race the reason he abandoned her? Both Aunt Peggy and Martin Dawes made it sound like the real reason, but that couldn't be true. "Please, tell me about her."

"I know very little. I sent the monthly checks for her care. That's really all I know, I'm sorry."

"Did he ever visit her?" Alex asked, thinking about the photograph she'd found.

"From time to time, I believe, in the beginning. Alex, you must ask your father these questions."

Alex thanked him, gave him her e-mail address, and hung up. The muscle under her eye pulsed.

An old photo of the Lawrence girls sat on her desk. Each of them stood slightly apart, dressed in their designer best; Alex, the tallest of the three, held Pigeon's hand and clutched a miniature purse in her other hand. Even then, Vanessa looked detached and Pigeon sad. Once again, Alex conjured up the image of the woman and the little girl, Kara. Not only did he visit her, but also, more troubling, he had taken Alex with him. Alex called Vanessa.

"Are you still up for a trip to the Bronx?" Alex passed the cigarette under her nose and breathed in its dry, sweet smell.

Out of the corner of her eye, Alex saw Sean's head poking into her office. "Everything okay with Jonas?"

She lowered the phone a fraction and whipped the cigarette behind her back. "Damn it." Then she lifted the phone back to her ear. "Oh, not you, Vanessa. Listen, I gotta go. See you at the hospital this evening." She placed the phone down slowly, reluctant to face Sean's unforgiving scowl.

"Tell me you called him."

She gave him an embarrassed shrug.

"Some of us have to make a living. Some of us don't have Daddy's money waiting in the wings."

"I can't believe you said that to me."

"As if it isn't true."

"You know the only way I get the money . . ." She couldn't finish the sentence. Sean knew she would inherit a chunk of money when her father died, but why would he bring it up at a time like this?

"I didn't mean to be insensitive." His face turned bright red. "Call him, Alex, before we have *no* work." He slammed out of her office.

Damn it. It was so easy to hurt him back. But of course he wasn't implying anything about her father dying. She pushed up from her chair to apologize to him, but halfway out the door, she stopped—the thing to do was make the call.

As she waited for a connection, she took a deep drag on her unlit cigarette. Bits of tobacco went into her mouth and made her cough.

"Jonas Frankel."

"Hi, Jonas, it's Alex."

"I expected your call yesterday, and my package today."

"My father had a heart attack."

"I'm sorry. Unfortunately, that doesn't change my financial needs."

"I'll have it for you by the end of the day."

Alex hung up, wondering how she'd manage that.

CHAPTER ELEVEN

Danny pushed into the shop, his partner close behind. Danny's hat was pulled low, his hand on the butt of his holstered gun, his jacket glistening with melted snow. He frowned, his eyes bright with concern. His partner, a short, square-shaped woman, blue-black hair tucked under her cap, checked out the shop and the people passing outside.

Kara waved and he came over.

"Let's get you out of here." He steered her to the warm squad car waiting out front, and the three of them climbed in, the female officer in the backseat.

"Kara Lawrence, Dawn Teagle."

The woman barely acknowledged the introduction.

With a notepad in hand, Danny said, "You sounded terrified on the phone . . . Tell me what happened."

Kara told him about the man at the bar, on the street, in the subway, and then today. As she explained each encounter, her anxiety rose.

"What are you doing down here?" Danny knew her school was uptown.

"I told you this morning, I had an errand to run." It felt like a lie. He stared at her. Maybe he could tell she hadn't told the whole truth, cops probably knew. She glanced away and then at her watch. "I'm going to be late for class."

"I'll drive you." The notebook snapped closed. Over his

shoulder he looked out the back window and then shoved the Crown Victoria cruiser into reverse.

There was something in his voice that made her feel bad, disappointment perhaps, as if she'd let him down.

Officer Teagle muttered, "Shit."

Kara could see the reflection of her pale, unmade-up face in the rearview mirror. Officer Teagle caught her eye.

"Waters, we'd better make time. We're way out of line here, and I'm not gonna get busted for her."

"I'm sorry. I didn't mean to cause you a problem."

"Nothing to be sorry for, Kara," Danny said. Then to his partner, "Give her a break."

The woman grunted but didn't say anything more.

Danny wove through the crowded streets and made their way uptown. Kara stared out the water-streaked window. Bits of slush accumulated along the window's edge. She went over in her mind the times the stalker had appeared: it started on Thursday, the day Zach gave her the envelope. Except she'd had the same feeling days before. She tried to remember when she'd first felt it. Was it when Zach had asked her to deliver the first package? Zach should have taken her call, he should have been the one rescuing her. Once again, her eyes filled up.

Kara missed the morning briefing at school. All the teachers from each grade met once a week to discuss the students, share their progress, discuss any special needs or worries. Kara knew each of her students well. She met with their parents or guardians on a regular basis and understood each child's likes and fears. Only once before—when she had the flu—had she missed the weekly session. But today, thirty minutes late, she'd run to her first class and plunged right into the lesson.

Now, she sat in the teacher's lounge, crammed with four

computer workstations and swivel chairs, long folding tables, and all the makings of a kitchenette. The room felt chilly. Kara pulled her sweater tighter around her shoulders. Her cell phone rang.

"Baby, what happened this morning? Sam said you didn't show up."

"I called you, Zach. Twice."

Joyce, the receptionist, stuck her head through the door. "Want some company?"

Kara gestured to her phone.

Joyce, gold earrings swinging, mouthed, *Is it him?*

Kara nodded yes. Kara and Joyce were friends. Not to the point of sharing secrets, of course, but enough to let Joyce know she was seeing someone special.

"When did you call?" Zach asked.

His surprise sounded genuine—the secretary hadn't told him. With only a slight quaver in her voice, Kara managed to tell him about her morning.

"Oh, princess, I'm so sorry; you must have been terrified. But this is all crazy. Why would anyone follow you? Are you sure?"

"I am. Too many coincidences, don't you think?"

"Listen, baby, let's have dinner tonight and talk about this. I'll send a car for you just to be safe."

"I'm exhausted."

"We'll have the dinner we missed last night. I should have stayed with you all evening. I kept thinking I should be with you, gazing into those golden eyes of yours, instead of sitting in meetings."

"Maybe."

"It's decided. We're not taking any chances. The car will pick you up from school at five, that'll give us plenty of time. And Kara, bring the envelope, okay?"

Joyce, still in the doorway, peered over her sandwich. Not eavesdropping exactly, but watching Kara.

"Okay."

"I love you."

"I love you too."

The minute Kara hung up, Joyce said, "Well, Miss Popular, Danny called you at the front desk. That's what I came in to tell you."

"Danny?"

"He wanted to know if you were doing all right. I told him you were fine." She handed Kara a pink message slip. "Why wouldn't you be okay?"

"It's nothing."

"Doesn't sound like nothing."

"I had a scare this morning, that's all."

"Two men worried about you. Sounds like a good day to me."

Zach and Kara sat across from each other holding hands. The restaurant thrummed with the conversations of the after-work crowd, interrupted by occasional bursts of laughter. Kara rubbed her thumb across the hairs on the back of Zach's hand. He slipped out of her grasp, brought her left hand to his lips, and kissed each fingertip.

"Was your salmon good?" he teased, his plate still half-full.

Kara ate fast—a leftover habit from foster care. She used to have to eat with her shoulders hunched, arms practically wrapped around the plate, to protect the contents from the bigger kids. She'd had to work hard at slowing down. "Guess so," she replied, matching his light tone.

"I tried to make it special for you."

"Everything was excellent, and the Fumé Blanc superb."

Their waiter refilled their water glasses. Live piano music

floated over the chatter, lavender orchids and votive candles decorated the table.

"Are you feeling better?" He held her hand again, his blue eyes intense, roaming across her face as if searching for clues.

"Much."

Zach always made her feel good. Well, most times. Kara took another sip of wine.

"Do you want to tell me about the man you think is following you? Are you up for that?"

She stalled. "I'm easily spooked these days." How could she ask him about the envelope and his friend Sam without sounding suspicious, as if she didn't trust him—which she did, but maybe she was too trusting. Maybe Sam was a bad person.

"I noticed." He cocked his head to one side. "But just in case there is something to all this, tell me about him. Can you describe him?"

She bit her lower lip.

"Humor me." He sat back and crossed his arms.

"Last night, right before you arrived, I saw him at the bar, mean eyes staring at me from the entrance. He didn't bother me or anything," she said quickly, in response to his expression.

"I should have stayed."

"It's okay, really."

"What happened next?"

"He was on the street; tall, narrow face, buzz cut."

She'd gone over this so many times now, first in her own mind and then for Danny. "He was on the subway, and then near my house. Finally, this morning, he was in the doorway of Sam's building. That's when I called you."

Zach appeared to listen intently.

"Danny came and got me."

"How did your cop friend get into the picture?"

"I called him after I couldn't reach you."

His tone changed. "Poor baby," he stroked her cheek, "it sounds like a string of coincidences to me."

"That many?"

"Well, if you'd taken a taxi, like you promised—"

"I should have."

"Anyway, it all sounds harmless."

She stayed quiet. Why dismiss it? It probably was harmless, but he didn't know that. She could feel herself getting angry and hurt.

The waiter dropped off the check, and Zach quickly paid in cash. "Let's get out of here. Can we go someplace, spend a little private time?"

"Sure," she said, after an almost imperceptible hesitation. This was Zach's way of asking her to make love.

He stared at her. "Don't do me any favors."

Her voice brightened. "I'm just tired. Sure, absolutely."

Huddled closely together, they walked uptown. Zach kept an apartment on the Upper East Side for entertaining out-of-town guests, and he took Kara there whenever he could get away from home for a few hours. The streets—filled with clusters of people on their way to and from dinner, the movies, shopping, work, home—seemed to buzz, or maybe the buzzing was in her head from all the wine. Kara bit her lower lip hard enough to hurt.

Although the precipitation had stopped, the atmosphere was still raw. Clouds from their breath rose in front of them. They walked east on 82nd Street until they reached the building. Zach scanned the lobby, then steered Kara toward the bank of elevators. The security guard gave them a perfunctory, "Good evening." Within a few seconds, Zach punched the up button four, then five times. He kept his head low and faced away from the others entering the lobby. Kara's lip swelled; she tasted blood, swallowed.

The apartment was New York small, but nice. A living and dining area led into a bedroom with a king-sized bed and not much else. The closet held two terry-cloth robes, some of Zach's clothes, and an iron and ironing board—like in a hotel. The bathroom had a glass jar filled with Q-tips, and there was an unopened bar of glycerin soap on the counter. Zach's toiletry bag rested on the sink next to it.

Kara took off her coat and shoes.

Zach pulled the drapes closed. "How about some music?" *Quiet Storm*, a smooth jazz program, was a favorite of both of theirs. "Want something to drink?" He walked into the kitchenette. "I've got diet and regular Pepsi, spring water, there's also chardonnay and Merlot." He grabbed the corkscrew and jabbed it into the Merlot.

"No thanks." Her anxiety level had reached a feverish high and she'd already had several glasses of wine in the restaurant.

Zach walked to her. "Come here, my sweet princess." He pulled her close. Large hands stroked her shoulders, slid down her back, and landed on her buttocks with a squeeze.

She let him unbutton her blouse and slip it off her shoulders. He kissed her cheek, her neck, and then her shoulder. With practiced expertise, he unsnapped her bra.

"Mmm, you taste so good." He licked under the swell of each breast and sucked her nipples.

The strong tugs brought arousal, and then the familiar unwanted fear.

Kara admonished herself: *Just breathe; this is what adults do. Zach is not Big Jim. Zach would never hurt you.* She ran her fingers through Zach's hair and took a cleansing breath.

You love him. It's going to be okay—better than okay: good. Pain stabbed behind her eyes and in her groin.

Zach slid her skirt and panties over her hips and ran his tongue across her stomach. "So good," he said, his voice muffled. He nuzzled her pubic hairs.

With eyes clamped shut, Kara held her breath. The image of Big Jim's swollen penis loomed large in her mind: its purple head towered over her like a giant steel probe. She forced images of a sandy beach, the sun on her face, waves lapping against her toes. With concentration and years of practice, she could keep the beach images strong and the menacing penis would fade. Nothing, however, kept the pain away.

His tongue danced across the curls of her pubic hair. "I love the way you smell," he moaned, burying his face in her bush.

With practiced sensuality, Kara pulled his face back up to hers. She knew how to make it work. Between kisses on his nose and lips, she asked softly, "What would you like, Zach?" She wanted to please him, to be normal—but mostly she wanted to get this part, the hardest part, over with as soon as possible. It was always easier once she took control.

He pushed her down on the bed, rubbing her breasts and squeezing her nipples. Still standing over her, he removed his shirt and tugged off his slacks and boxers, his penis bobbing free.

Kara shut her eyes as tightly as possible as he sank down next to her. He rolled onto his back and pulled her on top, his breathing fast and loud, his penis glistening with droplets of semen. She knew it was going to hurt something awful. It always did, but that wasn't his fault—it was Kara's flawed life sentence, thanks to Jim Smyth.

How come they never noticed—not Zach, not Winston,

not loser Frank, her first boyfriend? She knew the answer: she never told them, never showed them. Pretending was something Kara knew how to do well. Once, she'd brought it up to Tuesday. They had an unspoken pact about not discussing their torture, but she'd felt crippled and trapped.

"Fake it. That's what I do, and so do 90 percent of American women," Tuesday had said, sagely nodding her head. "It's all overrated anyway."

So, that's what Kara did. There were many ways to make it bearable.

"Let me take care of you," she said in a husky voice.

Zach moaned, closed his eyes, and let her.

CHAPTER TWELVE

Although it was only four p.m., the sky outside Alex's office window was as dark as midnight. She flexed her cramped fingers, closed her eyes, and rotated her neck—trying to ease the tension. She still had another five or six hours of work to do.

The phone rang. Gracie had long since left for the weekend so Sean must have picked it up. Half a minute later, Alex could hear him making concerned sounds into the mouthpiece. It was probably Jonas checking up on her progress.

Sean walked into her office, the phone against his chest. "It's your Dad."

"On the phone?"

"He's had another heart attack. Your aunt needs you and Vanessa to get there as soon as you can."

Alex sagged. *Dear God, please don't let my daddy die.* She'd been speaking with God—the God she wasn't sure she believed in—quite a bit lately.

Sean squatted beside her. "It'll be okay, Alex. I'll drive you there."

She let him hold her, let the weight of the past two days soak into his sweatered shoulder. It felt good to let go and let someone else be responsible, even for just a few minutes.

The moment passed. "I'm fine now. I can drive myself, but thanks. I need to find Vanessa." She snatched a tissue from the box on her desk and blew her nose. "Call Jonas. I know he'll be disappointed but you can check out what I've completed so far—it's all here on my desk."

Without waiting for a reply, she waved a low fluttering goodbye, and left.

It had been four hours since they'd taken Worth into the operating room. Four hours and no word. Alex shredded a cigarette in her pocket.

"Do these doctors even know what they're doing?" Her mother had repeated this question with ever-increasing volume for the past two hours. "It's not like this is New York. We're in the boonies up here at the mercy of doctors who barely speak English."

Alex glanced around to see who might have heard. A brown-skinned man in blue scrubs with shiny black hair walked past. She hoped he hadn't heard her mother.

Judy plowed on, her voice loud enough for him to turn around: "If I had been with him when this happened, I would have gotten him to Mount Sinai or Columbia Presbyterian. But this is what he gets."

"Mom."

Vanessa put down her cell phone and walked over to their mother. "Dr. Minter is one of the best cardiologists in the country, Judy."

"Then what is he doing at this hospital?"

"I checked him out," Vanessa said in the stern tone she'd inherited from Judy, "and lower your voice. You're embarrassing all of us."

"What do you know, Miss Never-been-sick-a-day-in-your-life?"

Vanessa threw up her hands.

"You stay downtown, barely finding time for your parents—

those same parents, I might add, who paid for twelve years at Brearley and four years at Vassar."

Alex tried to remember a time when there were no arguments or drama, but she couldn't think of a single day. When she got married, if she ever did, there would be no fighting or yelling. Probably, she'd never marry. None of her sisters would either—why would they want to?

"I'm getting some coffee. Do you want something, Judy?"

The part that always puzzled Alex was how unperturbed both her mother and Vanessa were after a spat. There her sister was, dressed in a cream-colored suede suit that probably cost two thousand dollars, unruffled and pulled together, offering to get her mother a cup of coffee. Alex knew her mother would respond in kind.

"No thank you, dear. I'll just sit and rest here awhile."

The storm was over for the next ten minutes, fifteen if Alex was lucky.

She often wondered why the three sisters had turned out so differently. In many ways, she was the classic firstborn: dutiful, needing to please parents who hadn't gotten the hang of parenting yet. By the time Vanessa arrived, they had settled in. Vanessa was disdainful of them, not needing their approval the way Alex did. On the other hand, although she fought with their mother constantly, Vanessa stayed close and went along in the end. Pigeon was the real rebel—she rejected everything their parents wanted, including college. Now she was off to California with some musician. Alex held her head in her hands.

"Don't be so dramatic, Alex. Nothing is that bad."

They sat together quietly for several minutes.

"Mom, can I ask you something . . . sensitive?" Alex eventually said.

"You can ask me anything, you know that."

Alex must have made a face.

"Didn't I always tell you that no topics were off limits?"

Alex remembered asking many "off limits" questions and receiving unsatisfactory answers. When she was seven or eight years old she had asked, *Mom, who do you love best: Daddy, Nessie, Pigeon, or me?* The answer came swiftly: *None of you best, what a silly question.* Or the time Vanessa had walked in on their parents having sex one Sunday morning and Judy fainted. When the undeterred Vanessa had asked about it later, their mother's response was, *Busybodies get ignored.* The most typical reply to an unwanted question was, *Wild girls with no manners end up unmarried, alone, and poor.*

Nevertheless, Alex felt compelled to try: "Daddy told me about the child he put up for adoption."

Judy blinked several times. "There are things cultured people do not discuss; this is one of them."

"I need to know about her," Alex ventured. Finding out more had become increasingly important for reasons she herself didn't fully understand. The urgency was for her father's sake, but the interest and importance had become personal. "I'm not trying to hurt you. It was a long time ago. Why can't we talk about it?"

Her mother sat motionless. When she faced her daughter, she was frowning. "Today may be your father's last day on earth. We are not going to discuss the whores in his life, the bastard child he fathered, or the way he neglected and mistreated his family."

Why would Alex think this conversation could go any other way?

"We are going to remember all of the good things, and she, my dear, is not among them."

Dr. Minter approached them. "Mrs. Lawrence."

All of the clichés turned out to be real. Alex could feel her heart in her throat; she could barely swallow.

"He's resting comfortably. We just have to wait and see."

The doctor's eyes were bloodshot, his scrubs soiled. A surgical mask dangled from his ears and chin. In manner and tone, questions were not invited.

"You may look in on him in the recovery room. The rest of the family can see him once he returns to his room."

Dr. Minter shook Judy's hand and left.

Her mother cried, at first tiny sniffles, and then body-wracking sobs. Alex put her arms around Judy and let tears of relief flow.

CHAPTER THIRTEEN

The next day a taxi brought Kara to the First Avenue address. It was late morning, still cloudy but with slivers of sun, less chilly than the night before. Although it was Saturday, people packed the stores and streets. Kara paid the cab driver from the fifty dollars Zach had pressed on her the night before—a rare occurrence. It still felt wrong to take the money, especially since he gave it to her soon after they'd made love. But the scare from yesterday left her feeling vulnerable, so she'd accepted.

She paid the driver and asked him to wait.

The brightly lit lobby appeared deserted. Kara cleared her throat. Somewhere, behind closed doors, machines hummed.

A security guard dressed in a pressed navy uniform approached her. "May I help you?"

"Sam Westin, please. He's expecting me."

The guard went behind a stand near the bank of elevators and punched several numbers into his phone. "Your name?" He sounded bored.

"Kara Lawrence." She belatedly wondered if she should have asked Zach to give Westin a false name. Or she should have worn a hat to cover her distinctive curls, and maybe sunglasses. People always remembered her eyes. This line of thought made her feel guilty. There was nothing illegal or immoral going on beacause Zach would never ask her to do something that could hurt her.

The guard lifted his chin in the direction of the elevators. "Go on up. It's the third floor, suite 302."

Sam Westin swung open his office door the minute she stepped off the elevator and motioned her inside. Two rows of empty desks made a corridor down the center of the room. A copy machine, coffee maker, and refrigerator were jammed into one corner, and a paper shredder cranked through several documents.

Sam was shorter than Kara's six feet. A fringe of gray hair circled his otherwise bald dome. His round eyes were bright brown, and a neat black—and obviously dyed—mustache outlined his upper lip.

He closed the door and gestured for her to follow him into the room.

Kara handed him the manila envelope. "So," she said, trying to sound casual, "this is going to be better than the first, you think?" She wanted him to believe she was in on whatever the deal was.

He eyed her; Kara kept her gaze steady.

"Yeah, I think so."

She tilted her head with interest. "You do okay on the last one?"

He ripped open the envelope and grunted an affirmative.

"Me too."

He chuckled.

"Of course, not as well as our mutual friend, but good enough."

He flipped through the papers and then stopped on one. Kara tried to make out the upside-down words, but couldn't.

Seeming to notice her interest, Sam gathered the pages and returned them to the envelope. Then, with his arm on her elbow, he steered her back toward the door. "Thanks for the delivery. When you see our friend, tell him I said thanks."

"I will." She faced him. "How long before it all comes together?"

"Couple of days, I guess. Make sure you pick up a *Wall Street Journal* and keep an eye out." Westin winked at her, hand on the doorknob.

Kara stepped through the threshold and asked the question she'd wanted to ask for days: "You don't think we'll get caught?" If this was legal, on the up and up, then his answer should be one of surprise or puzzlement.

"Nah, there's no direct path." He frowned. "You were careful, right?" He broke eye contact and peered up and down the hall. "Right?"

"Absolutely." Her heart bounced against her rib cage.

Kara hurried down the hall, took the stairs to the lobby, and went out the front door. She waved to the waiting taxi. Her anxiety remained at threat level orange as the driver took her back to Harlem. She thought about the conversation with Westin. There was no mistaking it—Zach and Westin were doing something illegal, and now she was involved. She clenched and unclenched her hands. The minute she got home, she would confront Zach. What would she say? It was important not to accuse him of anything. She replayed the conversation again in her mind. Maybe there was a simple explanation. It sounded shady, but maybe it was just business and they were cautious because of enemies. If that were the case, then why would he say there was no direct path? She knew why.

As the cab made a right onto her street, Kara saw the flashing lights of a police car parked in front of her brownstone. An officer stood behind a crooked line of yellow posts that blocked their way.

"Lady, I gotta let you out here." The cab driver sounded irritated.

Kara settled the bill and gave him a large tip, which was what Zach would have done, and it was his money. She climbed out of the taxi. People stood around in small clusters on the opposite side of the street from her house, small children darting around. A woman much younger than Kara held a baby on her hip; she grabbed one of the running boys.

"Excuse me, officer." Kara approached a middle-aged street cop in a bulky jacket. "I live here. What's going on?"

"There's been a homicide. You got ID?"

She dug out her driver's license, something she used only for ID since she didn't own a car. He scrutinized her face and waved her through the barricade. The sky was lighter than when she had left as the wind-nudged storm clouds had uncovered the sun.

The young woman with the baby on her hip said to an older woman wearing a tightly twisted scarf on her head, "I can't believe this happened."

"Can happen anywhere. I don't let my kids outta my sight."

Kara approached her home, spotting Danny and his partner talking to some of the neighbors.

"Hi."

Danny swung around. "Hey, girl, you doing okay?"

"What's happened? Is Mrs. E. all right?"

His face scrunched. "Mrs. E.? Yeah, she's inside." Then his expression registered understanding. "She's fine. They shot a kid—ten-year-old boy. Looks like an innocent caught a stray; we're waiting for the homicide guys."

Relief swept through her. Then she felt horrible because a child was dead. "What's his name?"

"Barry White, believe it or not."

Kara felt her knees sag.

"You know him?"

"He was one of my students. He lives in the group home on 127th. What was he doing over here?"

"Don't know."

"He was a good boy." A picture of his sweet face took shape—one of the children her imaginary fund would help. She'd signed up for DonorChoose.org, the online charity that helps teachers buy supplies. "Barry wrote the nicest thank you note with illustrations and—"

Danny grabbed her just as she began to sink. "Let's get you inside." He led her to their stoop. "You gonna be okay?"

"It's so unfair."

"Yeah."

She sat down.

"So, no folks?"

"Waters," Danny's partner Dawn interrupted, glaring at Kara.

"I gotta go talk to more neighbors, find out if anyone saw anything." He raised his hand to Dawn, two fingers asking for time. "I'll be back as soon as I can. We'll find the idiot who did this."

Kara watched the two officers move into the crowd.

Sweet Barry White. Who would hurt him? Danny had called him an innocent. He was. She stood and trudged up the steps to the door, pulled out her keys. The neighborhood was quiet, safe. With trembling hands, she shoved the key into the lock. Could Barry's murder have anything to do with her stalker? The door cracked open. Hairs on the nape of her neck rose—she turned. There he was, standing among the throng of black and brown neighbors, the man from the street and the subway. This time he was in a jogging suit, with a red sweatband encircling his head.

Kara searched frantically for Danny in the crowd but he'd moved farther down the block, out of earshot. The man appeared unconcerned that she'd seen him. He stood there watching, as if he was waiting for her to do something.

"Is that you, Kara?" Mrs. E. called from somewhere inside the house. "Come inside and close that door."

Without thinking, Kara ignored her and walked down the steps, her keys still in her hand. She was so tired of being afraid. All her life, she'd been frightened: afraid of her mother's illness, and then her grandma's; afraid of the children at the group homes; afraid her family would never come and claim her; afraid no one would ever adopt her; and, mostly, afraid of Big Jim Smyth. Well, this man, this stalker, was not going to intimidate her anymore. She wasn't sure if Barry White's murder was motivating her, or if there was even a connection, but it didn't matter. She moved around the barricades and crossed the street. Out of the corner of her eye, she saw a uniformed cop approaching her.

"Hey you, get back."

Kara kept walking.

The jogger had his arms crossed in front of his chest, legs spread wide. He stood a few feet from a small group of elderly neighbors who were friends with Mrs. E. The cop must not have cared too much because he didn't interfere as Kara moved toward the jogger, her blood pumping. Then an amazing thing happened: without breaking eye contact, the man backed up. Determined not to lower her gaze, Kara stared, in what she hoped was an angry, unafraid expression. In spite of the cold, sweat trickled from her armpits, but Kara didn't stop. The man backed up faster, bumped into one of the women, muttered sorry, and then turned and jogged away from the crowd. She saw him round the corner onto Lenox Avenue, the wide boulevard half a block away. For several moments, she watched the corner, saw the traffic light change from green to yellow to red. Should she follow him? Her body answered her. Now that the immediate danger had passed, so did her courage. Her mouth had gone dry, and her heart was still racing. She took a deep breath. It still had felt good, even for just a few minutes. It had felt powerful.

Kara walked back to the house. It was time to confront Zach.

As Kara put the kettle on, the doorbell rang and the grandfather clock chimed four o'clock. Although the sun hadn't quite set, it was pretty dark out, so she had already switched on all the lights in the house, which comforted her. She walked to the front door curious rather than worried, cracked it—leaving on the chain so that no one could force their way inside—and peered into a face she knew well.

This time he was dressed in a navy-blue suit. No sign of the jogging outfit or gray raincoat—an unbuttoned black topcoat had taken its place. Up close she could see his buzz cut was sprinkled with gray, and his eyes—the dark eyes that had stared at her in the bar—were inquisitive, and more intelligent than evil. Standing next to him was another man, shorter, also dressed in a navy suit, with a white shirt, striped burgundy tie, and open topcoat. He had smooth Asian features marred by a jagged scar on his left cheek.

The temperature had dropped. Kara pulled her sweater tighter around her shoulders and waited for him to explain himself.

"Good evening, Ms. Lawrence." He held up a large identification pack encased in plastic. "I'm Special Agent Boyd, and this is Special Agent Woo. May we come in?"

The FBI. Kara scrutinized the photos and then the faces of the men. Whatever trouble Zach was in, it was bad—and she was in it too. She removed the door chain, stepped back, and let them enter.

The courage she'd felt a few hours earlier didn't surge back as she led them into the living room. "May I take your coats? Would you like some water? I have the kettle on, would you prefer tea?" Without waiting for an answer, she left them in the living room and walked into the kitchen. Over her shoulder she said, "I'm sorry we don't have any real coffee. Would you like some instant?"

"Ms. Lawrence," Special Agent Woo spoke in a commanding voice, "we don't want anything, thank you." They were standing in the center of the living room, still wearing their topcoats. "We only need a few minutes of your time."

Kara lifted her head and squared her shoulders.

"We have reason to believe," Special Agent Boyd said, "that Mr. Zachary Lowe is involved in insider trading, along with a man named Sam Westin." Steam hissed from the radiator. "We're not sure how many others are involved—we're hoping you can tell us."

Special Agent Woo approached her, stepping into her personal space. "Do you want to sit down?"

"No." She brushed strands of hair from her eyes.

"We've been following you for some time."

Kara tried to swallow but her throat had closed. She forced her mouth open to breathe.

Agent Boyd watched her. Said nothing, didn't move.

Should she "lawyer up," as they said on cop shows, and demand to see her lawyer? What attorney? Maybe she should wait for Danny to come home, tell the agents she had a friend who was a police officer. She took a deep breath, hoping they couldn't sense her fear, but she knew that generating alarm was their intention.

Agent Boyd said, "I know you were aware of us. We wanted you to know we were there. We have times, dates, photographs."

Of what? She hadn't done anything.

"We need your help," he continued.

Agent Woo walked around the living room, as if searching for something.

"There is nothing you can do to help Mr. Lowe," said Agent Boyd in a matter-of-fact voice. "We know what he did, it's just a matter of time before we arrest him. We need to know the names of his accomplices."

Kara found her voice. "I didn't do anything wrong."

"Everybody's always innocent. Funny how that goes."

Special Agent Boyd's eyes darkened. They now had the menacing quality Kara remembered from the bar. "Tell us the truth, Ms. Lawrence: you're either guilty or you'll be a protected informant. You need to decide and you need to do it now."

The front door slammed shut and Danny strode into the room. "Boy, what a mess. Whole neighborhood's on edge." He pulled up abruptly. "What's going on?" His hand was on the grip of his holstered gun. "Kara, you okay?"

Thank goodness he was here. At least he'd know if she needed a lawyer. Kara's face flushed. What would he think of her, getting into trouble with the FBI because of Zach?

Agent Boyd ignored Danny's entrance. "Here's my card."

Kara took it.

"Don't keep us waiting."

She examined its official lettering, his name, phone number.

"Call no later than Monday night. After midnight on Monday, both this offer and you turn into pumpkins."

"You guys on the job?" Danny asked.

"Ask Ms. Lawrence." Agent Boyd brushed past the policeman.

Agent Woo followed him, but not before turning back to Kara. "I wouldn't mention this visit to Mr. Lowe if I were you. If you do, you're as guilty as he is, and you'll be treated accordingly."

The two agents left.

"Who the hell are they? What did they want with you? Are those the guys who were following you?"

He was using his interrogator voice. Kara knew she was in real trouble, so she told Danny about the two envelopes Zach had asked her to deliver.

"What were you thinking?"

"He said it was a business deal."

"Why would you do it? He could have hired a courier, or sent someone from his office."

"I trusted him."

He paced around. "You have until Monday to do what, snitch?"

She winced.

"What happens after that?"

His words pounded down on her like the blows from out of nowhere whenever Big Jim got mad. She felt stunned and bruised. Did Danny think she was guilty of some crime? He obviously wouldn't help her now. She had to take care of herself. Without another word, Kara sprinted up the stairs.

"Wait, damn it. Let's talk about this."

She reached the third floor, ran into her bedroom, closed

and locked the door behind her. What made her think Danny would or could help her? Why should he believe her? The power she had felt earlier was not even a memory.

Kara lay down on her bed and stared at the water stain on the ceiling. All her life, the only person she could rely on was herself—except for one time. Liz Kennelly, the social worker in charge of Kara's case, had come and removed all the children from the Smyth house. She'd placed Tuesday, Flyer, and Kara in the group home, which was an awful place. But at least no one was beating and raping them.

Tears pooled. She thought about Barry White. At least Flyer, Tuesday, and Kara had each other. When bad things happened, they figured out ways to cope, to stay alive. She'd have to do that now.

Marty jumped on the bed, rubbed against her, and purred. She stroked his fur, reached for the photo of her family—her real family—pulled off her glasses, closed her eyes, and used the one coping mechanism that had worked for her all her life, like whenever Big Jim had climbed on top of her or shoved his penis her mouth. Tears brimmed over. She conjured up her imaginary life: she was with her father and Alex; her mother and grandmother were both alive and well; Tuesday was there and Flyer was healthy, happy. She remembered how warm and safe it had felt in her mother's arms, resting against the cushion of her breasts. The sun shone in her imagined world, and her father—tall and wiry, his bow-shaped lips curled into a crooked smile—came and snuggled next to them. She couldn't hear his voice, but she felt the hardness of his muscles and believed the love in his eyes. Alex crawled onto his lap too, and their father held them both close.

Kara's comfort was short-lived. Special Agent Boyd's threats shoved her fantasy world aside. Escape needed to happen in the real world this time. Kara opened her eyes. She'd have to find out the truth from Zach without letting him know about the FBI, but how?

Kara got up from the bed and changed into her workout clothes—there was too much to think about this evening; tomorrow was another day. She mounted her stationary bike. Pedaling as fast as she could, she tried not to think about anything but the next programmed hill.

CHAPTER FOURTEEN

Alex loved Saturday mornings when she could sleep in without feeling guilty. She would lie in bed, click on the television, and watch an old movie she'd seen at least fifteen times. Last Saturday she'd rewatched *Love Actually*, a story about relationships woven together with humor and pathos. Often a cold slice of Friday-night pizza and a glass of orange juice held her over until she struggled up, surveyed the chaos of her three-room apartment, and debated cleaning up or going to the gym. Most Saturdays she chose a trip to Starbucks instead.

This Saturday, however, was different. First, she had to get up early because she and Vanessa were going to the Bronx in search of Kara. Also, the day before had been rough. While her father had made it through the night without incident, the hospital staff was still cautious about his prognosis. Alex was also worried about Vanessa.

They had left the hospital together the evening before, each going to their separate cars. In spite of the raw evening air, Alex had watched her sister climb into her BMW, start the car, sink back into the leather seats, and close her eyes. Clearly unaware of Alex's scrutiny, Vanessa reached to turn on the radio, shook pills from a vial, popped them into her mouth, and washed them down with bottled water.

Ever since the incident six months earlier, Alex had become increasingly concerned about Vanessa. Watching her swallow those pills brought Alex's fears back.

Vanessa worked as a personal shopper for some of New York's wealthiest men. She found just the right clothes for them, their wives, and their girlfriends, at the very best stores. Tailors accompanied her to her clients' homes, making adjustments on the spot. Business boomed. On the downside, Vanessa was having an affair with one of those customers, George Arthur, a divorced corporate executive who was three times married.

One night last September, Vanessa and George had a fight, a rare occurrence in Vanessa's orderly world. In fact, Alex couldn't remember ever hearing Vanessa raise her voice. It wasn't worth it, according to Vanessa. Their mother always screamed; Vanessa opted for quiet control. Not this time.

Alex had received a frantic call in the middle of the night.

"Come get me." Vanessa's words were slurred.

Alex had picked up her alarm clock and peered at it—three o'clock in the morning. "What's the matter? Where are you?"

"In the street."

"What street?" Alex sat up and tried to focus. "Are you hurt?" Vanessa sounded drunk. Alex expected this kind of behavior from Pigeon but not from the middle sister.

Alex dragged on her sweats and went to pick up her sister. It was an obscure location but Alex's GPS got her there. She'd found Vanessa sitting on the dirt road, her heels and shredded stockings in her hands, the neon lights of the blues bar—the letters *u* and *r* missing—blinking in the background.

During the ride back, Vanessa explained that she and George had gone away for the weekend. On the way back to Manhattan, he'd asked her to move in with him. "We're alike, you and I—eyes wide open. I know I'm older than you, by many years, but we're cut from the same bolt of cloth. World wise, sure about who we are." He had pulled over and stopped the car, turned in his seat, and reached for her.

"What are you talking about?" Vanessa jerked away from him. "Why are you messing everything up?"

"I'm trying to make a commitment, to say something important."

"Don't bother." She'd opened the car door. "Men don't make commitments. They just use words and play out their own selfish shit."

"How can you say that?"

"I'm not like your other women, and I'm nothing like you." She'd climbed out of the car. "If you ever want to see me again, never bring this up."

Vanessa walked for at least a mile in the middle of nowhere, in three-inch heels on a deserted road, with no idea where she was going.

George trailed along for a while. He'd begged her to get back in the car, but she'd kept walking. When she reached the blues bar, George drove off.

In the bar, Vanessa met a guitar player. They'd gotten high on speed and had sex in the back of his truck, her skirt hiked up and legs wrapped around his waist. She'd sworn to Alex this was the first time she'd ever done anything like that, including taking drugs. She'd promised, slumped against the door of Alex's Jeep, that she'd never do it again. Last night, watching Vanessa pop pills in her BMW, rattled Alex's confidence in her.

The phone rang, bringing Alex back to the present—it better not be Vanessa calling to cancel. Caller ID told her it was Pigeon.

"I'm so glad to hear from you." Alex had been up long enough to shower and find an outfit still wrapped in plastic

from the cleaners. She took a deep drag on a phantom cigarette. "It must be early in LA."

"I couldn't sleep."

Alex tugged her fingers through her matted curls; she
needed a haircut. She knew she was using her mother's singsong voice and tried to sound more normal. "So why can't you
sleep?"

Pigeon's response was wet and husky, the way people
sound when their salvia goes down their windpipe. "Yesterday was such a crazy day, nothing like I thought it'd be."
Alex waited. "There were so many of them. I can't keep them
straight."

"This is Cool Breeze's family?"

"Yeah—his cousins, aunts, uncles, sisters and brothers,
nieces. They cook together and everyone talks at once except
nobody gets mad."

"And this is a *bad* thing?"

Pigeon didn't joke back. "They're regular, Alex. The kind
of family we used to pretend to be when we were kids."

Alex walked into the kitchenette. She needed coffee. She
rummaged through the refrigerator. "So why isn't it great, being with a family like that?" Her hand snagged an orange juice
that had expired a week ago. "Do they like you?" She opened
the carton and sniffed.

Pigeon's voice dropped to a whisper: "I guess."

Alex poured as she glanced at the clock on the microwave. Vanessa would be there any minute. "Help me understand what's wrong."

"It's Breeze—he's really sweet with me and his mom is nice."

Juice in hand, Alex walked back into her bedroom. "So?"

"She's a giant and kind of a hippie."

"A giant, you mean taller than I am?"

"Bigger. She dresses in long skirts and has a braid down to her butt. When we landed, she grabbed me and hugged me. I just met her and she's already welcoming me to the family."

Alex could picture Mrs. Cole, dressed in tie-dye, holding onto to little Pigeon, who wouldn't know where to put her arms. "What's so terrible about all of this? Is Cool Breeze pushing you to get married or something?"

"No . . ."

"Do you like them?"

"It's complicated."

"Give me the number where I can reach you." Alex searched around for a pen and paper, finding them on her dresser under some bills that needed attention. "Vanessa will be here any minute, we have something important—" She caught herself. This was not the time to tell Pigeon about Kara. "I really want to discuss this with you, though. Can I call you back later?"

"How's Daddy doing?"

"Okay, he's holding his own." She would give Pigeon a better update later, not now.

"I think I love him."

"Daddy?"

"Breeze."

"You just met him." The doorbell rang; confident it was Vanessa, Alex pushed the buzzer that unlocked the lobby door. "If you want to come home, I can send you money."

"Thanks, but I'm okay, I'm just all mixed up."

Someone pounded on Alex's door. "I'll call you back." Pigeon could be impetuous. Actually, that was an understatement— she was always winging it. "Maybe coming home would be good. Think about it." The knocking grew more insistent. "I gotta run. I love you."

Alex pulled opened her front door just as Pigeon said, "Love you too," and hung up.

Vanessa looked clear-eyed and annoyed. "It took you long enough."

"Sorry." She stepped aside to let Vanessa in. "I was talking to Pigeon—trouble in paradise."

"Let's get moving, you can tell me on the way."

"I need my coat." Alex yanked her coat off its hanger. "I did a quick search on Google, LinkedIn, and Facebook."

"For Kara?"

"Yeah. Just in case she's still a Lawrence. You know, maybe the people who adopted her kept her name."

"That doesn't make sense."

"There are a lot of them—one's an author, they all blog and tweet. None seemed to fit."

Vanessa pursed her lips. "I'm hoping this grandmother has the answer so we can put this behind us." She gave Alex a once-over. "You look nice." She sounded surprised.

Alex had made an effort to look professional. She wanted Kara's grandmother to trust her, so she wore a black pantsuit and a cobalt-blue collared shirt—an "ask for the order" outfit she used for sales pitches. She'd put on makeup—foundation, lip gloss, and mascara—something she seldom did. Her tumble of curls looked tidy tied back in a ponytail. Vanessa, of course, was dressed in a perfectly tailored camel coat and Alex knew that underneath was a designer outfit.

Alex shrugged into her nondescript winter coat. "I want to make a good impression."

"In the Bronx?"

Alex laughed aloud, which felt good and unusual. She laughed far too infrequently. Ninety percent of the time, she was worried about something—her father, work, Pigeon, Vanessa, her mother. Now she added one more person to the list. Kara Whatever-her-new-name-was.

CHAPTER FIFTEEN

The familiar ring tone of her cell phone pierced the air. Eyes stinging from sweat, she grabbed it. It was Zach.

"Hey, babe, how'd you make out today?"

At first, Kara thought he had learned about the visit from the FBI. Relief swept over her. It was going to be all right, it was a mistake; Zach would fix it.

"You got the envelope to Sam, right?"

He was checking up on her. She rubbed the sweat from her eyes.

"Did you deliver it?"

"I did. But I had a bad feeling about it." Kara paused, waiting for Zach to say something, but there was only quiet from the other end. "Is everything . . ." she searched for the right words, "on the up and up?"

"What kind of question is that?"

Zach seemed to be whispering into the phone. In the background, she could hear the clattering of dishes and the high-pitched voices of young children—he was at home. A new sadness descended upon her.

"I'm worried. Sam implied . . . Well, do you think you can trust him?"

"Implied what? What are you trying to say?"

Distant laughter came over the phone line. Kara heard a woman say, "Stop it." A child responded, and more peals of laughter followed.

"Kara?"

"I'm still here."

"Meet me at the apartment in one hour, we can talk then." His whisper was urgent.

Kara didn't want to go. Maybe the FBI would follow her there. "Why not now, on the phone?"

His tone changed, his voice turned warm, soft. "Now's not a good time." Then, sounding vulnerable, the way he sounded when he talked about his kids, he said, "Listen, sweetheart, I can tell you're upset. I am too. It's funny, you asking me about Sam. I'm worried about him, like maybe he's not playing straight with me."

It was Sam, not Zach. "That's what I was thinking."

"Baby, I need your help on this one. If something's going on—and it's probably nothing—we should compare notes, think this through together. Please, baby. I need you."

The FBI could have it wrong. Sam Westin was probably the one doing something illegal. "I'm not sure."

"Talking to you really helps me."

Could she sneak out and make sure the agents weren't following her? Was that even a good idea?

"I wouldn't ask if it wasn't important. Give me an hour and then meet me at the apartment."

"Sam made it sound like you knew exactly what was going on."

"Trust me. One hour."

Kara caved. "Okay."

She disconnected the call. The phone was wet with perspiration. Kara rubbed her hands against her black workout shorts and took several deep breaths. Why would Sam have said *we* each time he spoke about the deal, as if Zach were 100 percent in on it? On the other hand, Zach was trusting;

that's how his wife hurt him. He had believed her when she lied about where she was going, who she was with—he could have misjudged Sam too. Kara pressed her fingers against her forehead to ease the stabbing pain in her temples. Of course, Zach could be the one lying.

She walked into the bathroom, stepped into the shower, and scrubbed as hard as she could without tearing her skin. How could she uncover the truth? She toweled off, put on skin lotion, dressed, applied makeup, grabbed her tote, and went down the stairs. Danny and Mrs. E. were watching a basketball game. She could tell by their grim expressions that their beloved Knicks were losing again.

"I'll be back," she said in their general direction, not slowing down enough to invite questions. Danny called her name as the door closed behind her with a solid *thunk*.

At the corner, a gypsy cab rolled by. Kara waved it over and climbed in. She gave the driver the Upper East Side address.

"Nice night." The cabby caught her eye in the rearview mirror. "Can't wait for spring. All this cold makes my arthritis act up, you know what I'm saying?"

Kara murmured politely.

"Hurts bad. 'Course, you're too young to be worried about an old man's aches."

She nodded politely at his reflection.

"Me and the missus, we both got it, but she doesn't seem to mind as much. 'Course, she isn't driving no cab fourteen hours a day, shaking up her insides. It backs you up, if you get my drift. Kneels in church a lot though. That can hurt an arthritic knee—least that's what you'd think. But you wouldn't know it from her. She's a come-to-Jesus sort. No offense."

Kara closed her eyes, hoping he'd take the hint.

"She's always praying. Wish she'd pray me into retirement," he chuckled.

Kara kept her eyes closed and the driver finally stopped talking.

The street in front of Zach's apartment building was filled with couples and laughing families. Seeing them brought a familiar ache to Kara's stomach and moisture to her eyes. Whenever she thought about parents with their children, she felt sad. It had eased in recent years due to hard work under the gentle guidance of her psychologist, Dr. Marci Nye. But ever since Big Jim died . . . She shuddered. She had to banish him from her thoughts.

Zach was waiting. Dressed in jeans and a sweater, a ski jacket hanging from his arm, he looked rumpled.

"What's all this about?" He pushed the elevator button several times. "What made you wonder about Sam?"

Kara, her eyes wide, opened her mouth in surprise. The kind voice from the phone call was now a low growl. The elevator doors opened. Zach grabbed her arm and pulled her inside. His grip hurt.

"I'm not sure you should trust him." She tugged her arm away and rubbed it pointedly. "He said some things that worried me."

"Let's talk inside."

He walked ahead of her, reached his door, and pulled out his keys. She could see his hand trembling as she followed him inside. He dropped his jacket onto the recliner in the living room.

"Tell me exactly what happened. What did Westin say to you?"

Kara picked through her memory.

"So?" he prodded.

"After he opened the envelope, Sam said you were always careful. That you've never gotten caught." She waited, watching his expression.

"Then what?"

"Then there were those guys on the street stalking me." She described the scene outside her house during the murder investigation, failing to mention the subsequent visit by Special Agents Boyd and Woo. "They could have been anyone, but they seemed more like private detectives." It was close to the truth at least. "Could they be your competitors? You know, someone trying to learn more about your business deal?" Kara raised her eyes to his. "Is your wife suspicious, do you think?" Now she was not only lying, she was being mean. Kara could feel her cheeks getting warm.

"I doubt it's Lori," Zach replied after several beats. "It's not her style. She's up front, more likely to pitch a fit than investigate."

Kara let that piece of information settle for a second. "Wouldn't it be hard for her to accuse you, since she committed her own transgression?"

"What?"

"Since she cheated on you, she might choose to hire someone to follow me instead of confronting you." Of course, Kara knew it was the feds, but now she doubted everything Zach had said to her. Maybe he'd lied about Lori's affair.

"It's not Lori, okay." His voice was hard. Zach sank down on the couch. "Sit." He patted the seat next to him. "Sit next to me."

Still wearing her coat, she sat on the edge of the couch, her knees pressed together, her gloved hands folded in her lap.

Zach pulled his sweater over his head and tossed it next to

his jacket. In his normal voice, one that hinted at a childhood in the South, he said, "I'm thinking your first instinct is probably right. Either it's nothing, or maybe it's somebody trying to get in on our deal." He paused, pondering. "Maybe Sam is double dealing—I'll find out. Don't worry about it anymore."

Kara stayed quiet.

"I won't let anything happen to you—ever." His eyes, much warmer now than when she'd entered the lobby, searched her face. "If it's the competition, they're only trying to scare you."

"They've succeeded."

"I'll take care of this."

Zach leaned closer and stroked her hair. His hand drifted from her hair to her neck, and then with three fingers he stroked her cheek. Kara sat stiffly, her hands still in her lap.

"On Monday," he said, his hand resting on her neck, "I'll put someone on this and we'll get to the bottom of it."

"What would your competitors gain by following me?"

"How about you stay here tonight and tomorrow?" He lowered her coat from her shoulders. "You'll be safe here, just in case it is something. I'll stay with you."

He kissed her neck, his hot breath warming her, his hand rubbing her breast through her sweater. She wasn't getting the information she needed. "What will be different on Monday?"

He lowered his head to kiss her covered breasts, not responding to her question.

"Maybe you should just tell me what this is all about. I might be able to help."

"I need you to trust me—I said I'll take care of it and I will." His hand slipped under her sweater and he squeezed her nipple with his fingertips. Then he pushed her back against the couch and kissed her hard on the mouth.

She wanted to believe him.

He pulled the cotton sweater up over her breasts and kissed each of them in turn through her lace bra. Kara closed her eyes and let the heat of his kisses ease her fears. Against her thigh, she could feel the hardness of his penis. Fear rippled through her. Once again, she got aroused, but she knew that terror would quickly take over and her dull headache would turn to a throbbing one. *This is what normal people do. This is what couples who love each other experience. It's all going to be fine.* She took a deep breath and imagined a beautiful cascading waterfall with a rainbow arching over it. Rays of sun made the water sparkle. Zach sucked one of her nipples, and she kept the images strong.

"I have to make a few phone calls," he said between nips and kisses. "Why don't you get undressed and pour us both a glass of wine. There's a nice Merlot on the counter and a chardonnay in the refrigerator, your choice." He got up and walked over to the phone. "I'll order takeout from that Thai place you like."

Kara went into the kitchen, opened the red wine, and poured two glasses. She walked into the bedroom, listening to the quiet murmur of Zach's voice in the other room. She tried not to listen, but she could tell he was speaking with his wife. The conversation ended and he made a second call—this one sounded confrontational. Finally, in a louder tone, she heard him call the Thai restaurant. She waited.

He entered the bedroom. "You're still dressed."

"I'm enjoying the wine." Her ever-present headache was heating up.

Long after Kara's pain from making love had subsided, after eating their takeout dinner, after Zach had fallen asleep, she had a startling thought: they were spending the night together—something Zach always said he couldn't do. This time, with one phone call, here they were. Moreover, she still didn't have an explanation about Sam Westin and the FBI.

CHAPTER SIXTEEN

The woman stood behind the storm door, arms akimbo. She peered at Alex and Vanessa from narrowed eyes.

The sisters had driven in Alex's Jeep to the Northeast Bronx and, using the GPS, had easily found the house. Semi-attached, two-story brick homes lined both sides of the street, each with a postage-stamp patch of grass in the front adjacent to a set of stairs—known in New York as the "stoop." Shared driveways separated each set of houses.

"Can I help you?" The woman shouted her question peering around the edge of a frosted-glass door, her smooth skin the color of cashews. "I ain't buying anything, and I'm a Christian woman in case you're one of those Jehovah's Witness people."

Vanessa stepped forward. "Good morning. My name is Vanessa Lawrence and this is my sister, Alexandra. We're sorry to disturb you, but we've come on a rather urgent matter."

Vanessa's smile, an almost perfect V shape punctuated by dimples on either side, rarely failed to charm. The woman, however, appeared unmoved.

Alex jumped in: "We understand Mrs. Ruby Strand lives here, or she did."

The woman stared at them for several seconds. "She's dead. Miss Ruby's been gone for a long time now."

Alex said, "We're looking for her granddaughter, Kara."

"Why?" She opened the door a little wider. The muscles of her face eased.

Vanessa spoke up: "She's our sister."

Our sister, from Vanessa?

The woman opened the door wide. "That near-white child is your sister?"

She invited them in, made coffee, and served them still-warm-from-the-oven homemade biscuits and strawberry jam while they explained to Mrs. Wilson—*but you can call me Cora*—about their quest.

"Brenda—Kara's mama—and me were friends as children, but then she went off to college. Miss Ruby made sure of that."

The sisters waited.

"She got a job in Washington, DC, to work for some big-shot politician." Cora peered at the sisters over her mug. "So you're the children of that white man that came sniffing around Brenda. I never got to meet him, but Miss Ruby fretted about him all the time."

The room was dark and smelled like Pine Sol, bleach, coffee, and bread. There was a round blond-wood table and four matching chairs in the eat-in kitchen. The rest of the narrow room was lined with counters and cabinets and ended with a bar-covered window

Alex sipped her coffee. "Do you know much about their relationship—Brenda and our father?"

"Not really. He'd swoop down on her every now and again and take her to fancy places."

"Did they know each other for long?"

"Long enough to get pregnant. 'Course, he disappeared after that." She wagged her finger in their direction, fellow sisters in an unfair man's world. "Paid her regular money, though, which is more than most do."

She looked at Alex and Vanessa for affirmation and both obliged.

"Far as I heard, he didn't come around but once or twice to see the child." She crossed her arms on top of apple-sized breasts. "Miss Ruby wasn't one to say I told you so, but there was Brenda, alone with a child, and that was that." Cora's head bobbed up and down to underscore both the end of Brenda and the end of the story.

Alex needed more. "Why was she put up for adoption? Do you know the name of the agency?"

"Adoption? Who's gonna adopt a six-year-old black girl?" She made a dismissive sound deep in her throat.

Alex's heart rate increased. "That's what we were told."

"Well, you were told wrong. No, Miss Ruby tried to care for her after Brenda got the Big C," the woman whispered. "Her breasts, they cut them off," she made a slicing gesture with the edge of her palm, "but it didn't do any good."

Cora Wilson had a flair for storytelling.

"I know, awful, right? She died anyway. Then Miss Ruby had a stroke and she just couldn't care for Kara. I had my own babies, and me and Malcom—my sweet late husband—we just couldn't take on another one." Cora leaned back in her chair. "Adoption? No, that sweet little thing had foster parents up in Co-op City last I heard. I don't know what happened after that."

Alex and Vanessa thanked Cora for her help, the coffee and biscuits, and promised to come again.

The sisters stepped onto the stoop, the woman right behind them holding the door open.

Cora said, "I do recall her coming here once, now that you got me thinking 'bout it."

"When?" Vanessa asked.

"Awhile ago, maybe ten years. I was outside tending my little garden; I grow herbs for healing and such. She and that white woman, the one with bright red hair from social services, at least that's what the card she handed me said—they came around."

The wind picked up and Cora wrapped her thin arms around her frame.

Alex barely noticed the change in weather. "What did they want?"

Vanessa, ever practical, asked, "Do you still have her card?"

"Connelly or Kingly. I didn't keep the card." Her face scrunched in concentration. "Kennelly. That was it."

Alex tried again: "Did they say anything?"

Cora's face folded again and then lit up. Even, white teeth showed against pink gums. "Kara must have been eighteen or so," she said in a spirited manner. "Real pretty, almost as fair as you, with light hair, big loopy curls." She pointed at Alex. "Tall like you too; and she talked educated like Brenda. I invited them in for refreshments but they said no, they were just passing through. Kara was kinda skinny, and she seemed sad."

"Can you remember anything else? Even a scrap might help us." Alex was almost begging.

"Never saw them again, though I thought about Kara for weeks afterward. It was the pain in her eyes. They were the color of that stone—you know which one I mean, goldish-brown, like a fine piece of glass?"

"Amber," Alex offered, remembering the photograph she'd found.

"Yeah, that's the one. She had these big, sad amber eyes. Haunted me."

The sisters thanked Cora again.

"Here's my card with all my contact info. Please call if you remember anything else," Alex said.

"Sure, glad to help."

Alex slid into the car and slammed the door. "Foster parents in Co-op City, could that be right? Someone misinformed Daddy."

Vanessa made a derisive sound. "Misinformed? Did he bother to follow up?"

"Of course he did."

"You don't get it, do you? He dumped her, just like he dumped us."

"He wouldn't do that."

"You keep defending him in spite of all of the evidence in front of you." Vanessa's voice was uncharacteristically agitated. "He is a piece of shit. He shat all over us, and evidently he did worse to his other offspring. And all of your denials and fantasies can't make it otherwise."

Alex started the Jeep. Vanessa was right: if their father had bothered to check, he'd have known the truth.

Vanessa's voice returned to its normal, controlled volume. "Did Dawes tell you the name of Kennelly's agency?"

"Nope." The Jeep's heater kicked in and fogged the windshield. "I didn't ask about the adoption. Obviously I should have."

Vanessa pulled out her cell phone and dialed the lawyer's number. When he picked up, she filled him in.

"He's checking," she said to Alex. The silver-and-gold pen tapped the dashboard.

"New York Family Services." She jotted notes. Her voice edged with sarcasm, she asked, "How do you know if the child was adopted? Do you have information on the adoptive family?"

Alex watched Vanessa's face: mouth turned down, her eyes squinted slits.

"Thank you," Vanessa clicked off, "for nothing."

"What did he say?"

"Surprise, surprise. No follow-up. No checking in. God bless the children."

"Crap." It was impossible to explain away their father's neglect.

Vanessa said, "Let's go find Ms. Kennelly."

"Will the agency be open on a Saturday?"

It wasn't. Alex resolved to call back on Monday morning and try to track down the caseworker.

After dropping off Vanessa at the Woodlawn Metro North station in the Bronx, she made a U-turn and headed north toward the hospital.

What was her father thinking? Did he truly abandon his daughter, never finding out if good people adopted her or not? Vanessa said Alex always defended him. Well, that was because Vanessa and her mother constantly attacked him. Maybe they were right.

The CCU was quiet, with empty gurneys angled here and there along the corridor. No one was in the visitors' lounge. Alex rubbed her stomach. It was already two p.m. and she hadn't eaten anything today except Cora's biscuits and jam.

Two women chatted at the nurses station; neither glanced at Alex as she walked past and entered her father's room.

"Daddy?"

His time was running out—she could feel it. The doctors had said it was still touch-and-go for another twenty-four hours.

"Hmmm," he murmured under his breath, his violet eyes half-opened. "How's my girl?"

She looked down at his unshaven face, dried saliva etched at the corners of his mouth. She had wanted to confront him, but now it seemed like a bad idea. "I'm fine, Daddy. Do you need anything?"

He lifted a hand, waving off the question. "Have you found her?" He tried to push up on his elbows but failed and sank back on his pillow.

"Not yet. I did uncover some things, though." She hadn't intended to sound so accusatory. "Did you know she was never adopted?"

He blinked several times.

"Did you know she probably grew up in foster care?"

His eyes opened wide.

"Daddy?"

A muted groan.

She couldn't stop herself. "Did you bother to investigate, to find out what happened after you abandoned her?" Alex's voice rose with each question.

"No."

"Look at me, Daddy." She was crying now. "Well, that's what we found out so far." Hot tears streamed down her cheeks and ran along the sides of her nose and into her mouth. "She was just as much your girl as I was—we were both six years old. She belonged to you as much as Vanessa and Pigeon. How come, Daddy? Tell me how come!" Alex sank next to him on the bed; her shoulders sagged, her head hung low. "Would you have sent me away?" This last question floated between them. "What if it were me, would you have left me to grow up with strangers?"

With the back of her hand, she swiped at her tears. She searched in her jacket pocket for a tissue, finding only a used one, but blew her nose in it anyway.

"I'm sorry, kitten."

"Sorry isn't good enough."

"I'm trying to make it right."

Alex blew her nose again into the sodden tissue. "Did you love her?"

"I loved them both."

Alex thought about that for a second. Her mother claimed to love her daughters; her father claimed the same. His clouded eyes penetrated hers. "Not enough, Daddy. You didn't love any of us enough."

CHAPTER SEVENTEEN

On Sunday morning, wet snores woke Kara up: Big Jim was in her room, ready to tear into her body. "No," she cried, and then in a softer whisper, "Please, no."

Someone was speaking to her; his words were slurred. The voice was familiar but she couldn't quite place it. "What? Kara, what's the matter?"

He grabbed her. She pulled away as hard as she could and rolled over, dragging the covers with her as she tried to wrap them around her body. With a hard thump her right elbow, then her shoulder and hip, hit the floor.

Nausea rumbled through her bowels and stomach as she gained her footing. With her feet still tangled in the sheets, Kara lurched forward, stumbled, and heaved. Vomit ran down her naked chest onto the bedsheet, and ended in a humiliating puddle.

"You're sick." He sounded disgusted.

"Please don't hurt me." She pulled her knees up to her chest and curled her body around them, her face buried into the folds of the sticky bed linen. "I'm sorry." She knew the vomit would make him angry. It wasn't the first time.

"Hurt you? Baby, what are you talking about? C'mon, get up."

Kara opened her eyes, but just a slit. Where was she? She opened them a little wider and peered sideways at the man squatting next her. It wasn't Big Jim—it was Zach. His eyes bleary, his hair matted against his head in haphazard spikes, his beard hairs angled oddly. Another wave of nausea swept up her throat, into her mouth, and then down again, leaving the taste of bile on her tongue. The next surge was stronger. She untangled the sheets, scrambled up, and ran to the bathroom, both hands clamped over her mouth. This time she made it to the toilet and emptied her stomach of the rest of Saturday night's meal.

What was the matter with her? What was happening? For so long she'd pushed the memories away—Big Jim in her room, night after night, pressing his penis against her vagina, shoving it into her mouth; drops of blood would trickle down her thighs as his thick fingers twisted the skin of her buttocks, leaving them black and blue for weeks. Now, here they were, not just as metaphorical nightmares, but alive in her wide-awake consciousness. She could smell the cigar smoke that clung to his clothes, hear his voice as sharp as a wasp's sting: *You better not tell anyone, you hear me, girl? No one's gonna believe you. Ever.* Kara couldn't speak. He grabbed her, dug his thumbs deep into her small arm, and squeezed until she cried. *You remember what happened to those kittens? That's what happens to bad girls who tell lies.* The dead kittens floating in the bathtub filled her mind's eye. She'd nodded her head, braids swinging forward and back. *That's my girl. You be nice to me and I'll take care of you.*

Urgent raps on the bathroom door brought Kara back to the present. "Let me in, baby. Let me help you."

Kara lifted her head from the toilet bowl, grabbed the edge of the basin, and pulled her body up. Embarrassment added another layer to her pain. "I'm sorry, Zach—just a bad dream and an upset stomach. Give me a few minutes."

The cold water from the tap ran through her fingers and she splashed some on her face. She pulled a washcloth from the rack and washed the vomit from her body. Steadier now, Kara found the guest toothbrush she'd used the night before and brushed her teeth, scrubbed her tongue, and then swished with mouthwash, trying to erase the bile taste and the memory of Big Jim's semen.

By the time she emerged, a towel wrapped around her, she had showered and washed her hair. Strange. It wasn't that she didn't know what Big Jim had done to her, but she'd never let it come to the surface before, never consciously remembered it. Why was it happening now?

"You had me worried," Zach said. His words were somewhat negated by his tone.

"I'm sorry." Kara turned away, dropped the towel, pulled on her panties and slacks. "I didn't mean to worry you." She found her bra on a chair, but where was her sweater? The vomit on the floor made her groan aloud.

"Are you going to be sick again?"

"No." She twisted to face him for a nanosecond and gave him a small smile. "I'll clean up this mess and go home to rest. I'm sure I'll be fine, probably a twenty-four-hour stomach thing or food poisoning. Are you okay? Does your stomach feel okay?" This strategy often worked.

"I don't think it was food poisoning."

She found her sweater and pulled it on. "Might be."

Zach frowned. "You're not pregnant, right?" Again, the accusatory tone. "You're being careful?"

"Of course not." He sounded more worried about himself than for her well-being. Damn. Her head buzzed. She surveyed the room; she needed something to clean up the mess. Unable to dredge up the energy to go into the kitchenette, she used the bath towel to mop up the vomit on the floor. Again, shame welled up. She had to get home.

Zach snatched the towel. "You can't leave."

She picked up her coat and bag, then stepped into her shoes. "I'll stay home, out of sight." Her resolve felt stronger than her shame or the need to please Zach. "You can straighten everything out tomorrow, like you said."

Kara walked backward toward the door, her eyes on his face, tote clutched close to her chest. In the most reassuring tone she could muster, she said, "I'll slip into my house and I'll make sure no one sees me."

"You don't know how to."

"Don't worry. No one will follow me and if they do, I won't tell them anything."

"You don't know what you think you know."

"Right, so there's nothing to worry about."

"You're staying." He grabbed her left shoulder and pulled her toward him. Her bag fell to the floor, its contents spilling out across the rug.

"I have to go."

His grip tightened.

She pushed him as hard as she could, tried to dodge around him. He shoved her. Her cheek hit the arm of the couch, her breath knocking out of her with a cry of pain as she landed on the floor.

"Baby, I'm sorry! Are you hurt?"

She pushed up onto her hands and knees and crawled toward the door. This was not going to happen to her again. No one—not Big Jim, not Zach, no one—was going to do this to her again.

Zach reached out, sank to the floor next to her. "You know I wouldn't hurt you on purpose."

The door was seconds away.

"You've got to give me more time."

Kara pressed her back against the door. The effort left her mouth dry and her heart thudding. She placed her hand on the doorknob and pulled herself up.

"I think you might be in danger. The man following you, there might be something to that. You're safer here with me." Zach stood up as well and put both his hands on her shoulders. "I can fix this in the morning. Please, Kara, let's sit and talk."

The yell that emerged from her throat sounded like a wild animal. She didn't recognize her own voice. It welled up from the core of her being and came forth full-throated, piercing the air. "No, no, no!"

Zach dropped his hands, pulled back. "What's the matter with you?"

"I'm going home." She reached down and picked up her bag. With her toes, she moved the spilled contents closer, stooped down, her eyes still on him, and shoved her lipstick, wallet, comb, and keys into the bag. "I won't tell anyone anything." Her tone was firm, sure.

She pulled open the door and stepped into the hallway. Her last image of Zach was his mouth set in a straight line, his arms at his sides, his fists balled.

With compact motions, Kara looked up and down the hallway, her breath coming in short gasps. The elevator bank was to her right and the stairs to the left. Waiting in the hallway for the elevator didn't seem like a good option, so she headed for the exit sign at the end of the corridor. Once there, she opened the door and started down the steps. After each flight, she paused and listened, and hearing nothing, she staggered down to the next floor.

Danny spun around. "Hey, girl." He sounded tentative, questioning, as if he were unsure if she was glad to see him. As tall as Kara, similarly thin and fit, Danny's bittersweet chocolate-colored skin glistened in the hallway light.

"Hey, yourself."

Kara felt exhausted. Time had crawled as the 2 train had banged its way north. At first, she tried not to think, but thoughts came anyway. She'd heard about flashbacks. Some war vets suffered from them. Images swarmed, taking the vets back to some life-or-death fight. Her dreams were like that. When she was with Zach tonight, was that like a daytime flashback? Marci Nye, her savior-therapist, would know what to make of them. Once Kara got the FBI behind her, she'd make an appointment.

By the time Kara was eighteen, she was still a virgin—well, not a virgin, but the only woman her age she knew who had not had consensual sex. When she took a chance with a boy a few years older, it had hurt like hell, not just inside her vagina but also through every muscle in her body. The migraine that followed made waves of red undulate in front of her eyes.

"Contrary to the images in the movies," Tuesday had responded when Kara asked her about it, "most women hate sex."

That didn't seem right, so Kara sought help. Post-traumatic stress disorder was the diagnosis. What had happened to her as a child—the loss of her mother; being put into foster care; the physical, verbal, and sexual abuse at the hands of Big Jim—had left her traumatized. Weekly sessions with Marci Nye helped her heal. Marci made it safe to talk about everything. They were working on sex, helping Kara find ways to have a normal sex life, and she'd mostly stopped thinking about Big Jim. But now memories of those nights bubbled up and spilled over like a pot of pasta left too long on the stove. Did this happen to Tuesday? Did she experience flashbacks like this?

Danny brought her out of her thoughts: "How are you doing?" He searched her face. "We were worried about you."

"I didn't mean to trouble anyone."

"I was way out of line the other day. I'm really sorry."

What was he apologizing for? Had they had a fight? She couldn't remember. "No problem."

"So, what are you going to do?"

What was he talking about . . . do about what? Then she remembered—he knew about the FBI.

"Mrs. E. thinks you might need a lawyer."

She shook her head no, she had probably just needed a lawyer the first time the agents came to her. How could a lawyer help her now?

"Someone who knows the ropes, could watch your back." He moved closer to her, his eyes wide. "Kara, what the hell happened to you?" He reached out and gently touched her check. She winced. "Did someone hit you?"

"I think it's too late for a lawyer."

As if reading her mind, Danny said, "A good lawyer might convince the FBI to leave you out of the investigation."

That made sense. After all, when she delivered the envelopes, she didn't know what was in them. She still didn't. Agent Boyd had said Zach was involved in insider trading, but Kara hadn't benefited from trading of any kind. No money had come her way.

On the other hand, when Zach asked her to deliver the second package, he had said there was a big merger afoot. In his business, Zach was probably privy to information about lots of mergers prior to the public knowing. He could buy stock at lower prices through Sam Westin just before the price went up. As his courier, even though she wasn't in on it, she might be culpable—the agents had pretty much said so. Nor could she say she was unsuspecting. Westin had confirmed her worst fears, but that was after the fact, after she'd made the second delivery. Yet a lawyer might be able to show the FBI she couldn't help them. All she had were suspicions and no facts.

None of this, however, did she say aloud. Danny was still staring at her as if she had said or done something ridiculous.

"Do you know someone?" she asked.

"Mrs. E. has a friend willing to help. What happened to your face?"

"Did she say how I could get in touch with this friend?"

Danny took a big breath. "I'm on my way to church and Mrs. E. is at Mass. Why don't we get together around noon and we can ask her to give the guy a call."

He was still watching her, as if waiting for something, but she couldn't think what that could be.

"Do you want to come to church with me?"

Church. Peace. Music.

"I find when I turn it over to the Lord—"

"Noon sounds good," she cut in. "Thanks." Kara turned and dragged her body up the stairs to her rooms. She could feel Danny's eyes still on her. She should go with him. Maybe next Sunday.

At first Marty had acted uninterested in seeing her. She'd been gone since Saturday afternoon. Of course Mrs. E. had fed him, but his litter box needed changing, and his gaze felt accusatory. Kara was too exhausted, however, to make amends. As if he sensed her stress, Marty seemed to forgive her. He leaped onto her lap, his gimpy half-leg tucked against his underbelly, and stretched and purred against her. The vibrations from his rumbles had their usual calming effect on her, lowering her anxiety with each second.

She wasn't sure how long she'd sat there, curled up with Marty, trying not to remember or yearn. The barely there March sunlight warmed her face through the window.

Mrs. E.'s voice disturbed the quiet: "Kara, you up there?"

Startled, Kara jumped; Marty did too. "Yes." The grandfather clock chimed twice, so she must have fallen asleep. A chill moved through her. She was supposed to meet Danny and Mrs. E. around noon. The growling from her stomach reminded her she had not eaten since the night before, and had thrown up all of that.

After washing her face and brushing her teeth, Kara headed downstairs, Marty at her heels. A man about five feet six, of indeterminate age, with caramel skin and a mustache, watched as she descended.

"Kara Lawrence, meet Norman Green."

Kara learned that the eighty-two-year-old Norman was the Edgecombe family lawyer summoned on her behalf.

Despite her natural reluctance to open up, Kara decided it was in her best interest to tell Norman Green everything. As her tale unfolded, she found it was a lot easier than she thought it would be. At first hesitantly, and then with greater clarity, prodded on by Mr. Green's questions, Kara explained about the envelopes, visits to Sam Westin's office, the FBI following and threatening her. Throughout the narration, the lawyer nodded his head and occasionally jotted notes in a steno pad with a pencil stub.

"Zach said he would clear it all up tomorrow. Special Agent Boyd said that I have until midnight tomorrow to agree to help them. After that he wouldn't make any deals with me, and they'll assume I'm an accomplice." Her stomach put a period to her tale with a growl so loud she was sure everyone heard it. "Excuse me."

"Hmmm," the lawyer said in response.

"Can you help her or not?" Mrs. E. asked.

"Of course I can." He sounded like an expat Englishman rather than a Harlem native. "They have nothing, we'll give them nothing, and they can do nothing."

Danny asked, "What should she do when they come back?"

Norman Green gathered his overcoat. "They won't." He fingered Agent Boyd's business card. "I'll reach out to the agent and report back to you sometime tomorrow." He shrugged into his coat, bowed to Kara, shook Danny's hand, and kissed Mrs. E.'s cheek. "Good afternoon to you all."

Danny, Kara, and Mrs. E. finished their grilled-cheese-and-tomato sandwiches and downed the last cups of hot cocoa. Kara's spirits were rebounding.

"How old is that guy anyway?" Danny wiped his mouth on a napkin. "He's gotta be at least a hundred."

Mrs. E. didn't take the bait.

"You two old lovers or something?"

"Mind your manners, officer."

Danny chuckled. "Friends, I meant."

"Indeed, an old friend. And he is not one hundred."

"So, how'd you meet him? What's his story?"

"If you really want to know . . ."

"Absolutely."

"His grandfather and mine were friends and colleagues."

Danny sliced off a hunk of iced-chocolate cake and put it on his plate. "Here?"

"No, they lived on Harlem's famous Sugar Hill on Edgecombe Avenue—and no, the street was not named after my family, nor my family after it."

"Wouldn't surprise me if it were. Want some cake, Kara?"

"What?"

"Cake?"

"Oh, no thanks." Kara was hardly listening; her mind was on her own troubles.

Danny's brow creased. Several beats passed, then he turned back to Mrs. E. "You were telling us about how you and the not-one-hundred-year-old Mr. Green came to be friends."

Mrs. E. made a sucking noise under her breath, but proceeded: "My grandmother came here from British Guyana, from a home staffed by servants. She landed in Manhattan and had to work as a lady's maid for wealthy Upper East Side women." She took a sip of her tea. "Not a lot of opportunities for black women back then."

"I bet."

"She struggled home every night, tired, took the elevator up to the fifth floor to her slice of heaven. Their apartment overlooked the Harlem River, with what was then the Polo Grounds in the foreground and a park on the other side. Every night she'd gaze out on what she called her *jewel box*; she could see for miles both east and south; the Triborough Bridge was her string of pearls, the bend in the highway making a perfect loop; the red and blue lights of La Guardia Field, what they called the airport back then, way in the distance, were her rubies and sapphires; and all the other lights made the rings and pins."

"Your grandmother was a poet," Danny said.

"Indeed. But not the only accomplished person in the family. My grandfather had migrated from North Carolina. He had an undergraduate degree from Shaw University and a law degree from NYU."

"When was this?" Danny asked through a mouthful of cake.

"Around 1920, when a black man with a law degree was a rare thing indeed. Well, Grandma couldn't believe he was working as a waiter. Badgered him to quit and open up a practice. Together they did okay. Mr. Green's grandfather and mine became law partners."

In spite of her misery, Kara now focused on the story. "When did your family move here, to this house?"

"Harlem was a dazzling place—jazz clubs, literary salons. Still is, or should I say it's back to being so. The law practice blossomed, but so did the family. Children arrived at a rapid rate. They had six, one every other year, including my father."

"I get it." Danny wiped his mouth. "They needed more space."

"They found this grand mansion, at least that's how my father remembered it. Been in the family ever since."

"That was pretty rare too, right?" Danny cocked his head to one side. "Most of these old houses fell into disrepair."

"Many did. Blocks and blocks of them, cut up into rooming houses, fireplaces boarded up, parquet floors damaged beyond repair. When the neighborhood got too rough, my parents lived in Riverdale for a time, up in the West Bronx, but they never sold the old girl. As things in Harlem started to turn around, we moved back."

Kara asked, "So Norman Green comes from a long line of successful attorneys?"

"Yes. You don't have to worry."

Kara nodded as if she agreed. She wanted to believe Mr. Green could make it all go away, but she had her doubts. "What a wonderful story."

"Oh, I have many more," Mrs. E. said. "I'll save them for another time, when all this upset is over."

When might that be? Kara wondered.

Danny, his cake finished, peered at her. "You gonna tell us what happened to your face?"

Kara studied Danny's worried features. "I bumped it on the edge of a couch when . . ." She tried to think. "I fell. I've not been feeling well."

Mrs. E. asked, "Did you faint? Do you need to see a doctor?"

Kara couldn't continue the lie so she ignored the inquiry. "Thank you both for helping me and believing I'm innocent."

Mrs. E. tilted her head to one side, her eyes wide. "I prayed for you today. I pray every day for the both of you."

CHAPTER EIGHTEEN

Alex lay on top of the covers in her plaid flannels, her left arm across her eyes, the right one flung high above her head. In less than sixty minutes, she was supposed to pick up her mother for Sunday brunch at a diner near the hospital. She was definitely going to be late, and yet she still didn't move. It was always hard for her to get up in the morning, and today she wanted to stay in bed until dinner. For the third night in a row, she hadn't slept—but that was only part of it. She was living a Lifetime movie drama. Freaking crazy and mortifying. Damn, she needed a cigarette.

Yesterday, after leaving the hospital at five, she'd gone by the office and worked for several hours. She didn't get home until well after ten. The Wendy's hamburger she'd picked up on the way smelled delicious. The minute she pulled off her jacket, she took three quick bites of it, the juices dribbling down her chin. She popped open a can of Heineken, icy cold, just the way she liked it. The burger disappeared with her fourth bite. Neither the beer nor the food, however, picked up her spirits. Then she remembered she'd promised to call Pigeon back.

"You won't believe this," Pigeon said after a quick hello.

She sounded happier than she had earlier that morning, which did make Alex feel a little brighter.

"We played softball and I got a base hit—me, the anti-athlete."

"Wow, congratulations. To what do you attribute this incredible feat?" From her perch on her bed, Alex clicked on the television but kept it on mute; the newscasters' mouths moved and pictures of floods from some other state filled the screen.

"That's the thing. I've always been the kid nobody picked."

"Sports were not part of our home life, that's for sure." Alex and her father rode horses, but that was about it. She took another pull on her beer. "So, did you win?"

"No, but we still had a blast."

By Pigeon's account, Saturday had been a warm, sunny day in Los Angeles, and everyone was at Griffith Park in Los Feliz, near where Tommy and his extended family lived. She described the blazing heat, the picnic tables covered with flapping paper tablecloths and chicken and potato salads in plastic containers, bikers and skaters, many dressed in bikini tops and super-short shorts, gliding by, along with couples pushing baby carriages.

"It felt like a vacation," she said. They were playing softball and there were enough Cole family members to fill the roster for two teams.

"*Two?*"

"For real."

Alex took a pull on her second beer.

Pigeon's voice remained animated: "When it was my turn to hit, I held my bat high and tucked in my chin the way Breeze taught me."

Alex pictured little Pigeon, who barely reached Alex's shoulder, her dark hair shining under the sunlight. "This is not the Pigeon I know."

"Right? Ronnie, Cool Breeze's oldest sister, must have known because she kept yelling, *No batter!*"

"Ouch."

"She's super competitive and looks just like her mother, right down to the braid hanging to her butt—what's that about?"

Alex laughed. The answer was probably as complicated as the answers to all of the Lawrence family's mysteries.

"Ronnie was a few steps away from first. E.J., she's a sister-in-law, danced on and off first base as if she was at a club. I could tell she was itching to run."

"And?"

"Ronnie kept slapping her mitt with her fist and yelling at me, *You're going down, New York!* Alex, I was so nervous."

"I would be too."

"But Cool Breeze reassured me: *Don't let them rattle you. Lean into it like we practiced, and swing hard.*"

Alex could visualize the entire scene as Pigeon, in a voice as excited as a kid describing a birthday party, called the action. The first pitch was a strike and the second pitch missed the plate. Pigeon lowered her bat and wiped her sweaty palms on her shorts. She could feel perspiration soaking her tank top. Ready for the next pitch, she lifted the bat. *Whack.* Without watching to see where the ball went, she dropped her bat and sprinted to first. In her peripheral vision, she saw the outfielder, another cousin, trotting backward, trying to catch the ball. E.J. sprinted to second, her short legs pumping. The cousin scooped it up after one bounce, and threw it to Ronnie.

"What did you do?"

"I remembered how the pros did it on television. I threw out my legs, pointed my toes, and slid into first. E.J. hollered from second base, *She's safe!*"

"Were you?" Pigeon playing softball and getting a base hit—wait until Alex told Vanessa!

"Yep. You should have heard the cheers from the peanut gallery. Then Breeze came up to bat and everyone quieted down."

"Is he good?"

"The golden boy." Pigeon sounded a bit in awe.

Alex could understand this after witnessing Breeze conquering their mother. "So?"

"With me on first and E.J. on second there was a chance for three runs to tie the score. I could see the sweat dripping from Cool Breeze's head."

"Now there's an image—a wet bald dome."

"He's not bald! He shaves his head. Besides, he looks cool in his wraparound sunglasses."

Alex hadn't found the man remotely attractive. "Sorry."

"Whatever. Anyway, he gave E.J. and me a look, as if to say, *Get ready to run.*" Pigeon was jazzed again as she relaunched into the story. "The first pitch was a ball, so was the second. My calves and ass hurt from my crummy slide—and I later found out you're not even supposed to slide into first base. Alex, I can't believe how out of shape I am. I've got to give up beer and start working out."

Alex glanced at the now-empty can in her hand. "I'm with you, kiddo. We'll both hit the gym. So what happened next? Did Cool Breeze bring you all home?"

"Not exactly. On the third pitch, Breeze hit the ball and it flew straight up the middle, past his wheezing brother John—the pitcher—and deep into the outfield. I took off, head down, sweat blurring my vision. E.J., unfortunately, was still on second base, jumping up and down."

"Why didn't she run?"

"No clue. But you have to picture this: E.J. is top-heavy, and she's jumping up and down and her gigantic breasts are just swinging wildly."

"Oh my goodness."

"She's not paying attention, so I yelled, *Run!* but E.J. just kept cheering me on. No way could I stop in time so I plowed right into her, knocked her over, and landed on her boobs."

Alex laughed so hard that tears filled her eyes. "Were you hurt? Was E.J.?"

"No, but I was out, according to the ump—who of course was another cousin."

"Oh. You did say earlier you didn't win, but I was still hopeful."

"Ever the optimist in spite of evidence to the contrary."

"Hmmm." Was that true? Vanessa had just said something similar to her.

"I was lying on top of E.J. and I heard Breeze laughing. In fact, everyone was laughing. That got me laughing too."

"What a good day you had."

"That's the thing: E.J. and I were so hysterical we could barely get up. All of my muscles ached, my legs were scraped and filthy, but you know what?"

"What?"

"I felt fabulous." Then Pigeon got quiet.

"Isn't that a good thing?" Alex broke the silence.

"You'd think so, but the strangest thing happened."

Alex heard the shift in Pigeon's voice, the cautious, glass-half-empty tone.

"I kept laughing until I cried, and then I cried some more, and I couldn't stop. There I was lying on the ground with everyone laughing around me, and I'm sobbing."

Poor baby. What's wrong with us? Is the whole family crazy?
"Why do you think that happened?"

"Beats me. All those beer-hazy nights with no-name men, and shitty jobs . . ."

Alex heard Pigeon's quavering intake of breath. Alex hugged her knees to her chest and waited for her sister to continue. While her own situation wasn't the same, the hollowness she heard in Pigeon's voice sounded familiar. In fact, all three Lawrence girls had a hard time being happy. Even when they were, they questioned it, never trusting it would last, or that it was even real. Did Kara feel the same?

Pigeon said, "I used to think I was destined for the streets. Now, I have that Alex-hope. Maybe I can get it right, have what Breeze has, and not be Pigeon-the-loser."

"Oh, sweetie." Alex clicked off the muted Jimmy Fallon, who had followed the news. "You are way better than the worst name Mom ever called you."

"Am I?

"Yes. We both are."

CHAPTER NINETEEN

A couple from Bangladesh owned the small East Indian restaurant next to Tuesday's apartment in Morningside Heights. In fact, the owners had explained, Bengalis owned most Indian restaurants in New York. It was a perception issue, they said. People wouldn't come to a Bengali restaurant, but an Indian establishment felt familiar. The three friends—Tuesday, Flyer, and Kara—often met there on Sundays to catch up.

Today, the aroma of curry and meat filled the air. It was after the church crowd and before dinner so the place was almost empty. Jammed in with ten or twelve other tables, theirs was covered with a white tablecloth and stood close to the kitchen. One of the owners took their order.

Tuesday sipped her water. "What happened to your face?"

"I fell."

"On your face?"

Kara didn't want to talk about Zach or the FBI. "I'm fine." She had other things on her mind. She couldn't stop thinking about Barry White, wondering what his short life had been like. As troubled as theirs? Plus, the nightmares and daytime flashbacks were wearing her down.

Their food soon arrived. Each dish in a separate bowl for easy sharing. For the next few minutes, the trio focused on filling their plates and sampling different dishes.

"What's with all the urgency?" Tuesday tucked into her

spinach, lamb, and potato casserole. "Why aren't we meeting for dinner like we usually do?"

Kara needed a point of entry so she decided to take an oblique approach. "I was thinking about the first year we all moved to the group home—how scared we were."

Tuesday asked, "Why were you thinking about that?"

Flyer reached for a slice of warm naan. "Good thing we had each other. Some of the older kids were crazy mean."

"What brought this up?" Tuesday put her fork down. "You've been acting all weird lately, jumpy."

Kara wasn't sure where to go next. She was waking up exhausted every morning with little strength to deal with Zach or the FBI. Did Tuesday have nightmares as well? She never hinted at it, but then again neither had Kara. How did Tuesday deal with them? Did they start recently like Kara's, or did Tuesday always have them? Kara also wondered about Flyer. He seemed unwell, and his life was haphazard. Her therapist, Marci, told Kara that sexual abuse in families sometimes happened to children of both sexes: it was about power—not sex, control, and violence, like rape. They weren't exactly a family, but still. Maybe if they all admitted it to each other, they could get better together.

"I remember being frightened all the time," she repeated.

Flyer's head bobbed up and down. "We must have had a fight a day on the school bus, not to mention in the dining room."

Tuesday jumped in: "They picked on us because we were the newbies."

"We were a great team," Flyer chuckled. "Tuesday worked the shins with her lunch pail and I had the intimidating shove down to a science."

Tuesday's scowl deepened. "We still got beat up."

"True," said Flyer.

"But why are we talking about ancient history? Who wants to remember those crappy days?" Tuesday peered at Kara. "You look like hell, and not just the new bruise. What's really going on?"

Kara took the plunge into taboo waters: "I was wondering if you remember why they took us from Big Jim and Nora."

"Because he was a sadistic moron." Flyer tapped a rhythm with his fingers on the edge of the table, his spiky dreads dancing to the beat. "And Nora let him. She never made him stop."

"He beat her too," Tuesday protested.

"Still, she could've reported him. Did something." His voice became hushed. "They were both evil."

"Yes, but how did they find out that he was—" Kara pulled back the word she was about to say, "beating us?"

Tuesday pushed out her breath in exaggerated annoyance. "It was the social worker's job. Didn't Liz check up on us?" She took a slice of flat bread and dipped it into one of the sauces. Chewing with her hand over her mouth, she said, "This can't be why you insisted on meeting up early today."

"I've been having dreams about when we were kids."

"Nightmares, more like," Flyer said.

"Yes. Flashbacks, you know, like war vets."

Dwarfed by the taller Flyer and Kara even when sitting, her dark skin as shiny as patent leather, Tuesday dropped her eyes. Flyer shifted in his seat.

"Big Jim did more than hit and yell at us, and I just thought it might be time to talk about it." Kara held her breath, her eyes shifting from one to the other. Her friends sat in silence, but Kara decided to wait them out. She stirred her food; still nothing. "He sexually molested us." Her mouth felt dry and she could feel tears filling her eyes. "Night after night for years." A voice in her head screamed, *Never tell anyone, ever!*

Tuesday was sitting opposite her, Flyer was diagonal to her right. Kara couldn't read Tuesday's reaction, and Flyer wouldn't meet her eyes.

The pain in her head throbbed. "I think it's harmful, you know, keeping it all in, keeping his secrets."

"Damn you, Kara." Tuesday spat out each word, her saliva and bits of food flying out with each one. "We agreed."

"We didn't."

Flyer bounced up from his seat. "He said he'd kill us if we ever told." He took a swallow of his Coke, sat back down. "Then he drowned the kittens."

Flyer had brought home the cat, who they named Splash—because her coat had splashes of colors, as if someone had spilled paint on different days. They were all excited when they realized Splash was pregnant, and even more so when the kittens were born.

"Why did he drown them?" Kara couldn't remember anything except seeing them floating in the bathtub.

"Because he was a sadistic bastard," Flyer said.

Tuesday stood up. "I can't believe you're talking about this now. It was a zillion years ago, who cares?" She ran both her hands through her short Afro. "He's fucking dead. Why are you doing this?"

"I've been seeing a therapist," Kara said.

"How's that working? You're going crazy and now you want us to feel the same way."

Tears rolled down Flyer's gaunt cheeks. "I told him to stop. I tried to help you girls, but then he killed the kittens and said he'd kill all of us and I couldn't do anything. I tried, I did, but he was too big."

Kara grabbed Flyer's hand. "It wasn't your fault. You were just a kid."

"I was supposed to protect you girls."

Tuesday paced around in tight circles. "Flyer, you were the baby." She pointed a finger at Kara. "It was your job to take care of us."

"We were all children." Kara's voice trembled; she could hear Marci Nye's tender voice in her head. "They were the adults."

"You didn't save us." Tuesday's dark skin was purple with fury. "You were the biggest. You were all we had, and you didn't save us."

"I'm sorry." Tears streamed down Kara's face.

Kara put her arm around Flyer. "Did he hurt you too?" Her voice was a hoarse whisper.

"He used you girls like whores."

"Did he do the same to you?"

Flyer's tortured eyes pierced her even more than Tuesday's accusation.

Tuesday flopped back in her seat, wiped her face with a napkin.

They sat in silence, except for Flyer's sobs. Finally he lifted his head. With his two index fingers, he beat out an angry rhythm on the edge of the table before he wiped his nose and eyes with the backs of his hands. "Nah, not like that. What do you think? No way, just you girls." He swiped at his tears again as they continued to flow. "I used to wish I had a sword or something, maybe a gun, something to make him stop hurting you. I would've killed him for sure, if I could've." He drummed his beat again. "No, no, he never touched me like no girl."

CHAPTER TWENTY

The diner, packed with an after-church crowd, had a long line of waiting patrons. Fortunately, Alex and her mother had gotten there just before the rush.

Dressed in a mixed—but not matched—jogging suit, hair smoothed back from her face with a headband, Judy addressed Sharon, their wizened waitress: "I asked for buttermilk pancakes," she said in her best mistress-to-lowly-servant voice. "These cardboard disks are made of something powdered and fake."

Sharon appeared bored.

"Go ahead, taste them." Judy lifted a forkful toward Sharon's mouth; the woman pulled back like a two-year-old refusing a spoonful of peas. "They're as dry as dust."

"Mom, just order something else." Alex caught the eye of a woman in the opposite booth. She gave Alex an empathetic nod.

"Something else? If they can't make decent pancakes, why would I believe they are capable of making an omelet or French toast?"

Alex grabbed her things. "Come on, I'll buy you brunch somewhere else." She spoke to Sharon: "I'm sorry, can we just get our check?"

"I'm starving, so this place better not be far."

"Argh." Alex wrapped her scarf around her neck and picked up her mother's coat from the seat next to her. The desire for a cigarette welled up—five weeks smoke free and counting. She was not going to make it.

Sharon returned. "You have to pay the full bill," she said, her hands on her hips. "Just 'cause you're picky don't mean you get away without paying."

"Get the manager," Judy ordered.

Alex lifted a hand to stop Sharon from walking away. "We'll pay," she said, digging into her bag and pulling out her wallet. Out of the corner of her eye, she glimpsed her mother, mouth agape, staring over Alex's shoulder. *What now?* Alex shifted her gaze in time to see a large black carpenter ant scurrying across the backrest of the booth.

"Oh dear," said Sharon, "we just sprayed." With gnarled fingers, she gripped her order pad and swatted the bug, knocking it off the back of the plastic-covered booth and onto Judy Lawrence's lap.

Her mother's screech startled the other diners. She struggled to get up and out of the narrow space between the seat and the booth table, glasses and cutlery rattling. "This sort of thing doesn't happen in Bedford!"

Alex couldn't help it—her shoulders rocked from suppressed laughter. Typical Judy-theater: on the one hand humiliating, and damn funny on the other.

"Do you see what kind of place this is?"

Alex helped her mother into her coat, fighting to hold in the laughter now shaking her entire body.

"Styrofoam pancakes and ants to boot." Judy eyed Sharon. "Not to mention incompetent help."

"Come on," was all Alex could say between clenched teeth as she continued to hold the guffaws at bay.

The moment they stepped outside, Alex exploded with laughter. Her mother stared at her, her heart-shaped face still scrunched.

"You should have seen your expression, Mom. It reminded me of the carpenter ant invasion we had at home, remember?"

Judy's face relaxed. "They marched across the kitchen floor and in and out of the cabinets, feasting on spilled honey."

"You chased them with the broom and screamed at them as if they would listen to you."

"Remember how Pigeon kept trying to eat them?" The two women walked to Alex's Jeep in the crowded parking lot. "Your father called the exterminator and checked us into the Rye Hilton until they were gone." Judy chuckled. "We had an antless picnic in our room and watched *I Love Lucy* reruns."

"Vanessa and I love telling that story to Pigeon." *Why was it so memorable?* Alex unlocked the car and the two women climbed in. She started the engine, backed up, and pulled out of the parking lot, the memory still with her. Their father wasn't even upset, and although Judy was in full-force agitation, the day had ended with all of them together, sharing a meal in their hotel room.

They drove in silence for several minutes. The recollection of the ant invasion fused into the conversation she'd had with Pigeon the night before. Had the Lawrence family ever had as much fun as the softball game Pigeon had described?

"We did have good times, Mom, didn't we, back then? We were happy some of the time, weren't we?"

Her mother didn't respond.

"Did we ever play games as a family?"

"Stop talking nonsense."

"Weren't there other times when we just laughed?"

"What does that have to do with anything? How does that change things?"

"I'm just wondering."

"You learned to speak fluent French, you rode thorough-breds, you took piano lessons and ballet."

"Mom, I'm not ungrateful."

"Not that Monica ever cared. How is she, anyway? I suppose you've heard from her."

"She's fine. Happy, in fact."

"Happy? While her father is on the precipice?"

"Of course she's worried about Daddy, and about you."

Her mother snorted.

Alex wanted to get back to her original query. "So, what *was* the best time we ever had as family?"

Judy uncrossed her arms, smoothed out her gloves across her lap. "Life is not supposed to be fun; it just *is*."

"The Cole family seems to have lots of fun."

"I did my best, Alex."

"Were you happy?"

"Do you think I don't know you and your sisters wished you had a different mother?"

"Not true."

"You thought it was my fault—your father's philandering, his utter neglect."

She was right. Alex did blame her mother for Worth's absences; she had seemed to drive him away.

"I gave you girls every advantage, all the opportunities I never had. Not that you used them wisely." She put on her gloves, carefully smoothing the leather over each finger.

"What happened to you and Daddy?"

Judy closed her eyes and pressed her head against the backrest. "In the beginning, it was fine."

Alex pulled over and half-parked in a metered spot. She needed to hear this story, to sift out the real meanings hidden in her mother's words. Judy, for all of her bluster about straight talk, never shed light on anything.

"Your father was charming, handsome, Yale-educated, from Central Park West. I was Judy Colonie, daughter of a housewife and a high-school dropout, twenty-two years old with a Hunter College education and a Bronx accent—a cliché."

Afraid of what she might learn, but also scared her mother would stop, Alex stared straight ahead, willing her to continue.

"Not that Hunter was a bad place, but it was already changing. Still lots of Jewish girls, you know how they are, always pushing to get ahead of everyone else."

Alex groaned. Her mother's list of prejudices and hateful stereotypes was long.

"I'm not saying anything wrong."

"You are."

Judy pursed her lips.

"Finish your story."

"Where was I? Oh yes. By then the college had started letting just about anyone in. Not like the old days when you had to have the grades. Blacks, Hispanics, and foreigners crowded the classrooms." Judy's body shuddered.

Alex bit her tongue.

"But what could I do? It was what we could afford and Hunter's reputation was still solid."

"Okay, you're at Hunter, then what?"

"My parents couldn't afford the kind of education we gave you girls." She gave Alex a pointed look. "I'm not saying I didn't have things going for me—we lived in a nice place and Mother made sure I learned all of the right things, just as I made sure each of you did. She took the Bronx out of me and helped me be the kind of girl Worth Lawrence would covet for a wife."

"You met at a party, right?" She'd heard this part a dozen times or more. "Your friend Sheila introduced you," she prompted. What she wanted to hear was how they went from a Cinderella story to *War of the Roses*.

"Correct. Sheila and I were at a party of a friend, when this handsome, smooth-talking man with smoldering violet eyes walked right up to us. I knew right away he was old money." Judy chuckled. "He spent the whole evening wooing me. Mother was beside herself when I told her. This was what she had dreamed for me, a man like your father. I have to admit," she added with a wistful tone, "he was what I had dreamed for me as well."

Alex could tell this part of the tale verbatim. It often came up after a tirade against Worth, after a terrible night when he didn't come home. Alex would sit and listen as her mother recounted the night they met, the courtship; the wedding— paid almost entirely by the Lawrences—cost fifty thousand dollars, *which was amazing back in the day.*

"It wasn't just the money," her mother continued. "It was also the power. He made things happen. Important people listened when he spoke, as young as he was, and even older people paid attention." Judy took out a tissue from her purse and pulled at her nose. "He was good to me at first."

This was the point in the story where she usually stopped. "What happened?" Alex twisted around. "Why did things change?"

Judy's tone became matter-of-fact: "Who knows? . . . Work, travel, kids, and your father's legendary lack of self-control." She waved her hand for Alex to start driving again. "I'm hungry. Where are we going?"

Alex eased out of her parking spot and searched for another open restaurant. She knew her mother didn't want to discuss it anymore, but Alex wasn't satisfied.

"Did it happen slowly, or did something big happen?"

"Well, if you must know the truth, it was his terrible upbringing."

"He was abused or something?"

"Don't be stupid. No, his parents spoiled him and Peggy . . . Thrice-married Peggy, now there's a story. First the Spanish accountant—well, really, that had no chance, nor should it have. And then she married the backwater jazz musician who was as bad as the blacks he consorted with. Sorry, I forgot, I'm not allowed to say things like that."

Alex dropped her head forward with a silent sigh.

"Her last marriage lasted less than a minute—a personal trainer of all things." Her mother threw up her hands. "Anyway, it just happened."

"How? Tell me."

"Your father is self-centered, if you haven't noticed. What do you want to hear? That I did something terrible and sent him into other women's arms? Well, I didn't. I tried to be a good wife."

It was clear her mother was not going to provide any real insight. She never did. Maybe she herself didn't know what happened nor did she understand the roles they had each played in the withering of their marriage. Just ahead, Alex saw another diner and pulled into the parking lot. The two women sat for several minutes in silence.

"Men are like that, Alex. You'll see if you haven't already. They just are."

They lucked out. The young woman who seated them was solicitous. Once they settled in, Alex decided to try one more question she'd always been afraid to ask.

"Mom, why did you stay with Daddy after he started fooling around? Why didn't you pack us up and leave?"

With clear eyes, her mother leveled her gaze on Alex. "Your father loved me. He still does." Her hands fluttered in the air. "Men are weak and rich men are the worst. Besides, divorced women, like unmarried women, die bitter and lonely." She wagged a finger in Alex's direction. "So you be careful, young lady. You're not so young anymore."

"I take care of myself."

"If your father dies—when he does, someday—each of you girls will get a bundle."

"I don't need it. I'm making my own way." Was that true? Sean certainly thought she was just playing at being a struggling business owner until her inheritance came in, a loan a mere request away. She replayed her mother's words in her head. The explanation didn't make sense. Did he really love her? Was that enough? All the anger, suicide attempts—it just didn't add up. Hoping her mother would say more, Alex stayed quiet.

Finally, her voice as low as it was when she was talking to Aunt Peggy about private things, her mother asked, "Have you ever been in love, Alex? Crazy in love with a man who made it hard to breath every time he touched you?"

Alex only had to think about it for a fraction of a second. "No."

"It's a funny thing . . . I loved him so much, I believed he would change." She looked at her daughter with moist eyes. "After he got that woman pregnant, he swore to me never again."

"Did he stop?"

"Of course not."

"Did he honor his promise for a while, at least?"

Judy shrugged. "Besides, where would I go? The trick is to find someone who'll provide for you, someone who'll be there when you get old."

"I don't believe that." Alex lifted the menu and pretended to read it. Like her sisters, she never let men stick around long enough to fall in love. There was no way she would ever put up with the life her mother had chosen. If she didn't find someone who wanted to be with her and only her, then she would stay single. She didn't need a man to fulfill her. Her mother was wrong—it was better to be alone than to be unhappy with someone who didn't love you enough.

They ate their breakfast in relative silence, occasionally making comments about the quality of the food, her mother pronouncing it *passable*. Then Alex drove Judy home and tucked her behind her electric gates. Before going to her own home, Alex swung by the office and put in a few hours on the Frankel job. By the time she closed up shop, she was pooped. All she wanted to do was watch mindless television, wash her hair, soak in the tub, and turn in early.

After parking the Jeep, she walked toward the lobby, her head down, keys clicking in rhythm with each step. When she reached her door she saw Sean in front of her, his hands deep in his pockets, shoulders hunched, a wool cap pulled low over his ears. His handlebar mustache glistened in the fluorescent light.

"What's wrong? I just spent three hours catching up at work and I got a lot done last night. Has Jonas called again?"

"No, no." He sounded flustered. "I just wanted to say I'm sorry, and to let you know I'll take care of everything at the office."

"Oh."

"I know you're under a lot of pressure with your dad and all. I should have been more understanding . . ." His voice trailed off.

"It's okay." She reached out her hand and touched his. "I know I haven't been holding up my end."

He grasped her hand. "No, I've been a jerk. Listen, I wanted to let you know that you should do what you need to do, and I'll take care of everything else. So, things are a little tight. We've been through worse."

"Thanks, Sean." As much as she appreciated the effort, she was bone tired and needed to end this conversation. "It would mean a lot to me if I could take a few days off to help my family."

"Sure, stay home and tend to stuff. When you're ready, when you can . . ." His voice trailed off again.

She unlocked the door. "Did you want to come up for a cup of coffee?" She hoped he'd say no but felt guilty.

"Don't want to bother you." He moved away from the front door. "Let me know when you're ready to come back." Then, in typical Sean fashion, mustache moving up and down as he spoke, "When might that be, you coming back when you can?"

Alex was almost amused, Sean never knew when to stop talking. "A couple of days. I've practically finished the Frankel project and emptied my e-mail inbox." She was too tired to placate him more than that, and he must have sensed her exhaustion because he said goodbye.

It was clear—if she were honest, it had always been since the day they met—that Sean loved her. Would he make a devoted husband, the kind Alex dreamed about when she let herself think about it? Didn't she need to love him back? Didn't he need to love her even more than he appeared to?

Alex walked to the elevator and pushed the button. Her mother's words came back to her as she rode up to her apartment: *Have you ever been in love, Alex? Crazy in love with a man who made it hard to breathe every time he touched you?*

CHAPTER TWENTY-ONE

In spite of only a few hours of sleep, Kara woke up early Monday morning: today was the day. The FBI agents had said she had until midnight to make a decision about helping them trap Zach. She needed a plan, but it was hard to think. All night memories kept flooding back, sometimes in flashbacks, sometimes just in feelings and aches in her body. She covered her face with the bedcovers and cried out, "Stop!" to her empty room, to the recesses of her brain—it didn't work. The minute she closed her eyes, slices of memory, the fragments of sexual violence, came to her.

Tuesday's accusation still stung. It was unfair. What could Kara have done? It was true that she was the oldest, they all ran to her whenever Big Jim was swinging his belt at them, his wife included. Kara would scoot the other kids under her bed and hold both of them close.

A sob caught in her throat.

It was six thirty a.m. "Get up," Kara said aloud. Her body didn't respond. She closed her eyes for a second and then tried again. This time, the internal message worked. First, she sat up, and then with effort swung her legs over the side. She shuffled to the bathroom and washed up. Feeling better, she dragged on jeans and a sweater, dabbed makeup over the bruise on her cheek. Red capillaries spread out from the amber irises of her eyes. A few drops of Visine helped.

She decided to call in sick, something she hadn't done since a year ago February when she had contracted the flu. It didn't feel like a lie when she called her friend Joyce, the school receptionist, at home. She felt crappy enough physically and emotionally to qualify as too sick to work.

"Do you want me to drop by later, bring you some soup or something?" Joyce asked.

Kara declined. She didn't intend to stay home. Even though she still had no idea how she was going to get out of her trouble with the FBI, she knew she had to see her case-worker, Liz Kennelly. Had Liz known about the sexual abuse when she removed all three of the kids from the Smyth home? Had Big Jim hurt Flyer as well? Did Liz have all three of them examined? Did Liz—or anyone—do something to keep Big Jim from hurting other children?

"Where are you off to, missy?" Mrs. Edgecombe watched Kara finish her tea and toast in a matter of minutes. Still in her bathrobe, her white braids hung down to her waist.

"I'm coming down with something so I'm going to the doc-tor instead of work." She hated to lie to Mrs. E.—she hated to lie, period, but it seemed she was doing a lot of it lately. "I'll be back soon." She coughed for added effect. "I had a rough night." At least that was the truth.

"Is that why you fainted and hit your face? You've got the flu or something?"

"Could be."

Mrs. E. reached over and stroked Kara's arm. "There must be something going around."

"How are *you?*"

"*Phish.*"

"I'm glad."

"I heard they caught the guy who killed that little boy. Did Danny tell you?"

"Barry White?"

"Was that his name? You knew him, right?"

"Was it someone from the neighborhood?"

"No, an outsider." She picked up their plates and balanced them on a tray across her lap. "Just as things were getting so much better around here, safer for sure, something like this happens."

Kara's life had always been like that: two steps forward, three steps back. Something bad lurked around the corner, no matter how well things were going.

"Danny thinks the neighborhood is still pretty safe."

"And murder can happen anywhere," Kara added.

"Does."

"Did your grandniece's parents, your sister, live here with you?" Kara remembered Mrs. E.'s story about her family.

"We shared the house."

"And she died? How?"

"Car crash. A drunk driver, upstate."

"I'm sorry."

Another *phish* sound. "Me too."

"How old was their daughter, your grandniece?"

"Same age as that little boy, ten."

"You're a good woman, Mrs. E."

The old woman looked embarrassed. "So, you're off to the doctors. I'll have some chicken soup waiting for you when you get home."

Everyone was entitled to secrets.

Kara stepped into the hall that connected her three rooms. She planned to brush her teeth, retrieve her coat, and take the subway south to see Liz. Then her phone rang.

"It's me, Zach."

"What do you want?"

"We need to talk."

She let the coldness she felt toward him reflect in her voice: "Were you able to straighten things out?"

"No, not yet, that's why I need to see you."

Kara stayed quiet. If he had an explanation, a real one this time, she would listen.

"I'm sorry you got caught in the middle of this, baby. I really am."

Still, she waited.

"Are you there?"

"Yes." She sat down on the edge of her bed, opened and closed her fist, her fingernails digging into her palms with each flex. "So, what do you want to tell me?"

"I've got a plan, and I need your help."

He sounded like the old Zach, his tone kind and loving. But Kara knew she had to be strong.

"It seems the SEC might be investigating me—nothing serious."

"*Sounds* serious."

"They're always investigating traders. In fact, I don't know one guy on the Street who hasn't been a target at some point in his career."

"Really?" She switched the phone to her other ear.

Her response must have sounded skeptical because Zach's tone took on an edge. "They investigated my friend Chris three times and he's super clean. Sometimes they do it themselves, and sometimes they use the FBI."

"When they think it's something big?" Marty jumped on the bed next to her and Kara stroked his fur.

"They should be going after the money-grabbing bigwigs."

"So, why go after you?"

"They shouldn't harass innocent citizens."

"Okay, but why you?"

"I think maybe it's the FBI following you. They're at the investigative stage, casting their net."

Finally, the truth. "What are you going to do?"

"Have they approached you? You need to tell me."

Despite Agent Boyd's threats, she was tempted to tell Zach everything. How could he clear them both if he didn't have all the facts? To ease some of the tension she felt, Kara held the phone in her left hand and rubbed her left shoulder muscles, which were tight and bunched. She pressed harder and tried to think. What would Zach do if she told him about the FBI? He said he had a plan. He must have a team of corporate lawyers who take care of things like this. Would his lawyers also help her? She stood up, switched hands again. All her instincts told her to be honest with him, but still she hesitated.

"Kara, have they threatened you? Because if they have, they have no right. They have nothing on us—nothing." His words flew at her. "They use scare tactics to get people to turn on each other. When people stick together, the feds come up empty."

She noticed his use of the word *us* and began pacing around her bedroom. "I don't know anything, and I didn't do anything."

"Of course not, you're innocent. We both are."

Who could she trust? Not Zach.

"Too bad that won't stop them from making our lives miserable. Kara, you have to level with me. Have you spoken with them?"

"No."

An audible sigh came over the line.

"What if they do approach me? What should I say?"

"Be up front. Tell them you delivered an envelope, and before handing it over you examined the contents. Tell them it was a contract about insurance for Sam to sign. That's what Sam does, he provides all kinds of corporate insurance."

Kara realized she was holding her breath. She let it out as quietly as she could.

"You saw Sam open the envelope, watched him sign it, and you returned the envelope to me. I have a signed and dated copy as proof." Then, as an afterthought: "This will protect you too."

There it was, beyond a reasonable doubt. He was guilty. He had done everything the FBI said, and he wanted her to lie to them. Then she *would* be an accomplice. "I have a lawyer," she whispered.

Zach's response was explosive: "A lawyer?"

"I have to go."

"So, they *did* get to you."

She deserved the accusatory tone.

"When did you get a lawyer? They only get in the way, Kara." Now he quickly changed up his tactic: "Sweetheart, let's meet and talk this over. Poor baby, this has to be so hard for you."

"I'm hanging up now, Zach."

"Don't—"

"Goodbye." She clicked the red symbol on her smartphone.

The pain in her neck and shoulders was getting worse. She could barely turn her head right or left. With effort, she walked to the bathroom and downed three Motrin with shaking hands. *Breathe.* It only took a few minutes for the drugs to kick in. The pain began to subside, but not the hand tremors.

"Kara, are you up there?" Mrs. E. called from the foot of the stairs. "Special Agent Boyd wants to see you. I told him you were sick."

"I'll be right there." She glanced at her watch. It was only eight a.m. *What now? Don't I have until midnight?*

CHAPTER TWENTY-TWO

When it happened, it happened quickly. One minute Alex was embroiled in a fruitless search for her father's missing daughter, and the next minute she had a Harlem address a mere cab ride away. Her good fortune had not stopped there: not only did she know how to find Kara, she also had a date with a fascinating social worker named Michael Rosen.

The day had started out with a quick check on her dad, who was holding his own; the zapping of yesterday's coffee in the microwave, knowing it would taste like burnt dirt but downing it anyway; eating a slice of cold pizza for breakfast; looking for a social worker with the last name Kennelly.

New York Placement, a private, not-for-profit adoption agency that worked as a subcontractor for New York City, was located on Broadway and 66th Street. Managing Supervisor Elizabeth Kennelly had time to meet with Alex. If Alex's luck held, she was *the* Kennelly.

The man who greeted Alex in the waiting room was as tall as Alex would be in her stocking feet. Damn, he was good looking. The softness of his brown eyes, fringed with eyelashes women must envy, worked for him. That and the way his smile reached his eyes before his lips caught up.

"Liz asked me to meet with you until she can join us," Michael had said.

The room was sparse. Wood floors, white walls, and glass partitions made it feel cool rather than a welcoming place for potential parents or women giving up their children. Michael's well-modulated Brooklyn accent, however, made Alex feel warm nevertheless.

"Thank you." Alex could see her reflection in the glass. She should have combed her hair after her shower. Drip-drying left it an explosion of curls. She smoothed it down as best she could.

Michael led her into a small conference room. "How can we help you?"

Alex launched into her story, speaking faster and less coherently than usual. With each sentence, she twisted a strand of hair around her fingers. By the time she came to the trip to the Bronx, she was sure he saw through her juvenile nervousness.

"I know information about adoptees is confidential. I'm hoping, however, that Ms. Kennelly, if she is the same person, will give me some clue about what to do next."

Michael had listened attentively, occasionally nodding encouragement. He was beautiful in a non-movie-star way. Crooked, bright-white teeth contrasted with his Mediterranean complexion. Every time Alex looked at him, she got flustered.

"The information *is* confidential," he said at the end of her story. "However, Liz knows your sister very well. That's why she agreed to see you."

Eureka! Not only had she found the right Kennelly, but she was also still in touch with Kara.

"Have you worked with Liz for a long time?" She wanted to ask if he was married. There was no ring on his finger, but that provided scant comfort. The thickness and length of his lashes gave his features an almost feminine quality. *Please don't be gay.*

"Since college, about eight years ago."

"I graduated eight years ago as well. Maybe we met at some keg party on a campus somewhere?"

He laughed. "Could be. I went to City." He was referring to CUNY, the same system from which Alex's mother graduated. "Where did you go?"

"Smith," she said, almost apologetically. Smith College was a small liberal arts school for women and one of the "seven sisters"—an elite and expensive higher-education club.

"I doubt we ran into each other." He seemed amused by the conversation.

So taken by Michael, Alex was disappointed when a short, curvy woman entered the conference room. That feeling changed quickly, however, as Liz Kennelly held out her hand.

"You must be Kara's sister."

With a firm handshake, Alex said, "Thank you for seeing me."

Liz perched on the edge of the conference table. Michael sat catty-corner to Alex.

"As I explained to Michael, my father is critically ill and wants very much to see her before . . ." She couldn't say it. "I hope you can help us."

"Do you have identification?"

Alex pulled out her driver's license from her overstuffed backpack as loose change clanged onto the tabletop.

"Kara will have to *want* to meet you," Liz said as she scrutinized the license. "All I can do is share your request."

"If I could just speak with her, make my case. Impress on her how important this is to him."

"To *him*? Kara is thirty years old, Ms. Lawrence. His urgency is rather late, don't you think?"

Of course it was. Alex realized how selfish she must sound. She glanced at Michael and chose to read his expression as sympathetic. "I would like to meet her as well. She has sisters, two others, who didn't know she existed until a few days ago. We're not late."

It was true. Somewhere along the way, the search had become personal. After all, it could have just as easily been her or one of her sisters. What made Alex more his daughter than Kara? What made it okay for Kara to grow up in foster care and Alex to live with her parents in Bedford? Was it all about race, or the illegitimacy, or both? "What's she like?"

"Why don't I call Kara and then we'll see where we go from there." With agility, she hopped off the table. "You can wait for me if you like." Liz left the room.

"You okay?" Michael tilted his head. "Want to get something to eat while we're waiting?"

"I'm not really hungry, but something to drink would be terrific." Alex heard how high-pitched her voice sounded and brought it down an octave. "It's been a bizarre couple of days."

"I can imagine. I'll let Liz know we'll be in the cafeteria."

CHAPTER TWENTY-THREE

Agent Boyd looked just as he had on Saturday: same navy-blue suit, same cropped hair sprinkled with gray, same truth-seeking eyes.

"Good morning, Ms. Lawrence."

Kara stuffed her trembling hands into the pockets of her coat. "Aren't you a little early?" She tried for a confident tone but wasn't sure she was pulling it off. "As Mrs. Edgecombe explained, I'm unwell and off to the doctor."

"I can understand why you're feeling poorly."

"So?" At least her bravado sounded authentic this time.

"I came by to remind you about the deadline, and to see if you've figured out yet that our deal is your only way out."

"My lawyer is on his way over."

Mrs. E. wagged her finger at the agent. "Be here any second."

"Besides, I have nothing to say to you and harassing me won't change that."

They were facing each other, almost toe to toe in the long living room with its high ceiling and dominating fireplace. The baby grand stood to Kara's right, the family photographs that graced it a counterbalance to the tension in the room.

"You may not believe this, Ms. Lawrence, but I'm not here to hurt you." He relaxed his stance. "In fact, I believe you."

Kara pulled her hands out of her pockets and put on her gloves. She knew Zach was guilty. She knew he wanted her to lie for him, which she would not do. But that didn't change her determination not to trap him for the FBI. What kind of person would that make her? Moreover, Agent Boyd using psychology and telling her he believed she was innocent was not going to work.

Agent Boyd did not back away; nor did Kara. Finally, he said, "It's not like he hasn't used women like you before as his illegal couriers. Why do you think we were following you?" He never blinked. "Some people call you mules."

Kara reached out her hand in search of the edge of the piano and, finding it, moved closer and sank onto the piano stool.

"What? Did you think you were the only one?" His eyes tracked hers. "Scum stays scum, in all aspects of life—that's been my experience." The implied question, *Hasn't that been yours?* hung in the air. "Listen to me, Ms. Lawrence: covering for this crook is stupid, and you're not a stupid woman. I can tell." He glared at her. Then, bending his knees, he squatted in front of her. "We'll make it easy for you, Kara. May I call you Kara? We'll be with you every step of the way."

It was all she could do to keep from screaming.

"Even if I believe you, which I do, I still have to do my job."

Kara stared at the tip of his nose.

He rose. "If you don't cooperate, we're talking jail time."

Mrs. E. made a distressed sound. "Jail?"

Kara couldn't focus. She wasn't the first woman Zach had used. Was she so hungry for affection she had become some kind of bag woman? Her stomach rumbled a metaphorical answer. Zach and Agent Boyd were both threatening her and both had promised protection; both claimed they didn't want to hurt her while doing just that. She couldn't trust either one of them.

The front door opened just as the grandfather clock began to chime. Dressed in a rumpled 1970s corduroy jacket and shiny black pants, the type only seen at funerals, Norman Green came in with Danny right behind, his keys dangling from his hands. The civilian clothes and the books in Danny's hands reminded Kara that he was studying for the sergeant's exam. She had been so wrapped up in her own personal issues that she had forgotten.

Mrs. E. made introductions as if they were at a social gathering. "Have you met our lawyer, Mr. Green? Do you remember Officer Waters?"

Norman Green said, "Are you charging my client with something, Agent Boyd?"

Mrs. E. jumped in: "He threatened Kara with jail."

"Not yet," Agent Boyd replied, his lips barely moving, eyes never leaving Kara's face.

With his cultivated accent, Norman Green said, "Then we have nothing to discuss, do we?" He pointed toward the door. "Shall we leave these good people?"

"Ms. Lawrence, lawyers get in the way," Agent Boyd said in much the same way Zach had. Then, in a softer tone, "Talk to me, Kara. Help me help you."

Kara almost laughed except she was so near tears. He sounded like Tom Cruise in *Jerry Maguire*. Danny cough-laughed into his hand.

"Remember what I said," Agent Boyd continued, unaware of the comic relief. "He's not worth it. You can get out of this mess unscathed."

"Sir," Norman Green said with pointed emphasis.

Boyd walked in front of the lawyer to the door. "Until tonight, Ms. Lawrence."

The minute the two men left, Kara jumped up from the

piano bench. "I have to go out for a little while." She buttoned her coat. When she looked up, she saw the puzzlement on Danny and Mrs. E's faces. "To the doctor," she added. The tremor was now in her voice. "Thanks for calling Mr. Green," she said to Mrs. E., then turned to Danny. "I'm sorry"—but she wasn't sure what for.

Danny stepped forward. "Let me drive you."

That sounded appealing, but since she wasn't really going to the doctor, she couldn't accept. "No need, but thanks." She snatched up her tote.

"Let me help you." The minute the words came out of his mouth, he laughed. "Help me help you."

This made Kara laugh as well—not a healing laugh, but it still felt good. Yet it didn't change anything. She had to see Liz and she had to do it alone. Besides, she needed time to think. Beyond Norman Green's assurances and Zach's meaningless promises, she needed a plan of her own, and time was running out.

Kara hadn't seen Liz Kennelly since Christmas. They had each sent the other a card and met in Midtown for high tea as a holiday treat. Today, they were in the Starbucks near Liz's office. Located on a corner in Rockefeller Plaza, the coffee shop was crowded with professionally dressed men and women, the grinding hum of the coffee machines mingling with conversation and laughter. The aroma of ground beans mixed with a woman's perfume and the wet-wool smell of the man closest to Kara.

Kara and her former caseworker sat opposite each other at a table jammed against the front window.

Liz's nail polish matched her fiery hair and lipstick. She'd gained a little weight over the years, but her classic Irish features and flawless skin were the same as Kara remembered from childhood.

"It's been too long," Liz said, taking a sip of her black coffee. "Didn't we say after our Christmas get-together that we'd do this at least once a month?"

For the first time in days, Kara felt safe. "I've been sick."

"Sick, or is something else going on?"

Liz always had a way of getting directly to the problem. After she had rescued Kara, Flyer, and Tuesday, she'd stayed in touch, checking on all of them weekly while they were in the group home. Once Kara was on her own, Liz provided practical help. When children aged out of foster care, usually there was little support—no family to help an eighteen-year-old find her way, no job placement, housing, assistance to finish high-school diplomas or get into college. Nothing. But Kara had Liz.

It was through Liz's efforts that Kara got a scholarship to Pace University after graduating from Bronx Community College. Liz took Kara, Tuesday, and Flyer out to celebrate the year Kara graduated. Afterward, Liz drove Kara to her grandmother's old home in the Bronx. Kara had wanted to see it, go inside, she wasn't sure why. Once she got there, however, she was too overwhelmed to go in.

Liz helped Tuesday and Flyer too, but she took a much stronger interest in Kara. Perhaps because Kara returned her affection. She remembered Liz's birthday, talked to her on the phone several times a year, and, on occasion, visited Liz's Brooklyn home. Liz's questions brought her back.

"Has something happened?" Liz's eyes reflected the color of her teal suit.

"I've been having flashbacks." Kara stirred her tea with the supplied wooden stick.

"From your childhood?"

"Yes, about what Big Jim did to me." Kara surprised herself with tears, which silently slid down her face.

Liz came around the table, pressed Kara's face against her bosom. "I didn't know when I placed you there. The minute I found out, we came to get you. I'm so sorry."

Kara didn't know for how long she cried against Liz's chest. When she pulled away, the silk teal suit was stained with tears. She blew her nose. "How did you find out?"

Liz cleared their table, threw the paper cups into the trash. Her eyes were wet. "This is not the time or place for this—you're not feeling well, and we need to sit somewhere more private."

"Tell me now."

Lines of sadness etched Liz's face. "We thought he was molesting you and the other kids. We had no proof, but the circumstantial evidence was compelling."

"Like what? It had been going on for a long time. What finally made someone . . . ?" Kara hesitated. "What finally made *you* realize?"

It was Liz's turn to cry, the tears rolling down her pink cheeks. "We should have noticed sooner. I'm so sorry, Kara."

"Flyer too?"

Liz raised her wet eyes. "Yes."

Flyer said that Big Jim had used Kara and Tuesday like whores. Now Liz was telling her he used Flyer too. Kara had let Zach use her. Was that what she was, a whore? In her mind, she heard Marci Nye's voice tell her no, she wasn't.

"Say something, Kara. What are you thinking right now?"

Instead of voicing her true thoughts, Kara patted Liz's hand. "Thank you for telling me."

"Are you still seeing Dr. Nye?"

Kara nodded. "Big Jim died."

"When?"

"Last week."

"Does that help at all?"

"Not really." In fact, things had gotten worse ever since she'd heard. Maybe she could turn things around now. Maybe the ugly truths, all out in the open, would let her move things in the right direction.

Kara and Zach sat in Mrs. E.'s living room; Kara in the rocking chair and Zach on the edge of the sofa. He was waiting for her when she'd arrived home from her meeting with Liz. Dark smudges edged his eyes and his normally sleek beard looked like a lawn in need of mowing, with gray roots she'd never noticed before. He wore an open-collar shirt and his usually pressed slacks were rumpled. Only his shoes hinted at the Zach she knew, each polished to a glass finish.

As Kara rocked, she pulled her shawl tighter around her shoulders. She decided to take the offensive. "I need your help: I want you to tell the FBI that I had nothing to do with whatever it is you are involved in. I had no knowledge; I made no money."

"I can't do that." His voice was flat, his arms crossed.

"If you love me, as you say you do, you'll do this."

"Not possible."

"It's the right thing. It's the truth."

Zach unfolded his arms and leaned forward, his legs spread wide, his forearms resting on his thighs. "Listen to me—you know I love you, but this is business and it's serious." He stood up and stared down at her the same way Agent Boyd had earlier that day. "I'm the target of a baseless SEC investigation.

Despite the case's lack of merit, the FBI is still dangerous. We have to hang together."

In that instant, Kara knew she had to cooperate with the FBI and clear her name. Zach didn't love her, he never had. Here was the evidence smack in her face. Why did she fall for bad boys? Dr. Nye said her "family-of-origin messages" were powerful, meaning her mother had made the same kinds of choices. In addition, childhood trauma ate away at self-esteem. Okay, but now she had to make her own way, *be the master of her fate*—Marci Nye's favorite phrase. It had merit. It was time for Kara to embrace it.

She stood up. "Of course I'll help you," she said in a dead-pan tone. Almost as tall as Zach, she squared her shoulders and looked him straight in the eye.

"When they come back, you'll tell them there was a contract in the envelope?" He didn't sound convinced.

"Don't worry about me. I'll do my part."

He blinked several times. "They have nothing on me."

"I'm tired, Zach."

"Okay, Kara, I'm going to trust you. Just remember: if I go down, you go down."

CHAPTER TWENTY-FOUR

Kara's phone vibrated in her pocket. She dug it out.

"Hey, Liz." The shawl slipped from her shoulders. "Thanks for checking up on me, but I'm doing okay." They had parted only a few hours earlier.

"I'm glad."

Kara heard something in Liz's voice. "Are you okay?"

"I have some news you might find startling, upsetting, or maybe wonderful, I don't know."

"What is it?" Kara's stomach rumbled.

"I have a visitor who says she's your sister Alex. She's asked for your address and phone number."

At first, Kara was too stunned to comprehend what Liz was saying. Alex had finally come for her after all of these years? She was with Liz? The timing of this was bizarre. Curled up in a chair in her sitting room, her legs pulled under, a cup of tea on the table next to her, Kara tried to sort out her feelings. "What's she like?" Kara finally asked. "Do you trust her?"

"I think so. She seems genuine."

"Are you sure it's *my* Alex?"

"She has your eyes, just a different color, the same cheekbones, and a head of curls. I'm sure."

Kara closed her eyes. She pictured the laughing four-year-old Alex in the picture, reddish-blond tangles spilling down her back. Her sister had finally come for her.

"Why now?"

"Do you want to see her?"

"Yes." The answer came from deep inside. "Please tell her to come today, right away. Liz, my family has finally . . ." She couldn't finish the sentence or thought. All these years of pretending and waiting. Maybe Alex had been searching for her all along.

"There's something else you need to know."

The other shoe always dropped. "What?" Her mouth felt dry; she untucked her legs.

"You asked why now? According to Alex . . ."

"What?"

"Your father is deathly ill."

The man in the photograph was young, the picture of health: blond, bow-shaped lips, tanned muscles, and eyes the color of irises. "What's wrong with him?"

"Massive heart attack."

The words floated in the air after Kara hung up. *He is mortally ill.* She walked in tight circles around her sitting room. In the background, afternoon street sounds of cars and delivery trucks reminded her of the here and now. Alex had emerged. Downstairs the grandfather clock chimed four times. They had finally come for her, and he was dying. Kara slipped to the floor and pulled her knees to her chest. All her life, she'd waited for this moment, and now it might be too late.

The cafeteria was more like a snack stand with a few tables and a television in the building's basement. Refrigerated containers filled with sodas and juices lined a wall. Self-service coffee and tea machines were standing along another wall. After Michael selected apple juice, Alex passed on the coffee she really craved and bought the same.

"Kara is a special person." Michael sipped his juice.

"Is she? Have you met her?"

"No, but Liz has stayed in touch with her all these years, since Kara was six or so. Anyway, Liz is protective, is what I'm saying."

It felt like a first date. They drank their juices and moved onto other "getting to know you" topics. No mention so far of a Mrs. Michael Rosen or a partner, not even a *we*, which was encouraging. The bad news was that they had nothing in common. He loved soccer, so much so that he got up at five a.m. to watch afternoon European matches. Alex, on the other hand, was a football and baseball fan. He was a vegetarian; Alex lived on hamburgers. He was Jewish. Alex was what? Not Jewish—her mother would have a fit. What would his parents think of Alex? She'd known him for thirty minutes and she was already worrying about how they'd celebrate Christmas, and who would officiate at the wedding. *Get a grip.*

Liz's arrival brought Alex back to reality: "Kara has agreed to meet you today."

Oh my God—there it was. It was going to happen. The search was over, just like that. "I can't thank you enough. What did you say to her?"

"I explained the situation just as you explained it to me." Liz held a mug of coffee.

"Was she surprised? Is she okay with this?"

"Yes and yes. She's at home not feeling well."

"What's wrong? I can't bring a sick person into my father's hospital room."

Liz's gaze was steady, judgmental. Alex realized her mistake. "I hope she's okay."

"Don't make me regret this." Liz handed over a piece of paper to Alex. "Her address and cell phone number."

"Thank you so much." Alex glanced down at the neatly

written note. She couldn't name what she was feeling—scared maybe, excited, relieved she'd completed her assigned task; she was still the daughter her father could count on.

"This is a good person who was dealt a shitty hand. Do not—do you hear me—do not mistreat her for the benefit of your father."

"I won't. I promise."

Liz gave her one last hard stare, turned, and left.

"I warned you, she's protective," Michael said with a soft laugh.

Still stunned, Alex scooped out her car keys. "Well, I guess I should get over there." She made no move to go.

"Would you like to have dinner afterward?"

Alex blinked. Was he asking her out on a date?

Michael seemed embarrassed, or maybe unsure. "You might need someone to talk to, you know, professionally, I mean."

Ah, *professionally*. She stood up and he followed suit. "Will that be okay with your wife or . . . ?"

When he laughed, it was a joyful sound. "No wife, no anyone. What do you say?"

It was definitely a date.

Alex's cab pulled in front of a row of stately brownstones, many with brightly colored doors glowing in the pale afternoon light. The wind had picked up. Children dressed in baggy pants and oversized coats played on the sidewalks. Several young men worked on a car parked a few doors down, its hood up, with a light fastened to it. A small knot of people in dark coats stood in front of a funeral home situated in one of the buildings. Parked cars crowded both sides of the street. To Alex's left, a man swept in front of his building.

Alex made her way between the parked cars to number 106. She was glad she'd left the Jeep in the garage near Liz's office and taken a taxi—this neighborhood might not be safe. She rang the bell and waited. A tall man with a high forehead and deep brown skin answered the door.

"Hello." In spite of her stomach doing flips, she tried for a cheery tone. "My name is Alexandra Lawrence and I'm here to see Kara Lawrence. I believe she's expecting me."

The man stared at her with a perplexed expression. He stepped back, gesturing her inside. "You're related to Kara?"

"If you could just let her know I'm here." Alex shifted from one foot to the other.

"I'm Danny Waters," the man said, still looking dumbfounded.

Danny went to the top of the steps and peered into Kara's sitting room. "There's someone here to see you."

It was real. Alex was here. Kara rubbed the dried salt from the corners of her eyes and licked her lips. She had waited what felt like a hundred years for her real family to come for her, to rescue her from Big Jim, from the group home, from belonging to no one. Now, here she was, her sister Alex ready to claim her.

"You've been crying." Danny extended his hand toward her, square-tipped fingers slightly curled, palm up.

She put her hand in his and let him pull her up. "I want to show you something." She grabbed the photograph of her imagined—now real—family. "This is all I had up until now."

He studied the picture. "You were mighty cute."

The corners of Kara's mouth lifted. "I don't know how to feel."

"Just *be*."

* * *

Alex was pacing up and down the hall. The place smelled like a bakery. Something wonderful was going on in the kitchen for sure.

"Hello."

The voice, as familiar as her own, made Alex whirl around—she would know her anywhere. She had the oval-shaped Lawrence face, with large eyes etched with thick, arching eyebrows. Although Kara's eyes were not violet-blue like her own and her father's, the almond shape was the same. Unsure of what she'd expected, she saw that Kara's skin color was a honeyed beige, fairer than Michael's.

Alex put out her hand and stepped forward. "Hello, Kara. I'm Alex."

Kara just stared at her, her hands in the pockets of her slacks. Alex let her own hand drop back to her side.

"Thank you for agreeing to see me," Alex said.

Now what? Kara didn't seem the least bit happy to meet her. Why should she? Liz had said she wasn't feeling well. That might explain her lack of animation. Kara was still staring; Alex couldn't think what to do next. An old woman in a wheelchair rolled into the living room.

"Welcome to our home, I'm Eloise Edgecombe."

"So nice to meet you."

"Have you met Danny Waters?" Alex was about to reply, but the old woman kept talking. "Danny, Kara, where are your manners?" She turned back to Alex. "Please, have a seat. I've made a red velvet cake and iced it. Would you like some?"

"That would be wonderful."

"Some tea or instant coffee?"

"Don't go to any trouble."

"You probably like the real thing."

"Instant is fine." Caffeine from any source would help. She felt in her pocket for a cigarette, but there were none left.

Eloise Edgecombe swung her wheelchair around and pushed it toward the back of the house. "No trouble at all."

Danny led Kara to a rocking chair as if she were an invalid. *Jeez, maybe it* was *something serious.* Alex followed and found a seat on the sofa. The three of them looked at each other in what felt like an excruciatingly awkward silence. In the heat of the search, Alex hadn't planned the conversation. Rarely at a loss for words, her brain failed her now.

Danny broke the ice: "I see the family resemblance."

Alex leaped in: "Me too. Don't you think so, Kara?" It was as if the woman was a deaf mute. Alex was tempted to speak louder and more slowly. "I didn't know you existed until a few days ago," she continued. "My . . . our father had a heart attack."

Danny squinted. "Is he okay?"

"For now." She waited, but still no response from Kara. "He's a good person. I mean he's flawed, but decent."

Danny said, "Where's he been?"

"He's trying to right the wrongs of his past. That's why he asked me to find Kara." Then, leaning forward, she said, "He desperately wants to meet you before . . . if anything . . ." Her words caught in her throat.

Pushing her wheelchair forward with both hands, Mrs. E. came in with a silver tray balanced on her lap; it was crowded with cups on saucers, slices of cake, forks, spoons, and napkins. The aroma of hot coffee and cake could lift anyone's spirits. For several minutes they were all distracted with serving, sipping, and chewing.

"Wow." Alex was impressed.

For the first time, Kara smiled.

Danny said, "Mrs. E. is known for her sweets."

"I can see why. You ought to go into business." Alex took another bite of cake and made appreciative sounds. "Do you two get to eat like this all of the time?"

"Every night." Danny licked crumbs from the corner of his mouth.

Alex changed the subject back to their father: "Do you remember him at all? He told me he hasn't seen you since you were four or so."

"Yes, and I remember you too."

Hearing Kara's voice again, Alex realized why it sounded so familiar: it was Pigeon's voice when she was scared. Alex swallowed. In spite of the coffee, her mouth went dry.

"I have a picture of all of us together in a park in DC—you, my mom, our father, and me."

That had to be the picture Alex had found in her father's desk when she was rummaging for the insurance cards. She could feel heat creeping up and she knew red splotches were forming at the base of her throat and would soon reach her cheeks. Two persistent thoughts echoed in her head: *How could he desert his own flesh? . . . It could have been me.*

Kara pulled a photograph from her pocket, leaned forward, and handed it to Alex. A three-legged cat joined them; first he circled Alex's legs and then brushed against them. Absently, Alex stroked him as she studied the picture. When she'd first seen the photo at the house, she had not remembered the day. Now, a flash of memory came to her. "I fell off your bike and your mom cleaned my scrape." She examined the bruise on her knee. "I didn't know who you were." A terrible sadness descended. "He never said."

Kara nodded. The somber music of the rocker against the wood floor added to the swirl of emotions in the room.

Alex knew she was about to cry. She ducked her head and pulled a fresh tissue from her bag. When she looked up, Danny appeared panicked, which made Alex laugh. "Don't worry, Danny, we'll get ahold of ourselves."

He chuckled.

"Will you come and meet him?" Alex passed the picture back to Kara.

"No."

"What?" Why wouldn't she want to meet him? "He loves you and I know he loved your mother—he told me so. Please don't let him die in pain. He's sorry."

"He doesn't know what he's sorry for," Kara said. "He doesn't know what happened to me." She shook her head, curls swishing left and right. "I appreciate your coming, Alex. I used to play a game—trying to find you on the street."

Alex had nothing left to say.

"I hope he lives, for your sake." She got up, and this time she put out her hand and took Alex's. "Be well." She went back up the stairs from whence she'd come.

Alex turned to Danny.

He hiked his shoulders in response to her unspoken question.

"Do you think she might change her mind?"

"It sounded kinda final."

It did to Alex as well. She pleaded with Mrs. E.: "Would you help me persuade her? She has sisters, not just me."

"Sisters?"

"Two others."

The old lady gathered the dirty dishes. Before Alex could offer to help, Danny took them and finished the job.

"I'm sorry for your troubles, young woman," she patted the crown of braids on her head, "but Kara holds her own counsel."

Feeling like she'd failed, Alex dug in her backpack and pulled out a business-card case. It took a few seconds to separate two cards from the others. "Here's how to reach me, in case she changes her mind." She gave one to Danny and one to Mrs. Edgecombe. "Even if she doesn't want to see him, maybe just to get together." They each took her card.

Not knowing what else to do, but feeling she'd somehow missed something important, Alex put on her coat, thanked her hosts, and left. Once on the front steps, she realized she had no idea how she was going to get back downtown. Did cabs cruise Harlem? It was almost dark; the side-by-side buildings blocked the setting sun. Alex surveyed the block. The funeral across the street must have ended because everyone was gone. She wished she had her cell phone with her, but stupidly she'd left it in the Jeep's glove compartment.

"Let me get you a cab," Danny said from behind her.

Alex jumped, recovered. "Thanks, I was starting to panic."

He gave her a look.

Alex felt embarrassed. Was she as bad as her mother and Aunt Peggy, being afraid because she was in Harlem? As it turned out, cabs did cruise around the neighborhood—all kinds—a few yellow cabs as well as private service cars, but mostly battered old cars called gypsy cabs. A dented Chevy responded to Danny's wave.

A cigarette was all Alex could think about as the car rode downtown. If she just had one, then she could sort through all she was feeling. People use the term *surreal* for the dumbest things. This experience, however, fit. She placed two fingers against her lips and sucked in imaginary smoke, held it deep in her lungs, and then blew it out in a stream.

Kara was strange. Yes, she had a tough life—Michael and Liz had both hinted about something but didn't say what.

Kara had said their father *doesn't know what he's sorry for.* Still, compassion should have moved her at least to meet him. Alex took another unsatisfying phantom drag.

It would be bad for both of them—Kara and their father— if this didn't work out. Besides, who wouldn't want to meet their real family after all these years? Alex pictured family Christmases . . . *Hmmm.* She could remember more than one conversation filled with disparaging remarks about black people. Did her father criticize them? Not that she could recall.

No matter, she wasn't going to give up—her father was counting on her. Kara would like Vanessa and Pigeon, and they would like her. There was no need to tell her dad about today's meeting. What Alex needed was a new strategy.

CHAPTER TWENTY-FIVE

Kara watched from her front window as Alex's taxi pulled away from the curb. In many ways, Alex looked like the little girl in the picture, but now there was seriousness around her mouth, with parentheses carved into her skin. People always commented on Kara's eyes; she bet people did the same to Alex—their color was arresting. It was Alex's hair, however, that Kara remembered the most. Red-gold with waves upon waves of squiggly curls going in all directions, framing her face and hanging down her back, just as it had in the picture.

She let her mind run through the encounter. The conversation had been positive: her father wanted to make amends, and Alex wanted Kara to meet her other sisters. Wasn't that Kara's dream? She replayed every aspect from the moment Liz had called. What was missing? Why did Kara feel so bereft? It came to her in a flash of insight from the child inside of her. She wanted Alex to run to her, to hug her, to weep and laugh, to tell Kara how long and hard she'd searched for her, how much their father loved her and wanted her. This was, of course, both childish and impossible. Nevertheless, without it the hollowness remained that Kara had lived with since the day her mother died.

With a mental head shake, Kara placed her treasured photo facedown in a drawer. The FBI and Zach were pressing problems. She could not continue barely sleeping, having nightmares, throwing up, crying all the time, and believing in a fantasy life that could never be. In addition, she had to find a way to help Flyer and Tuesday—especially Flyer. When they were small, she couldn't save them; today, she could do something. Alex and her father were no longer a priority. They were her past and she had to focus on a better future.

Resolved, Kara walked out of the sitting room and into the hallway just as Danny passed by on his way to his rooms above hers.

"Thanks for helping me today," she said. "It's been tough, and without you and Mrs. E., I don't know how I'd stay sane."

"No problem." His face muscles were tight; his mouth opened, then closed again.

So wrapped up in her own drama, Kara realized she didn't know how Danny was doing. Was he ready for the sergeant's exam, did he need help studying?

"I'm going to listen to some music," she said, gesturing toward her record player. "Would you like to join me?"

He hesitated and then stepped into her sitting room. It was six in the evening and dark, so Kara switched on the lamps. She tried to see the room through Danny's eyes: a ceiling-to-floor bookcase crammed with paperbacks and a few hardcover books stood against one wall. The mantle of the fireplace held a variety of inexpensive carved figures, some African, some Asian, some Native American. Several framed photographs dotted various surfaces—Kara and her principal in front of the school; Tuesday, Flyer, Kara, and Liz at Kara's graduation; her mom and grandmother. The jazz collection, stacked in a corner of the room, was one of the few luxuries Kara allowed herself. She wondered what kind of picture this room painted of her.

Danny walked over to the pile of albums and picked up a Sarah Vaughn. "Who introduced you to the great divas?"

"My mother loved jazz. As far back as I can remember, jazz and Motown were all I heard."

He lifted his chin toward one of the photos. "That her?"

"Before she got sick."

Danny flipped the album over and glanced down at the song list. "My dad was a jazz fanatic too." He slipped the record out of its jacket, careful not to touch the playing grooves. "Mind if I put it on?"

"Please do."

Soon, the ambient sounds of "Misty" filled the room. *Look at me. I'm as helpless as a kitten up a tree. And, I feel like I'm clinging to a cloud. I can't understand. I get misty just holding your hand . . .*

Kara sat down; she loved this song. She closed her eyes. When she opened them, Danny was watching her.

"Tough day, right?"

For reasons she didn't understand, Kara felt uncomfortable as Sarah sang about her longing. Kara tried to sound in control. "I've had better." And to move the conversation to safe ground, she asked, "What about you? How are things going? Mrs. E. said they caught the murderer."

He leaned forward and rested his chin in his hands, then scrubbed his face with his palms. "Yeah."

"You don't sound happy about it." Sarah's musical tale of being *too much in love,* plus the darkness with only two lamps providing focused light, made the setting feel intimate. This made Kara nervous, but also bold. "Is something else going on?"

Again, he seemed to hesitate. Then, not meeting her eyes, he said, "This morning I interviewed the foster parents of that kid who got shot."

"Barry."

"Yeah. They didn't seem . . . I don't know . . . as broken-up as I thought they would be. Should be."

"There are good foster parents out there."

"I guess."

They fell silent, listening to the piano riffs and Sarah's deep soprano. But the love song didn't change the mood in the room.

Breaking the silence, Danny said, "I didn't get to say good-bye to my dad before he died."

This caught Kara by surprise. First, she knew nothing about Danny's family. Until now, he'd never mentioned them and no relatives seemed to visit. "When was that?"

"A few years back."

"How?"

"Alone."

Sarah's love song ended. Kara waited.

Danny got up, lifted the needle from the record. "The last time I saw him alive, we had a fight. I screamed at him, asked him why he hadn't been a better dad. You know, been there for me more." Danny had his back to Kara as he spoke. He returned Sarah to her jacket. Absently, he shuffled through the rest of Kara's albums. "I wanted to know why he hadn't taught me how to throw a baseball, or dunk a basketball, or catch a fish—stuff like that."

Kara tried not to disturb the air.

"He said he did the best he could." Danny faced her. "But his best wasn't good enough. I wanted him to be the dad I needed, not the one he felt he could be."

Did everybody have a terrible childhood? Was anyone ever happy?

"Next thing I know, he's gone. He called me, said he

wasn't feeling well. I was still mad and he didn't make it sound serious. My dad wasn't a complainer, he was a self-sufficient person. I told him if he wanted me to, I'd take him to his doc first thing in the morning."

"What happened?"

"He died."

"You can't blame yourself, Danny. It sounds like you do."

His mouth twisted. "It's not rational, but yeah, I do." He paced in front of her for a second or two and then stopped. "The man worked two jobs, sometimes three, so I could get an education, live in a decent apartment, go to summer camp upstate, not grow up in the streets. Worked for the sanitation department during the day, cleaned and polished office floors in the evenings. Caught odd jobs on the weekends. He was gone all the time, and I was alone. He was strict: I had to come straight home after school and call him, do my homework and leave it out for him to check, cook us both dinners and save his. When he could, he called me while I ate alone. You see what I'm saying?"

"He sounds like a good man." Kara could feel the inadequacy of her words.

"He was."

"Where was your mother?"

"When I was ten, my dad came into my bedroom. I was already in bed. He said, *We can't stay here anymore. It's not safe. We have to go.* I hated leaving my mother, but even at a young age I knew she was crazy. I stuffed everything I owned into a backpack and duffel bag, took my dad's hand, and that was that."

Kara thought about her mother. One of the things that stayed with her, one of the things Marci Nye helped her hold onto, was what a loving mother she'd had—even if it was only for a few years. "You're lucky. You had someone who loved you, you had family."

Danny nodded his head. "He loved me and I loved him."

"Do you know where she is now, your mother?"

"Yeah, I hear from her sometimes, but I haven't seen her for years. She didn't come to my dad's funeral." He sat down in front of Kara. "Here's the thing." Fingertips steepled, Danny continued: "What if she dies? Will I feel bad like I do about my dad? He *was* a good dad, raised a son alone the best he could. Came home every night; never brought women over. I should have told him before he died."

"I'm so sorry, Danny. I bet he knew. I bet he knew how much you loved him and appreciated him. It was only one day, one fight."

Danny shrugged, his eyes shining with moisture.

She reached out and touched his fingers, and Danny gathered her hands into his. She said, "People *feel* love; they don't always have to hear it."

Several beats passed. Then, he pulled her gently up and close to him. She could smell spearmint and feel the heat of his breath. Danny brushed his lips against hers and she leaned into the kiss. His arm circled her waist and tugged her closer, his tongue slipped into her mouth. For a second, she let it happen. Then she pulled away.

"I'm sorry," he said, but it came out like a question.

She should say something, but she felt confused.

"You okay? I mean, was it okay I kissed you?"

"I kissed you back." What kind of woman was she, barely through with Zach and now kissing another man? "We're both overwrought," she added, trying to give it a safer spin.

"Right."

She looked away from his intense stare.

"Except that's not why I kissed you."

"All this stuff going on," she waved her hand in the air, wiping it all away, "it's just not the right time."

"Okay." Danny stepped back and edged toward the door. "The reason I told you about my family is that I've been thinking about going down to Virginia where my mom lives. Anyway, what I'm trying to say is, maybe you should take Alex up on her request. Make sure you have no regrets."

"Are you going?"

"You want me to?" Her confusion must have showed on her face, because Danny said, "Oh, you mean go to Virginia?"

She nodded. Several seconds ticked by.

"Yeah, I'm definitely going to go."

It wasn't that she didn't understand Danny's advice—she did. Her conclusion, however, was different. His mother could come to New York, and her father could have found her sooner. Only now that he was dying had Kara become important. His search was selfish and had nothing to do with caring for her. Well, Danny was right: she didn't want any more regrets. She had to deal with the FBI and then move on with her life. She had to take charge.

Danny eased closer. "What are you going to do?"

Now it was her turn to step back. This was no time for whatever had just happened between them. "Thanks for your advice and help, Danny."

He seemed hurt.

"Really, I appreciate everything, but I have to do what's best for me."

"I get it." For several seconds he just stood there, as if expecting her to change her mind or to say something more.

"I'll think about what you said."

Danny backed out of the room, his eyes still on her.

Marty wound around and between her legs, so she picked him up. "You, Mr. Marty, are the one constant in my life." She touched her lips with her other hand. She had to admit, Danny's kiss had felt good, safe. *No, no more of that.*

The phone rang. Still holding Marty with one hand, Kara picked it up.

Tuesday's voice was panicked: "It's Flyer, Kara. You've got to get over here fast."

CHAPTER TWENTY-SIX

Flyer stood on the narrow ledge of his apartment building, his arms splayed wide with his palms pressed against the brick, his overcoat flapping and billowing around his ankles.

Kara and Danny arrived on the scene less than fifteen minutes from the time Kara had hung up the phone. Tuesday had been almost incoherent. "He's out there and I think he'll do it. He said he wants to die."

"I'm coming."

She'd called for Danny and he appeared in seconds. "Flyer is trying to kill himself."

They wove through the traffic, Danny at the wheel. When they arrived, the crowd in front of the building was thick; one woman munched on popcorn as if she were at the movies. With her hand in his, Kara and Danny dodged through the crowd to the police barricade. Danny wasn't in uniform, but on the way, he'd hung his badge around his neck. Now he flashed it at the cop barring their way. "She's family," he said. The officer parted the posts and let them through.

They ran up the steps to the fourth floor. Kara tried to clear her mind. When they were children, she could send Flyer mental messages—get him to choose a certain card when they played bid whist, get him to turn around and look at her. At the time, they thought it was funny. As they matured, she realized it was the manifestation of the powerful bond between them. She prayed she could make him come off the ledge.

The building was located on 145th Street on the west side of Harlem. Flyer shared the two-bedroom apartment with two other men—Joseph and his partner Darrel. Both of them were in the living-dining-entranceway space, along with Tuesday and a police officer, when Kara and Danny arrived. Tuesday ran to Kara the minute she saw her.

"He's gone crazy or something. Joseph called me right after he phoned 911. I tried to get him to talk to me but he won't." Tuesday's round head barely reached Kara's shoulder.

"Where is he?"

She pointed to Flyer's bedroom.

Kara, Danny, and Tuesday entered the room. A man in a suit leaned out of the bedroom window. "Son, you don't want to do this. Why don't you come inside and we'll sit down and work through whatever's bothering you." He extended his hand. "It's cold out there. Just take my hand and come in, we can all get warm."

The muscles of Kara's thighs trembled; her heart beat erratically. "May I try?" she asked the man's back. "We grew up together, he might listen to me."

In a tear-clogged voice, Tuesday said, "Let her speak with him, let her try."

The man didn't seem to hear. "Can I get you something, Flyer? That's what your friends call you, right? Is it okay if I call you Flyer?"

A female officer joined them and approached Kara. "What's your name and relationship to Mr. Dresden?"

"We're practically siblings; please let me help."

Danny stepped forward. "Ms. Lawrence and Mr. Dresden grew up together. Why not give her a chance?"

The man leaning out of the window had evidently heard this because he said, "Ms. Lawrence is here, Flyer. Can she talk to you?"

"Kara?"

The man turned and Kara nodded.

"Yeah, Kara is here. That okay by you?"

Flyer must have indicated assent. The man pulled his head back in and welcomed Kara to the window with a gesture. "Keep your voice low, don't spook him. The goal is getting back inside. Got it?"

"I understand." She could feel the blood pounding in her head. "Flyer, hey, it's me. What's going on with you?"

At first, he didn't answer her. She focused on his sharply drawn profile, dreadlocks pointing in different directions. With deep concentration, she tried to connect the way they did when they were children. The wind stung her face. Nearby, a pigeon cooed and then swooped away. Kara put every ounce of energy she had into sending him a message.

Finally, Flyer spoke: "He didn't do anything to me, you know."

It was all her fault. She leaned farther out, her right hip on the ridges of the window frame, her left hand pressed against the closed portion of the window. With her right hand, she reached out toward Flyer. "I know. It was just Tuesday and me."

"I tried to make him leave you girls alone. If I had a real sword, you know, not the toy one, but a real one, I could have stopped him."

"You were just a boy."

"I prayed night after night that he'd stop. I prayed until I stopped believing."

"God heard you. He sent Liz."

"Took too long."

"There was nothing you could have done. It wasn't your fault."

"Sometimes I called on the devil and asked him to help—I promised him things."

"Flyer, we were children."

"Do you know why they call me Flyer?"

Kara was crying now. He'd been too little to save her, just as she had been too young to save him and Tuesday. She hadn't let herself remember the overwhelming helplessness she'd felt when she couldn't rescue them.

"You told me you wanted to be a pilot when you were a kid, isn't that how you got your name?"

"That's what I said, but it's not the truth."

"Come in and tell me the real story."

He seemed not to hear her or notice her hand reaching for him.

"When I was real small, I jumped out the window of our apartment."

Kara covered her mouth to keep her sobs unheard.

"Broke both my legs and cracked a few ribs. When they asked me why I jumped, I told them I wanted to fly."

Oh dear God, why didn't we talk about any of this before?

"The truth was I wanted to die."

She took a deep breath to steady her voice. "I know. I used to think about dying all the time, but I didn't do it. Do you want to know why?" He didn't say anything. "Because of you and Tuesday."

Flyer still didn't seem to hear her. Desperate, Tuesday's words came back to her: that Flyer used to do everything Kara told him to do. "Flyer, I want you to come inside and be with me and Tuesday. We're alive and Big Jim is dead."

She waited, but he still did not respond.

"We need you—I need you. Please come in."

Kara sensed, rather than saw, Danny standing behind her. He circled her waist and braced himself so Kara could lean out as far as possible. "Please take my hand, Flyer. I love you so much. You and Tuesday, you are the only family I have."

It was true. All her life she had held on to the dream of her father and sister, her "real" family—but they weren't. Her family was here. "Please, Flyer. We were kids. They were the grown-ups. It wasn't our fault."

Flyer's tortured eyes burned into hers. "He never did anything like that to me."

"He never did."

It seemed as if he was going to come in. He nodded to himself and said, "Okay," several times. Then he inched to the side toward Kara. Farther along the ledge and out of Flyer's sight, Kara noticed a police officer easing along the ledge. A heavy rope secured him to a cop leaning from what must have been a neighbor's window. The officer on the ledge placed his finger on his lips and nodded meaningfully at Kara.

Either sensing someone's presence or reading Kara's face, Flyer jerked his head to the left. The motion caused him to lose his balance.

"No."

As if in slow motion, Flyer began to topple over.

The officer flung out his arm and caught Flyer by his left forearm midair; Flyer's momentum pulled the man with him.

Kara broke free from Danny's hold and scrambled out the window on her knees. "No, Flyer, no."

Now both Flyer and the police officer dangled from the window, forty feet above the ground, as two other cops grabbed the rope.

"I'm going to drop him," the first officer shouted. "I'm losing my grip."

The two officers inside tugged. "Hold on, Tony, we've got you both."

Kara crawled out as far as she dared and watched Flyer's hand slip, second by second, along the officer's forearm, his topcoat still billowing around his lean frame. She could hear isolated voices from below.

"Let him die if he wants to."

"Hold on to him, don't drop him."

Behind her, she heard Tuesday sobbing.

They hung, suspended in air, Flyer dangling from the officer's hand as the officer gripped the rope in a deadly tug-of-war.

Kara held her breath. The two officers hoisted first the cop named Tony, and then Flyer, to safety.

Crawling, she backed up and climbed in through the window. Once inside, she stepped into Danny's arms.

He held her, her face mashed against his neck, as shudders convulsed through her body. He stroked her hair, patted her back, and rocked her. "It's okay, Kara. He's safe now."

It felt like the safest place she'd ever been.

She stopped crying and pushed away. "I have to go to him."

Tuesday, however, stood in her path. "Satisfied?" Spittle sprayed Kara's face. "This is your fault."

It was. "I'm so sorry."

"You're the one he liked the best. You're the one who got everything while we got shit."

"What?"

Tuesday hammered Kara's chest with her fists. "We said we'd never, ever say anything to anyone. Now look what you've done."

The blows rocked her, but she didn't even feel them. "What are you saying?" It felt like everyone in the room was watching them.

"Leave her alone," Danny said, catching Tuesday's fists.

"You think we didn't notice you were Big Jim's favorite?" Tuesday wriggled free from Danny's hold. "You and your white skin and light eyes. You think it didn't matter he made sure you ate the best, got the best, while we ate shit and got nothing but his belt?"

What was Tuesday saying? Big Jim *cared* about Kara? "He did the same to me that he did to you." The blank face of a flat-screen TV stared down at them from its perch on a wire organizer. "Same as you."

Tuesday ran into Flyer's bedroom. Kara followed.

She stood outside the door with no way to process what she'd just heard. Where to begin? She searched the faces around her, each as blank as the television screen, except for Danny's. He walked over to her.

"Don't think about it now," he said. "There's time enough later."

Tears pooled and slid down Kara's face. She squeezed Danny's hand and stepped into Flyer's room.

Flyer, curled in a fetal position on his bed, had visible tremors moving through his body. Tuesday had flung herself next to him. What could Kara say? What was the truth? What did it matter? Danny was right—think about it later. She looked at her brother and sister curled together. Tuesday's silent cries made her muscles tremble under her blouse. Kara went to them, lay down on the bed, and put her arms around them both. "I love you," she said. "Nothing happened, nothing ever happened."

CHAPTER TWENTY-SEVEN

Michael and Alex sat opposite each other in a Japanese restaurant on West 56th Street; its authentic motif was marred by the faux-celebrity photographs scattered across the walls. When he'd asked if she liked Japanese food, Alex had said yes. In fact, she'd never had it before. She liked Chinese okay, would it taste the same? It didn't.

"Tell me about your family." Alex, mirroring Michael's move, poured her Sam Adams down the inside of the tilted glass. She was usually a drink-from-the-bottle girl, but not today.

"Not much to tell." He took a long pull and then wiped his mouth with his napkin.

"Siblings?"

"I'm the baby. My brother Matt is eleven months older; Rebecca and David are ten, and eleven years older than I am."

Alex liked the sound of Michael's voice, his Brooklyn accent softened by education and probably from practice as well. As hokey as it sounded, his chestnut-brown eyes had amazing depth. Not to mention those eyelashes—women strive to achieve that length with mascara but rarely do. What had he just said? She lifted her glass, sipped, and swallowed. Oh yeah, ten and twelve years older. "Second marriage?"

The amused way he watched her made her think he knew

two separate conversations were going on: the one out loud about his family, and the other with her imagining him naked beside her in bed.

"Nope, Sid and Estelle have been bickering happily for forty-five years. Rumor has it Estelle cut him off after David was born and only let him back in the bedroom after David stopped raising hell."

Alex laughed. "With all the fights my parents had, I can't ever remember a time when my father slept on the proverbial couch." Not that she had any clue about her parents' sex life, or wanted to for that matter. It was just hard to imagine Judy, or anyone, saying no to Worth Lawrence.

"They're affectionate, so maybe that wasn't it."

A comfortable silence followed. Their food came and they both dug in. Between forkfuls, Alex asked, "Are your brothers and sister around? Do you see them often?" She was thinking about Pigeon who was clear across the country.

"I see Becca a lot. She has five kids, so I'm Uncle Mike. My parents live in West Palm Beach, the land of the seventy-year-old Jewish gentry from New York, the sixth borough. I try to get down there a couple times a year."

"Is your family religious?" She hoped her question wasn't too abrupt. She knew what Judy would think about "a nice Jewish boy," but what would her father say?

"Culturally, if that makes sense."

Alex nodded and took another forkful of her *rad na*, which was rice noodles in gravy with chicken and shrimp. "This is yummy."

"Glad you're enjoying it."

"So, you were saying about being culturally religious?"

"We celebrate the major holidays—Rosh Hashanah, Yom Kippur, Passover—but it's more about being Jewish than about

God." He took another bite. "I think I might feel differently if I had kids."

This time the silence felt awkward, or maybe that was a result of her carnal thoughts from earlier.

"Tell me about you."

"Like what?"

"I don't know, stuff."

Alex shrugged. How could she explain in a coherent way what it was like growing up in her family, or why at thirty she was still alone and, in fact, hadn't had a committed relationship with anyone, ever?

"What's your happiest childhood memory?"

The question caught her by surprise. "Happiest?" Hadn't she tried to remember happy times on Sunday with her mother? The ant invasion had been the only one that came to mind. Surely, Judy-drama hadn't filled every moment of their lives. Finally, she said, "I guess the year we didn't have a Christmas tree."

Michael's eyes glinted. This was crazy, she barely knew him, but she felt herself opening up.

"What happened?"

Alex searched for the details. "Christmas was important to our family—a time for reunion and sharing more than a religious occasion, like for your family. For my sisters and me, however, it was magical."

Michael put down his fork, kept his focus on her face.

"My mom would take us to the local Italian bakery and let us pick out all of the pies and cakes."

"No home baking?"

"She was only good at meat and potatoes." Just thinking about it brought back images of Judy pulling out the hardly used cookbooks and making roast lamb and beef with Yorkshire pudding and gravy. "Grandma Colonie, my mom's mother, loved to cook."

"Did you grow up with all of your grandparents alive?"

"The grandmothers outlasted the granddads."

"What's that about?" He was laughing at her again, but not in a mean way. "You ladies like to kill us off early and inherit the loot?"

"You guys never go to the doctor when we tell you to or take vitamins or—"

"I give, I give. Besides, I *do* take vitamins."

Of course he did.

"We've gotten sidetracked. You were telling me about the no-tree Christmas."

"This Christmas I could sense something was wrong. Usually, my dad would take us to a tree farm to get a freshly cut Scots pine, his favorite. He also took us shopping for Christmas presents for the rest of the family. It was already Christmas Eve and he hadn't been home for a week—no tree, no presents." Once again, images filled her mind's eye of how much she'd loved shopping with her father and finding the perfect present for everyone. Sometimes, he would drop off the younger kids and take just her along with him to find something special for her mother.

"How old were you?"

Alex tried to remember. What year would that have been? "Little, I'm not sure."

"So far, this is a sad story. How does it end up being your happiest memory?"

The waiter came over and took their empty plates.

"Want another beer?" Michael asked.

Alex nodded yes, then continued: "My middle sister Vanessa saved the evening. She'd made a tree at school out of evergreen branches and aluminum foil."

"Cool."

"For once, my mother said and did the right thing. We decorated it, acted like it was the best tree ever." Vanessa had been so proud and Alex was distraught—where was her daddy and the real tree? "But that's not the best part. The best part was when sleigh bells woke me up sometime in the middle of the night. I was positive it was Santa, and it was."

"It was, huh?" He was laughing again.

"Absolutely," Alex laughed too. "I climbed out of bed and crept downstairs, like in a movie, and there were silver bells hanging from red ribbons all over the living room. And in the center of the room was the most spectacular tree ever, with presents packed under it, and my parents—both of them— were holding hands and drinking eggnog."

"What happened to Vanessa's tree?"

"It had its own place and there were presents under it too."

"What a great story."

For a few minutes they just watched each other; they hadn't yet noticed that the waiter had brought them two beers and clean glasses. Eventually, Alex said, "My dad could always pull things together at the last minute." That's what he was trying to do now with Kara. A new thought suddenly occurred to her. "Now *this* Christmas memory doesn't feel the same."

"What do you mean?"

"I was about six that year, which means so was Kara." Michael nodded as if he already understood. He knew it was the year Kara's mother had died, the year her father chose Alex over Kara and put Kara up for adoption. Alex's voice dropped to a whisper. "I wonder what kind of Christmas memories Kara has from that year."

Michael reached across the table and took her hand. After a while he asked, "How did your visit with Kara go?"

Alex had pushed it to the back of her mind. For the first time since her father's request, she had been really enjoying herself. Now, the conversation with Kara came back like a too-spicy meal. "Awful. She said no. I did everything I could, but she wouldn't budge."

"I can't say I'm surprised, but I'm sorry."

Someone pushed past Alex and Michael's table heading for the restroom in the back. They both steadied their bottles and glasses, and simultaneously accepted the urgent diner's apology.

"Well, I was surprised. I could see my story touched her." Alex poured her second beer and took a sip. "She told me my father didn't know what he was sorry for."

Michael responded with a noncommittal noise.

"I asked the people she lives with—a cop who I think has a thing for her and a grandmotherly person in a wheelchair—I asked them to try and persuade her, but I'm not too hopeful." She took another pull. "Why aren't you surprised?"

"He abandoned her."

"I get it." She wiped the beer foam from her mouth with her fingers. Then, embarrassed, grabbed her napkin and redid it. Although she was unsure how she felt about Kara, Alex knew she had to see this through. Her father had asked, and she had to give him peace. But now she had met Kara; Alex saw another sister who needed her help, even if Kara didn't know it—everyone needs family. "Do you think Liz will help me?"

"Help with what?"

"Persuading Kara."

He shrugged. "You can ask her, but I don't know if Liz will go any further than she has. There's a lot about Kara's story you don't know."

"You think?" Then, regretting her tone, "Everyone keeps hinting at things but no one is telling me anything."

Michael pulled at his mouth with one hand, pinching his lower lip, his eyes moving across her face, and then he looked away.

"Please, Michael, what happened?"

"I can't tell you anything. It would be unethical."

Alex winced. Did he think she was asking him to commit some wrongful act? That's not what she meant.

"However, I will ask Liz if she'll help persuade Kara. I don't think it will work, but I can try."

"Thank you."

"You're welcome." He signaled to the waiter that he wanted their check. "I'll talk to her in the morning."

"I'd never ask you to do anything wrong. I know you hardly know me."

"I didn't think you were."

The waiter brought over the check and Michael peered at it.

"How much is my half?"

He had that amused expression again, which was starting to irritate her. "I got it."

"You're sure? Because I can pay my way."

"No need."

"Thanks." Well, not exactly irritating. "Thanks for dinner, and for listening and helping me."

Michael scratched the back of his head, his brow creased.

"We should probably get going," Alex said.

"I guess."

Neither moved. Finally, Alex grabbed her bag from the seat next to her and Michael jumped up and helped her into her jacket. He was close enough that she could smell the beer and onions, but it wasn't unpleasant.

Her cell phone rang. She didn't recognize the number but thought it might be Pigeon. "Excuse me," she said, then answered the phone. "Hello?"

It was a familiar voice. "Kara?"

CHAPTER TWENTY-EIGHT

Kara stood on the corner of 145th and Frederick Douglass Boulevard waiting for Alex to pick her up. She shifted from one foot to the other, both to keep warm and to help relieve her anxiety. The purple-and-white scarf wound around her neck helped keep the night chill out, but her nose and fingers felt frozen. Every few seconds, she glanced up and down the wide avenue searching for Alex's red Jeep.

It was almost eight p.m. and the street was crowded with people moving in all directions at a New York pace. The sky was dark, but the light streaming from the street lamps and storefronts helped illuminate Kara's vigil.

This was it. She was going to meet her father after all of these years. She stamped her feet and blew on her hands before shoving them back into her pockets. What would she say to him, ask him? What would he look like now? Would he even be able to speak? Alex said he was gravely ill. For that matter, maybe visiting hours were over and she wouldn't get to see him at all.

This was probably a bad idea; she should be with Flyer. She glanced at her watch again: 8:03. It had only been an hour ago when she had lifted her head from Flyer's bed and asked the policewoman what would happen next.

"They'll take him to Bellevue for assessment," she'd said, her face a professional mask.

Kara heard sirens approaching. "And then what?"

The officer shrugged.

Two paramedics from the city's largest psychiatric hospital had crowded into the bedroom and lifted Flyer onto a gurney. His eyes remained closed and she could hear his shallow breathing, his chest rising and falling in rapid succession.

Danny had put his arm around Kara's shoulder. "He'll be okay, it's not a bad place."

Tuesday watched from across the room. Although Danny's supporting arm felt good, Kara stepped away and approached her. "We have to talk."

"I was acting crazy," Tuesday said. Her normally smooth brown cheeks were mottled.

"Not crazy." Kara could still feel the sting of Tuesday's accusation that somehow Big Jim treated her better—better than what?

"I don't want to talk."

"Okay, but later, after . . ." Since Kara had no idea what would happen next, she'd been unable to finish the sentence.

Danny said, "I can give you both a lift home or to the hospital, but I don't think there's much you'll be able to do for him tonight."

That's when she'd made up her mind; the words came out before she really processed her thoughts: "Thanks, Danny, but I have to go somewhere tonight."

At first she didn't understand Danny's hurt expression, but then she realized he thought she was going to see Zach. "I've decided to take your advice and meet my father."

Tuesday said, "Your father?"

Kara nodded to Tuesday, but directed her words at Danny. "What you said about your dad and about going to see your mother—that all made sense to me after seeing Flyer on that ledge." She'd wanted Danny to know that she'd changed today.

Danny asked, "Can I help?"

Tuesday jumped in: "Help do what? What's going on?" She eyed each of them.

Kara leaned down slightly and hugged Tuesday. "Nothing—I mean a lot, and I'll explain everything. It will all be okay." She'd smiled at Danny but guessed from his expression that the result wasn't convincing. "I have to do this alone."

Clarity arrived at odd times. As she'd watched the ambulance drive Flyer away, with blinking lights and wailing siren, she'd seen the road ahead: meet her father and put the past to rest; deal with Zach and the FBI; help Flyer get better; move on with her life.

Now, as she stood on the street corner waiting for Alex, Kara didn't feel as sure as she had an hour before. A heavyset man walked past her; he appeared to check her out under the guise of looking into the shop window behind her. He could *not* be the FBI. Tonight was the deadline and they were awaiting her answer, so why follow her? The man rounded the corner. A group of teenagers in an illegally parked car blasted music and laughed on another corner. At that moment, Kara's eye caught the gaze of a woman standing just as Kara was, as if she too was waiting for someone. The way the woman kept peering up and down the street seemed exaggerated. This was a bad idea. Kara should have gone home with Danny or stayed with Tuesday. As she was about to abandon her vigil, a red Jeep Cherokee pulled in front of her. Alex opened the door and Kara climbed in.

The Jeep was warm. A vintage U2 album, *The Joshua Tree*, played on the car stereo. Alex lowered the volume. "I'm glad you called."

Kara watched the scene outside the window and squinted at the side-view mirror.

"What's wrong?" Alex asked.

"I think we're being followed."

"Followed?" Alex swiveled her head toward Kara and then back to the street traffic.

"I'm sorry, I'll get out if you want me to."

"Why the hell would any follow you?"

"You won't get in trouble or anything."

Alex's frown was deep. Kara decided that she had to explain about the FBI and Zach. She owed Alex in case she was putting her in danger. Keeping it simple, brief, and not mentioning her affair with Zach—or that he was married—Kara ended with, "I don't think he meant to get me into trouble, but here I am."

"Are you sleeping with this idiot?"

"I have until midnight to help them, or they'll prosecute me."

"Do you love him?"

They were going sixty-five miles an hour on the West Side Highway, heading north to Westchester County. Kara felt humiliated. She and Alex had only just met, and now Alex knew about her sorry history. From the side-view mirror, Kara saw a black sedan pull two cars behind them.

Alex said, "I thought you and the cop were a couple."

"Did you? Why would you think that?"

"He's crazy about you, anyone can see that."

"Danny and I are just friends."

They were speeding along the mostly empty highway with soft curves and three lanes. The faint sounds of U2 eased the tension.

Alex took her eyes from the road for a fraction of a second. "So, you love this Zach guy?"

It was a strange turn for the conversation to take. After

all, Kara was about to meet her father for the first time since she was four years old, and the FBI was following her. Plus, Alex was practically a stranger. Yet here they were discussing Kara's not-so-great love life.

"It's complicated," Kara replied. "I mean, I thought I loved Zach, but he betrayed my trust."

"Tell me about it . . . I just met this man for the first time tonight and I already have these crazy feelings I don't understand. Life is strange, that's all I can say."

Kara welcomed the diversion. "And?"

It was funny how easy it was speaking with her—it was as if they had known each other for years. In fact, Alex already knew more about Kara's current life than the people to whom Kara was the closest. Kara glanced at Alex's profile; it was like looking in a mirror.

Alex shrugged. "We'll see."

Kara shifted in her seat and twisted around to check out what the black sedan was doing. It was still there, now right behind them. They weren't even trying to be covert.

"How is your dad doing?"

Like Kara, Alex appeared nervous about the black sedan. She scanned her mirrors. "*Our* dad? It's touch and go. The second heart attack did a lot of damage."

"Will they let us go up?"

"They have to, he's desperate to see you."

"I want to see him too," Kara said, as much to herself as to her sister.

"Thank you. It will good for you both."

"You said I have other sisters. What are they like?"

"You seem sad, maybe meeting him will make you feel better." Alex was trying to delve deeper but Kara wanted to change topics.

"Didn't you say there are two others?"

The slate-gray Hudson River, to their left, had small whitecaps from the March wind. Occasionally they passed a crop of moored sailboats, waiting for spring.

"Pigeon is the youngest. She's rebellious, a lost soul." Alex clicked on her left signal and moved into the passing lane. The black sedan did the same.

"Why do you call her Pigeon?" Kara pictured someone small, with a flexible neck.

"Monica, but she's been Pigeon since she could walk. I think Vanessa—that's our middle sister—called her that because of the way she moved. Anyway, the name stuck."

"Tell me about Vanessa."

Alex seemed edgy; she kept tugging at her hair and shifting in her seat. "Sophisticated, but I'm worried about her. I think she may be using drugs." She clamped a hand over her mouth. "I can't believe I just told you that."

Kara sought to make all of this information real, but so far it was just conversation, like discussing characters in a novel. She tried for an empathetic tone: "It's been that kind of a day."

"Indeed." Alex peered at her sideways. "Can I ask you something?"

"Okay."

"What are you going to do about the FBI?"

"Help them. I have no choice."

Alex was amazed at how easy it was to be with Kara. The cold, unforgiving person she had met earlier today was not the woman sitting next to her in the Jeep. This Kara was warm, vulnerable, intelligent, and as mixed up as Alex was.

They had just passed the George Washington Bridge, its

lights strung across the Hudson River as if expecting a party. At this rate, they'd be at the hospital in less than thirty minutes. She turned up the music.

As nervous as Kara appeared to Alex, she seemed like someone who could take care of herself. Here she was meeting her birth father for the first time, while FBI agents followed her. Michael's words came back to her: who knew what else Kara was dealing with? Alex took a sip of water from an old bottle in the cup holder. She glanced at the rearview mirror. The FBI agents were still right behind them. She could see the male driver's hat-covered head and the female in the passenger seat. "They don't seem dangerous to me," she said to Kara with a shrug.

Kara cracked a smile.

For the first time since her search began, Alex was glad her father had asked her to do this.

CHAPTER TWENTY-NINE

The hospital lobby was busy even though it was well past visiting hours, which ended at eight thirty. Kara and Alex were not the only people who'd just arrived. Three adults, perhaps family members, walked in behind them, and an elderly man using a cane was only a few steps ahead. The woman at the reception desk appeared uninterested.

People were also leaving. Visitors stepped off the elevator. Some of them moved with speed, as if eager to get away from whatever or whomever they left upstairs; others lingered, chatting with each other the way family members did during the final moments of a reunion, reluctant for it to end.

As Kara took it all in, she wondered if Bellevue was this clean and bright. Did it smell like sickness, or more like an office building, the way this lobby did? Were the doctors and nurses taking good care of Flyer?

The steady *click-clack-click* of Alex's car keys pulled Kara back to the purpose at hand. Alex stood to Kara's left, her eyes darting around. Kara could feel her agitation, which matched her own. Since she was small, Kara had imagined this day a thousand times, but it was never like this. They were always at a house filled with family and pets: Kara not only had Marty, but a puppy; of course, she had a room of her own. Her father was healthy, looking just like he did in the picture, and he was ecstatic to see her. She braced herself for reality.

"Excuse me," said a hefty aide pushing a woman in a wheelchair. "Coming through." Alex and Kara stepped aside.

"Are you ready?" Alex asked.

How could she possibly be ready? "Sure."

Just to their left a voice interrupted, "Alex, Alex, over here." It belonged to a young woman with short black hair streaked with purple. She skirted a cluster of people and trotted over. "This place is crazy."

"You got here." Alex threw her arms around the woman and pulled her close. "Did you just land? Does Mom know you're here?"

This had to be Alex's sister Pigeon—not just Alex's sister, but hers as well. Kara searched for resemblances. It was strange meeting people who were blood relatives for the first time, people who a few days ago Kara didn't know existed. This sister was shorter than both Alex and Kara. Although by no means heavy, there was stockiness to her build, quite the opposite of Alex's leanness. She was dressed in jeans and an Angora sweater that shed wisps of wool with each movement; there were no similarities Kara could see in Pigeon's pointy chin or wide mouth to her own face. She decided Pigeon must take after Alex's mother.

As if she felt Kara's scrutiny, Pigeon took her gaze from Alex and stared back at Kara with equal intensity. There it was. Deep green eyes, one slightly darker than the other one, almond shaped and etched with arching eyebrows just like Alex's violet eyes and Kara's amber ones.

Following Pigeon's open stare, Alex said, "Oh, let me introduce you to—" Almost too late, Alex remembered she hadn't had a chance to explain the situation to Pigeon. She edited her sentence from *our sister* to just *Kara*.

"I'm pleased to finally meet you," Kara said.

In a quizzical tone, Pigeon replied, "Nice to meet you too." Her eyes pressed Alex for more information, but Alex was at a loss. Everything had happened so fast between Kara's call and the ride to the hospital and there had been no time to fill anyone in on the search. In addition, although she had begged Pigeon to come home, Alex was surprised to see her.

"Did you have a good trip?" she heard herself ask in that motherly singsong tone. She spoke to Kara: "Pigeon just flew in from LA." Back to Pigeon: "Have you seen Daddy yet?"

Pigeon appeared confused and Kara seemed expectant, making Alex's neck burn from anxiety. The lobby wasn't the place to have this emotional conversation. Surely Kara could sense the timing was off.

"The trip was fine, but too long." Pigeon peered at Kara. "Are you a friend of the family?"

"Not yet."

Alex shot Kara a look. *What kind of answer was that?* Just when she believed they were making progress. She led the way to the elevators and pushed the up button several times. It was going to be impossible to explain Kara to Pigeon once they were upstairs. Alex knew she should have thought this through.

The elevator doors opened and people pushed off.

"I feel as if I should know you," Pigeon said to Kara as the three stepped into the empty elevator.

Alex pushed the button for the CCU floor just as several people got on the elevator behind them.

Pigeon said, "I'm sorry if we've met before and I'm not remembering."

"I'll explain everything," Alex cut in.

"Explain what?"

"It's complicated."

The doors swooshed closed. Kara moved to the back so she was now standing behind Pigeon and Alex. Next to Alex, facing forward and watching the floor numbers go up, were the three strangers.

Pigeon leaned closer to Alex. "Explain what? What's complicated?"

From behind them Kara said, "I'm your half-sister. Today I'm meeting my father for the first time. How's that for complicated?"

Pigeon made a funny sound in her throat. The second floor pinged its arrival and one of the other passengers got off. Another peered curiously at the sisters. The doors closed again.

Damn, Kara—that was no way to handle it. Even though it was Alex's fault for not telling Pigeon last night, a little sensitivity would still have been nice.

They reached the fifth floor. "This is us," Alex said. She stepped out of the car and the others followed. Pigeon would not meet her eyes. "I'll explain, I promise. We need to focus on Daddy right now, okay?"

"She's our half-sister?" Pigeon twisted around and glared at Kara, who trailed behind as they moved down the narrow corridor.

"Yes. It's a long story."

One of the nurses who Alex recognized approached them in the hall. Alex greeted her but didn't slow down until they came to Judy, standing guard in front of their father's room, arms crossed, fists tight, lips pursed.

"It's about time." She stared directly at the now shrinking Pigeon. "I see you haven't completely lost your mind and decided to show." She opened her arms and leaned forward.

Barely stepping into the embrace, Pigeon kissed her mother's proffered cheek. "Where's Aunt Peggy?"

"Ladies," Judy said, and then lifted her chin to the left, "go on in. He'll be glad to see you."

Pigeon stepped around Judy and went into the room. Alex could hear murmurs of greetings. Worth was awake. That was a good thing, at least.

"So, are you going to introduce me or not?" Her mother eyed Kara with obvious distaste.

Did she know? Her mother had a nose for every misstep Alex ever made; it was impossible to lie to her or hide things. She felt like a soap opera character who hadn't read the script. Determined to prevent a scene, she tried to make Kara's introduction as businesslike as possible.

"Mom, this is Kara Lawrence. As you know, she's here to see Daddy. Kara, my mother, Judy."

Kara said, "How do you do."

Judy soundlessly worked her mouth.

Alex could feel the pending explosion and couldn't think how to divert it. "Kara, why don't you go in first and I'll be right behind you." Just then, Aunt Peggy emerged from the bathroom across the hallway. Her purple suit fit snugly over her round body, and her tortoiseshell glasses were sitting low on the bridge of her nose. A piece of toilet paper sticking to the bottom of her shoe followed her.

Relieved for a diversion, Alex grabbed Kara's hand and gave a slight tug. "Oh, and this is Peggy Lawrence. Aunt Peggy, Kara. She's Daddy's sister, so she's your aunt too."

"I do not believe what I am hearing," Judy said, her voice rising with each word.

Peggy stopped. Her head swiveled from Alex to Kara to Judy. "Oh my. Well, so, you found her." Peggy bobbed her head up down and patted her damp throat with her ever-present hankie. Much to Alex's relief, Peggy offered her hand and Kara took it. "Well, well. Nice to meet you, Kara."

"Same here," Kara said.

Then, in mirrored gestures, Peggy and Kara used the index fingers and thumbs of their left hands to adjust their eyeglasses.

Before Judy could say another word, Alex turned her back to her mother, took a deep breath, and said to Kara, "Shall we go in?" She could feel the heat rising from Judy as they stepped into their father's room.

CHAPTER THIRTY

Kara hung back and let Alex take the lead. She felt as if she was barely breathing. Her father lay propped up with multiple pillows. He seemed old. Pigeon stood next to him, her eyes riveted on Kara as if she understood whose drama this was.

Although a private room, it was crowded. A television stared down from one corner; a nightstand, cube of monitors, and two chairs flanked either side of the bed. Everyone's skin looked pale under the fluorescent lights, but his appeared almost translucent. Dried saliva was visible at the corners of his mouth, and two branches from a single tube delivered oxygen through his nostrils. There was a distinct smell in the room—illness, medicine, and the faint scent of urine.

He lifted himself up on his elbows. "Hey, kitten."

"Daddy, I brought someone to see you." Alex motioned to Kara to step forward.

Kara managed to say, "Hello." It was hard to process it all—Pigeon's confusion, Peggy's warmth, and Judy's ire. She felt overwhelmed, ill prepared, scared.

"How beautiful you are," he said as he sank back onto the bed. "Like your mother."

Kara's tongue felt thick and her brain, stupid.

"A whole lot of Lawrence in you too." He shifted under the sheet that barely covered him and inched over. "Come sit by me." As he moved, the corners of an adult diaper poked out and he tucked it from view. "Please." The effort brought on a raspy cough.

Alex grabbed a glass of water with a straw and gave it to her father. Pigeon tried to help by placing her hand under his pillows so he could lift himself a little higher as he took a sip.

Kara could not move her feet.

Still holding the glass, Alex spoke to Kara: "Just sit a minute, please. You've come this far."

Kara heard the words but she couldn't connect all the pieces. Heat suffused her bosom, neck, and face. Her breath felt hot in her mouth and her eyes watered like they did from spring allergies.

"Tell me about you," her father said.

Her mouth wouldn't move either.

"What do you do for a living? Are you married?" He cough-laughed. "Am I a grandfather?"

What was wrong with her? Of course he wouldn't look like the picture, or sound or smell like her fantasies. She knew he was sick. Why couldn't she tell him about Pace University, how she worked her way through, going to class at night, working days? Maybe he'd want to know about the Teacher of the Year award she'd received two years in a row. This was the moment of her dreams and a thousand reenactments. Instead, all she could feel was the heat. It took a few moments for her brain to name it: she was angry, and angrier as each second ticked by. It started at her mind's edge, and as she stood there speechless it built until it became a body-shaking fury.

"Kara lives in Harlem, Daddy, and she teaches school," Alex said, strawberry-blond curls in motion. "Her old caseworker gave me her address. Did you ever speak with Liz Kennelly? Very nice woman—she and Kara are friends and . . .

well, I'm talking too much." Alex turned to Pigeon: "Maybe we should leave these two alone."

The persistent ache in Kara's head seared. Finally, she found her voice: "Why didn't you come and get me after my mother died?"

Pain rippled across his face. "I thought it would be best for you to be with your own people."

"You weren't my people?"

"I didn't mean that."

"He raped me."

Someone in the room groaned but Kara only heard it as background noise, like the whir of the machines and the muted screech of a siren outside the window.

"I had a wife, children. They told me you were with a good foster family and that they'd find you a permanent home."

"Night after night, he raped me."

Her father pushed himself up on his elbows again, his voice as tortured as his expression. "There was no proof, just your grandmother's suspicions. If I had known . . . She was incoherent half the time. How was I to know for sure?"

"Every day, I waited for you to come and save me. I'd stand by my window and watch the road, thinking, *Today he'll come.*"

Alex was stunned. She could not believe this. Raped—that was the terrible thing Michael had hinted at, that Kara claimed, *He doesn't know what he's sorry for.* Raped.

"Daddy, what are you saying? Kara's grandmother told you someone was molesting her and you did nothing?" In the background, like music threading through a movie, Alex could hear Pigeon crying. Kara's tears ran down her cheeks, mucus slipped from her nose. Alex knew soon she'd start crying as well. "Tell me this isn't true."

Vanessa must have come into the room while Kara was speaking. "What did you expect, Alex? He deserted us, why wouldn't he desert her?"

"Not now, Nessie," Alex begged.

Still in her camel-hair coat, honey-blond hair twisted into a French knot, made up so you wouldn't know she had any on, Vanessa stood in the doorway, hands on her narrow hips. Her lids drooped and her words slurred. "He left us with a mad woman, why wouldn't he leave her to vultures?" She spun toward Kara, pressed her hand against the doorjamb, and steadied herself. "He didn't love us enough, and he didn't love you at all."

Kara made a strangled noise.

Alex couldn't focus. She heard Vanessa's words, could feel Kara's and Vanessa's anger and pain, but she couldn't reconcile it with her own feelings. All she had tried to do was fulfill her father's sickbed wish, to help both him and Kara.

"Only you never got it, Alex." Vanessa stepped farther into the room.

Pigeon's sobs underscored each word.

"Always Daddy's good girl, you never figured out he didn't give enough of a shit to be there for any of us. Not even you."

"Kitten, you have to believe me," their father pleaded.

Alex blinked, trying to clear her mind.

Worth Lawrence leaned on one elbow, reached his free hand out to Alex. "I didn't think it was true. Honest." He sank back.

Alex focused on his face. His eyes, up until now clouded from illness and drugs, were clear.

"The grandmother was forgetful, confused. I had to think of you and my girls. Your mother would have never given me custody. She'd never have let me see you." He coughed and beads of sweat dotted his forehead. "I had to think of what was best for you."

Alex swiped at her tears. "For me? Kara's grandmother called, and you decided it wasn't true?"

"I would have lost my family."

"It was true, Daddy. It happened and she was just a little girl, *your* little girl."

Alex could hear Kara's ragged breathing just to her right. Vanessa's breathing was also loud, adding to Pigeon's sob-music. Although Alex didn't know exactly when, Judy and Peggy had joined the ensemble, so now everyone was onstage. Everyone knew everything.

His voice was low and anguished: "I followed up, I did. After she wrote me, I told Martin Dawes to check. Ask him." He never took his wild eyes from Alex's face. His whole being seemed to beg her for understanding and redemption—forgiveness not from Kara, but from Alex.

Kara didn't believe him. She didn't believe he was sorry, or that he followed up, or cared about her now. This man was not her father—she had a mother and knew what love felt like. This man and these people were not her family—Tuesday, Flyer, Mrs. E., and Danny, they were her people. What about Liz? Liz had said there was circumstantial evidence. For how long did she wait? Worth said her grandmother knew—that means that she had deserted Kara as well. This was too hard to think about right now. Kara pushed past Vanessa, Judy, and Peggy Lawrence into the hall. As she moved down the corridor, her feet dragged more with each step. Finally, she reached the elevators and pressed the down button. To her right she saw the exit sign, so she moved toward the stairwell, stumbled down the steps, red waves of pain shimmering in front of her eyes.

With her fingertips, she wiped the tears from her face and sniffed up the mucus. Somehow, she reached the lobby. She needed a taxi, or maybe she should call Danny.

"Ms. Lawrence."

The voice was familiar but she couldn't place it.

"Ms. Lawrence, you have to come with us."

Who is this man? Then it came to her. It was Special Agent Woo, and it was Monday night.

Alex sagged onto her father's bed in the spot he had made for Kara, depleted and betrayed. A part of her felt humiliated. It was all so sordid. "How could you have done this, Daddy?"

Vanessa approached her. "What part of this don't you get?"

"Vanessa, please stop. Enough."

"He didn't want his dirty secret coming out and messing up his idyllic home life. How would Judy explain it to the neighbors?"

For the first time her mother spoke, her eyes so narrowed Alex could barely see the whites. "This is a fine picture— you've upset your father. What were you thinking bringing that person here? Where's your sense?"

"Mom, don't."

"Don't what? Don't call the filth Vanessa is speaking what it is? Shame on you both."

Anguish filled her father's face, but Alex could not comfort him. She couldn't understand him, or her mother, or even the depth of Vanessa's rage. For that matter, she didn't understand what she herself was feeling. Who were these people she had loved and protected for so long? How had she missed, ignored, disguised, and shored it up all this time?

Without saying anything more, Alex walked out of the room and Vanessa followed.

Alex said more to herself than to Vanessa, "She was raped and Daddy was warned."

"It happens."

"To whom? To whom does that happen?"

"Grow up."

"What is that supposed to mean?"

Vanessa was weaving back and forth on her three-inch heels.

"Are you okay?"

Vanessa straightened up, pulled her shoulders back, and stretched her Audrey Hepburn neck. "I'm fine." She sat in one of the chairs just outside of the room. "We're all *just fine*."

Alex took a step to sit next to Vanessa—then she remembered the black sedan.

She ran down the hall just as several men and women dressed in green scrubs were coming off the elevator. "Hold the door," Alex shouted, her cowboy boots clicking loudly on the tile floor. She bounded onto the elevator car and nodded thanks to the Asian woman who'd held it for her.

The elevator began its slow descent. It stopped on the fourth and third floors to let people in and out. Finally, it made it down to the lobby. Alex looked around: no Kara. She ran out the front door only to see the black sedan pulling away.

Kara felt a new calm. Special Agent Boyd sat in the front seat, his eyes catching hers in the rearview mirror as the car barreled south down I-684, a highway Kara recognized from the trip with Alex. The female agent she had seen on Frederick Douglass Boulevard sat next to him. Agent Woo was in the back next to Kara.

They knew. Her grandmother, her father, even Liz. They had evidence, and all the warning signs, and they left her there with Big Jim Smyth. Somehow, the threat from the FBI and whatever plan they had for her seemed inconsequential now.

CHAPTER THIRTY-ONE

lex watched the black sedan head into the distance. Her
Jeep was too far away to allow her to follow them. She
trotted across the driveway to the parking lot. What
should she do next? She had to help Kara, but didn't know
where they would take her. Maybe they weren't even the FBI.
Alex climbed into the Jeep and started the engine, glancing at
the clock which read 9:46 p.m. She backed the Jeep out of the
space, spun the wheel, and pulled out onto Route 172. She
dialed 411 on her cell.

"Say a city and state, or ask for other services," said the re-
corded voice.

"New York, New York."

"What listing?"

"Daniel Waters."

"Say business or residence."

Alex almost screamed, but since it was a recording what
would be the point? Instead, she did as requested as she
drummed her fingers on the steering wheel. "Residence."

"Please wait for an operator to assist you."

The street was empty, so Alex ignored the posted forty-
mile-per-hour speed limit. In minutes, she'd reach the junc-
tion for I-684 South.

Finally, a live operator came on: "We have several listings."

"He lives in Harlem, New York, around 130th Street."
Alex couldn't remember the exact address.

With ease, she maneuvered into the passing lane. Everyone was doing at least eighty miles per hour. Alex sped up while the operator connected her.

"Waters."

"Danny, this is Kara's sister Alex. She's in trouble. I think the FBI has her, and I don't know what to do." She sketched out what had happened. "Where do you think they would take her?"

Danny said he wasn't sure, but didn't think they'd take her all the way down to 26 Federal Plaza, especially at this time of night. "Probably to a branch office up there," he said. "What's the nearest big city?" He sounded as frantic as Alex felt.

"White Plains. I'll call information to see if there's an FBI office there, and I'll call you right back."

Danny gave her his cell number and told her he would start driving north and meet her once she had found something out. "I'm forty minutes away, I think." He also promised to call Kara's lawyer.

White Plains was about twenty minutes south. Her thoughts, like a drunk's feet, tripped over each other. In spite of the grandmother's suspicions, her father had left Kara in danger and he said he did it for Alex. In a way, she understood. She knew he was right about her mother's reaction. She would have sued him for divorce, taken the girls, and spent the rest of her life seeking revenge. Or would she have? How many times had her mother made derisive comments about divorced women, not from a moral point of view but out of pity? Her mother didn't work, and she loved the privileges of wealth.

Alex's mind jumped to Vanessa. Was she stoned? Did she drive wasted? Alex should have taken her car keys. Judy's face intruded, scrunched in rage, and Worth's words echoed in her head, *There was no proof, just your grandmother's suspicions.* It was as if every inevitable thing, the consequences of layers and layers of bad decisions, converged on this moment. Alex began to shake. Her fingers and torso trembled as her toes danced against the gas pedal. She had to get ahold of herself, one thing at a time: right now, she had to rescue Kara. Tomorrow, she would deal with Vanessa, and poor little Pigeon. "Stop it," she said aloud. "Focus."

The sedan pulled up in front of a stone building with a neatly lettered sign, which read, *United States Court House*. Special Agent Boyd held the door for Kara and helped her from the car. The trio moved toward the entrance, a street lamp lighting their path. No one spoke until the group, minus the female agent, reached a windowless conference room on the third floor. A picture of the president hung on the far wall.

"Ms. Lawrence, you're in a lot of trouble, whether you realize it or not," Agent Boyd said. With deliberate motions, he took off his overcoat and then his suit jacket. "You can still help yourself, but you have to do it now."

He seemed to be waiting for her to say something, but she had nothing to say. She could barely think. All the raw emotions from the hospital, the ire she had felt, had dissipated. Instead, she felt numb.

"Ms. Lawrence, look at me."

Kara tried hard to meet his unsympathetic stare, but it was more than she could manage. She dropped her eyes to her hands folded in her lap.

He bent over, his face close to hers, and spoke into her left ear: "I don't know what your lawyer told you, but even if we can't convict you, we can make your life difficult. What if we showed up at your school and questioned the principal and your colleagues? What if we subpoenaed your bank records? How long do you think it would be before people starting believing you were guilty of something?"

She raised her eyes and met his gaze. "What do you want from me?"

The agent straightened up. "Your help."

"So you said. But what does that mean?" In every crime drama she'd ever watched on television, the smart people didn't say anything until their lawyer came. Even though she'd decided to help them, she still might need protection, assurances.

"Do you know what this is, Ms. Lawrence?" He pushed an electronic apparatus toward her.

Kara studied it. Although she didn't recognize it, she knew where this was going. "You want me to record him, to trap him."

The agent leaned in close again. "If he's innocent, like he says he is, you're not trapping him, you're clearing him."

Kara opened her tote bag and pulled out her cell phone. She realized she didn't even have Mr. Green's number listed in her contacts. She would have to call Mrs. E.

"If he's guilty, like *we* know he is, he'll convict himself. You will have done nothing to harm him." With his index finger, Boyd moved the tiny piece of equipment around in a circle on the desk. "He'll be in his office tomorrow; he has an appointment with a potential new client—Agent Woo. All you have to do is call and tell him you have to see him. Tell him you'll help him, but he has to level with you."

It was almost ten p.m. Mrs. E. usually stayed up until midnight. Would Norman Green be up as well? Could he help her? He'd promised this would go away, but here she was anyway. Kara put the cell phone down. "No." She surprised herself. Yesterday she'd decided to help them. Moments ago, she was ready to do it, but now . . . *What kind of person gets out of trouble by pushing someone else into the muck?* She'd be no better than her father.

Agent Boyd's facial expression matched his disdainful tone. "What do you owe this guy? He set you up and used you."

"You said he used lots of other women. Go ask one of them."

"Do you think Mrs. Edgecombe will understand your decision?"

Kara's breath caught in her throat.

"Do you think your friend Mr. Dresden—what do you call him, Flyer?—do you think he'll understand?"

"What do they have to do with this? You leave them alone."

The man's face muscles and voice softened as he sat down. "The SEC wants this guy and it's our job to get him. We don't want to hurt you or your friends—"

"Then don't."

"But if we have to sift through the lives and finances of the people in your life, we will. Isn't Officer Waters up for sergeant?"

"You're just trying to scare me." It was working. She willed herself calm.

"We'll do whatever it takes, Kara, make no mistake." He waited a beat. "It doesn't have to be like this. Wear the wire, let him exonerate himself, save your friends, and walk away free and clear."

Kara shook her head no, but *Yes* was on the tip of her tongue.

Agent Boyd stood up again. The room was silent except for the sounds of breathing. His stare razor sharp, his voice once again hard: "Shake your head all you want, but this is real. Mrs. Edgecombe's medical-insurance claims could be scrutinized, payments slowed, challenged."

Can they do this?

"The breadth of our reach would surprise you. Your friend tried to commit suicide tonight. Life could get better for him," he paused, his stare never wavering, "or worse. It's up to you."

Kara tried to gauge his seriousness. His eyes were flat, his mouth a straight line. Stirring up trouble for her at school and messing with Mrs. E.'s medical claims sounded plausible. In fact, if he could pull off half of what he threatened, that was still a lot. She felt her face tighten and the pain behind her eyes intensify. All of them, everyone she loved, had few resources to fight back against such single-minded determination.

She stood up. "Okay," she said, knowing it wasn't, "I'll do it. But I want things in writing and I want my lawyer."

Agent Boyd appeared neither smug nor victorious. In fact, Kara thought she saw sympathy in his eyes.

The operator gave Alex the phone number and address of the FBI in White Plains. She was only ten minutes away. *Then what?* She called Danny and gave him the information. He was already only twenty minutes away, just pulling onto the Hutchinson River Parkway.

Alex saw the black sedan parked in front of the courthouse. She drove the Jeep alongside it and peered in, but saw nothing helpful. She looked around. Several car lengths down and across the street was a truck with white lettering. It offered cover for her smaller vehicle. She pulled in behind it and called Danny again.

"They're here. I've found the car."

After she gave him directions, she glanced at her gas gauge: forty-two miles to empty. She switched off the engine, drummed her fingers on the steering wheel. Even though she had nothing to fear from the authorities, she was still scared. She wondered how Kara was doing. If Alex was rocked by the hospital meeting, Kara had to be doubly so: if the FBI frightened Alex, Kara must be terrified.

It was odd, but just as Alex had gotten tired of taking care of everyone else in her family, here she was feeling responsible for a stranger. For a second, she thought about calling Michael. That made her smile. Who was she kidding? She just wanted to hear his voice.

She had pulled out her cell phone when something caught her eye. She scooted down low in her seat and peered over the dashboard. Two men were walking on either side of Kara, heading for the black sedan. Kara looked grim, her lips pressed together as if she held something precious or dangerous in her mouth and was determined it wouldn't escape.

Alex sat up. Maybe she was handling this all wrong. Maybe she should do something.

Kara knew it was close to eleven o'clock. The agents said they would drive her home. Just as they reached the car, Agent Boyd, palm on the door handle, turned to her. "Ms. Lawrence, the thing to remember tomorrow is to act natural, get him into a conversation about the deliveries. He trusted you enough to make the drops. He'll talk. We'll do the rest."

"What if he doesn't? Do you still keep your end of the deal?"

"You're a smart woman." He opened the door. "I'm sure you'll succeed."

Anything could go wrong—she could get tongue-tied and not get the words right; he might figure it out; the equipment could fail. Then she would have betrayed him for nothing. Her friends, her family—they would all still be in jeopardy.

From across the street, Alex watched them. What was there to fear? She threw her door open, hopped out, and ran across the street toward them.

"Excuse me," she said in as natural a voice as she could pull off. "I'm here to pick up my sister." To Kara she said, "Your lawyer is waiting for you and he said to bring you directly to him." She swung back to the agents, curls swishing across her back and falling into her face. "Alexandra Lawrence," she introduced herself. "Nice to meet you, but we have to go." She grabbed Kara's hand.

One of them stared her down, but Alex kept talking, walking backward away from them, Kara in tow. "Is she under arrest or something? Otherwise, we'll just take our leave."

Alex couldn't believe she was doing this. Her mouth felt dry.

The man stared at Alex but addressed Kara: "Nine a.m. tomorrow, Ms. Lawrence. We'll pick you up."

The two agents got in the car and slammed their doors behind them. Kara and Alex watched them drive off.

"Are you okay?"

Kara, her eyes glassy, said, "No."

"Come on. I'll drive you home."

Alex felt light-headed as they walked to her Jeep. She'd always waited for the light to turn green before crossing, even if no cars were coming; she passed only on the left, never kept library books past the due date.

Danny's Toyota came diagonally toward them, crossing several empty traffic lanes.

"Danny's here?"

"I called him."

They stopped and watched Danny pull up and leap out of the car. He was dressed in civilian clothes, his leather jacket unzipped. Alex could tell what Kara saw in him as he jogged over, athletically graceful, his angular face and even features quite handsome.

Alex said, "Hey, Danny, thanks for coming. I changed the game plan, I guess."

He didn't respond or even look at her; he was staring at Kara.

"I came as fast as I could," Danny said to Kara. His breath made a cloud in front of his face. "You doing alright?"

Kara was clearly glad to see him. She nodded yes, even though she was a mess.

With his right hand, he brushed away the hair that the wind had blown in her face. "You seem kinda shaky," he said in his late-night-radio voice.

"I'm okay." The March wind continued to dishevel her hair.

"What did they say to you?" Alex asked. She blew into her cupped hands to warm them.

Danny said, "Let's get out of the street, it's freezing. We can talk in my car."

"It's late," Kara said.

It was. Alex felt exhausted. "We just want to help."

This was such a new experience for Kara. Both Alex and Danny knew some of her secrets; in fact, Alex knew just about all of them. Instead of her world coming unglued, however, it actually had a chance, maybe, to get better. They were willing to go out of their way to help her. "Thank you both for everything."

Danny nodded in acknowledgment. "Do you ladies need to talk?"

"We do," Alex said, then turned to Kara. "You're welcome." She meant it.

Danny took charge: "Alex, you drive Kara home and I'll lead the way. Mr. Green, Kara's lawyer, promised to be waiting for us at the house. We'll all talk things through and come up with a workable plan."

As they made their way south, Kara let her new emotions sink in. For the first time in her life, she felt hopeful.

CHAPTER THIRTY-TWO

Alex kept Danny's car in view, changing lanes when he changed, slowing and accelerating in tandem. Knowing he was a police officer gave her a measure of comfort as they broke the speed limit. She glanced to her right to change lanes and caught Kara watching her. "Crazy night."

Kara nodded.

"I'm sorry about the meeting with our father, I'm sorry it went so poorly." The hospital scene came back to her. "I didn't know."

"You have nothing to be sorry for," Kara said. "I wanted to go, and I'm not sorry. Now I know."

Alex couldn't think how to respond.

"I used to look for you," Kara continued. "Not at first, but by the time I was eight or nine years old."

"So you said."

Kara shifted her body toward her sister. "I'd be on the playground and see a child with wild strawberry-blond curls and pretend it was you. Sometimes, I'd think you were someone I saw in a magazine or on TV. We'd have pretend conversations." She made a funny sound in her throat. "Did you ever have an imaginary friend?"

"Is that what I was?" Alex had been gripping the steering wheel so tightly her fingers were cramping. She took them off for a beat and flexed.

"Sort of."

They were doing seventy miles per hour, the Toyota ahead

by two car lengths. As they hit the New York City limits, Danny's car slowed to sixty, so Alex followed suit.

"I had imaginary parents instead of friends," Alex said. "Parents who didn't fight; a father who came home every night; a mother who wasn't nuts."

"Your parents fought?" Kara sounded incredulous and maybe a little disappointed.

"Constantly. We moved through maids and nannies at a record pace. Unfortunately, we kids had no such escape."

"Maids and nannies?" This time Kara sounded almost amused.

Alex shrugged apologetically. "I had a privileged life in that sense." *Maybe in every sense.* Listening to Kara's life story, Alex's family didn't seem so bad. "Did you look for our father also?"

"No. I was counting on him to find me."

Alex glanced at Kara, once again struck by the familiarity of her profile. She sounded so sad, as if the pain of her childhood was as real today as it was then. For that matter, that's how it seemed for Vanessa and Pigeon as well.

They pulled off the highway at 125th Street. There was so much more Alex wanted to know about Kara's life, the sexual abuse and its effects. She wanted to ask about the Christmas when Kara was six years old. Just as she formed the next question in her mind, Kara startled her: "Do you have any black friends, Alex?"

"Yes," she replied without thinking about it. But then, Alex reflected, maybe it wasn't really true. Her answer had been reflexive, almost defensive. Why should Alex feel defensive about the race of her friends? The truth was, she only had one black friend—Sonja, her roommate from her freshman and sophomore years at Smith, a friend she hadn't seen in two years and with whom she only exchanged e-mail updates, and birthday and Christmas cards.

"Why do you ask?"

They were heading east on 125th Street, Danny's car just ahead. In spite of the late hour, there was still activity on the streets. She could see people filling several bars and others exiting the Magic Johnson movie theater, heading home after a late show.

"No reason." Kara paused. "Well, a reason, but I'm not sure how to explain it."

Alex waited.

"All my life, I thought of myself as half-black, half-white; half-Lawrence, half my mother's child. I always knew I was different, that I didn't belong anywhere. Now . . ." Her voice trailed off.

"Now what?"

"Don't mind me, it's late and I'm exhausted. Thanks again for helping me."

They completed the remainder of the drive in silence.

By the time they arrived at Kara's home, Mrs. E. and Mr. Green were waiting for them in the kitchen. It was after midnight and everyone, with the exception of the dapper lawyer, appeared tired and frazzled. They listened to Kara's story, Danny and Alex jumping in now and then with a fact or impression. Mrs. E. clicked her tongue and Mr. Green took notes with his pencil stub. She told them about the FBI's threat to go to her school, and to make things harder for Flyer.

Kara was glad Mrs. E. was there for support but her presence kept Kara from mentioning the agents' threats about her insurance and Danny's chances of becoming a sergeant.

"I don't know what else to do except help them," Kara

said as she ended her recital. Earlier, she had felt optimistic, but now, after saying everything aloud, the situation felt impossible, just like life in the group home, just like life with the Smyths. Go along, or get iced.

The faces around her reflected her feelings back at her.

Kara asked Mr. Green, "What do you think I should do?" He'd promised to take care of things and make it all go away. Well, that hadn't worked so far. She examined his weathered face. For how long had he been practicing law? Maybe he was the wrong person to represent her. Maybe she needed some young hotshot with lots of connections.

"I think you are doing the right thing," Mr. Green said. He closed his notepad, his faux English accent high and nasal. "The only thing you can do. I tried reaching Agent Boyd's superiors earlier today but to no avail."

On Saturday, he'd made it sound so simple. Now, he was giving up on her.

"We'll just have to do what they want," he went on. "Get it over with and then you can get on with your life. I'll go with you, of course." He stood up but he didn't turn to leave.

Alex said, "I'm sorry you're in this mess, and I'm sorry our father was so shitty to you, and I'm just plain sorry."

All Kara could do was reach across the kitchen table and squeeze Alex's hand. The list of things for which Kara was sorry would fill one of Mr. Green's notepads.

Leaning against the refrigerator, arms crossed against his chest, Danny said, "Maybe, by cooperating, you can get rid of the mess and the bastard who dragged you into it."

Kara flinched.

"I'm just saying," he added in a softer tone, "you deserve better."

The grandfather clock chimed one time, reminding Kara

it was now Tuesday morning and she had to be ready by nine a.m. It was time to say good night. She rose from the table, shook Mr. Green's hand, and kissed Mrs. E. on the cheek with a thank you. She walked over to Danny and thanked him as well. She intended to kiss him on his cheek, but he turned his face and her kiss landed squarely on his mouth. Brief as it was, it was enough to taste the hot chocolate they'd shared and feel the softness of his full lips and the heat of his breath.

Feeling awkward, Kara spoke to Alex: "I read somewhere that children either make all of the mistakes of their parents, or they break the cycle—maybe you and I can break our cycles." She hoped Danny was listening as well.

Kara might be right about cycles, but Alex wasn't sure she was wise to take the advice of that useless lawyer. The FBI's plan felt like a big mistake, though Alex didn't have any ideas to counter it.

It would take her another forty minutes to get home. She checked her gas gauge—she'd need to fill up soon. Ahead of her, angled on the corner, was an open station. Reluctant to get out of the car, she pulled into the full-service island and asked the attendant to fill it up with regular. While she waited, she grabbed her phone and scrolled down the list of recently called numbers until she found Michael's number.

After several rings a sleepy voice said, "Yeah?"

"It's Alex. I'm sorry to call you so late, but you said you'd be waiting."

"Where are you? What time is it?"

"I have so much to tell you."

"Is Kara okay?"

"It's after one."

"Damn."

She could hear him moving around.

"So, what's the deal?" He sounded more awake.

"She's in a lot of trouble."

"What kind?"

In her mind's eye, she pictured him naked on top of the coverlet on his bed. Of course, it was thirty-seven degrees outside according to her car display, so that was probably unlikely, but maybe he kept the heat high in his apartment.

"Alex, are you still there?"

Embarrassed, she said, "Must have hit a dead spot. Yes, with the FBI."

"You're with the FBI?"

"No, I'm not with them, but she's in trouble with the SEC and FBI."

"Wow. Can I help?"

"She has a lawyer and the cop friend I told you about." *Plus, she has me.* "I'll fill you in tomorrow. I'm pooped and you don't sound awake. I'm sorry I bothered you."

"I'm not."

"It's late."

"Still glad."

"Me too."

They hung up after Alex promised to call Michael as soon as she got home, just so he knew she'd arrived safely. The gas station attendant stood by her window; she rolled it down and paid him.

Alex played the tape of the day over in her mind. She felt confused about her father. She loved him so much, but he had hurt his family. Her mother was right—he was selfish and self-absorbed—but there were also many good things about him. And he loved her, maybe more than he loved anyone else in his life. She felt equally confused about Kara. Tonight had been wild. In her gut, she didn't think there was a happy ending ahead. What if Kara helped the FBI and they still prosecuted her, or Zach incriminated her on the tape? It was hard to think through all the possibilities. Besides, she was exhausted. Her mantra from earlier in the evening came back to her: *Focus*. Tomorrow was another day.

Finally, she arrived. She pulled into the parking lot of her apartment building, locked up the car, walked to the lobby, and took the elevator to her floor. She opened her door and climbed over the piles of dirty laundry. The apartment smelled liked neglect—soiled clothes, unwashed dishes, unemptied trash. *What a day, what a night.* The blinking light on her answering machine told her she had messages.

"You have two new messages and no saved messages. Main menu."

She hit the play button.

"First message, received today at three p.m." It was from Pigeon. Her voice had a wet quality, as if she'd been crying. *"Daddy's okay, I guess; I mean for now. Aunt Peggy tried to explain about the half-sister thing but I don't understand why you're helping her."* Several beats of silence followed. Alex waited. *"I guess I don't understand anything. Cool Breeze called and he's on the red-eye. I told him not to come. Alex, I'm so mixed up."* The click of a hang-up followed.

It was too late to call Pigeon back. The muscle under Alex's left eye pulsed; she rubbed above her brow to soothe it. Then she pressed the button for the second message. She played it three times before dialing his number.

"Hi, Alex, it's Michael. Don't forget to call me, no matter what time it is. We don't have to talk if you're too tired. I just want to know you got home okay."

CHAPTER THIRTY-THREE

Danny and Mrs. E. hugged Kara goodbye when she left on Tuesday morning. They watched as she and Norman Green climbed into the black sedan that would ferry them downtown. It was nine a.m. The sun was out and the weather report had said that it was going to be in the fifties. Spring felt possible.

Like a kid reluctant to leave for summer camp, her nose pressed against the car window, Kara waved goodbye and Mrs. E. did the same. Danny gave her a thumbs-up. Knots tied up Kara's insides. She rubbed her belly to ease the pressure. Forty minutes later in the FBI offices, however, the knots persisted.

"Just get him talking," Agent Boyd repeated for the umpteenth time. Kara watched the technician slip a listening device into the lining of her raincoat and another into her tote. "Promise you'll help him, but tell him he has to tell you the truth so you can appreciate the entire situation."

Boyd made it sound easy, but of course it wasn't. Mr. Green nodded, but the pulled-down corners of his mouth contradicted his assent.

The agent picked up Kara's cell phone and handed it to her. "Call him."

They were in a conference room in 26 Federal Plaza—Kara, Mr. Green, the technician, Special Agent Boyd, and the female agent from the night before. Agent Woo was posing as a potential client at Zach's office to ensure his presence there.

The room was well lit, with beams of sunlight filtering through dried rain spots and dust on the windows.

Kara dialed his office. Zach's usually protective gatekeeper put Kara through immediately.

"Baby, thank God. I've been frantic. Where are you? We need to talk."

"I'm sorry I've been so distant, Zach." She closed her eyes in an effort to focus but she could feel the agents staring at her.

"No worries, what's important is that you've called. When can we meet?"

"I can come now, if that's okay."

"Absolutely. I'll clear my schedule."

"I'll be there in about—" she opened her eyes and looked to Boyd, who flashed the fingers on both his hands twice, "twenty minutes."

"You're alone, right?"

"I've been scared and worried."

"You're coming alone?" he asked again. It sounded less like a question and more like a demand.

It was strange. A few days ago, hearing his voice sent shivers of anticipation down her spine—not today. Still, she knew there was something there. Just as the morning air made her believe spring was near, a piece of her wanted it to all be a mistake; maybe the conversation she was about to have with Zach would clear everything up. Some of his story was plausible. Living in Harlem, Kara knew how often law enforcement grabbed the wrong person for the wrong reasons: some witness pointed the finger at an innocent man. The police, some all too quick to assume guilt, shoved his face into the sidewalk, locked his hands behind his back, and dragged him to the station, only to find out later it was another man—taller, lighter-skinned, heavier build. This could be like that. She'd ask her questions and it would become clear they had the wrong man. Then what? Zach would know she had betrayed him. Their relationship was over, no matter what happened today, but she still wanted him to be innocent.

"Yes," she lied, "I'll be alone."

As soon as she hung up, Boyd handed her the bugged coat and bag. "Keep them near you, we'll do the rest."

Kara took her possessions with her fingertips.

"There's nothing to worry about," Agent Boyd assured her as he helped her into the raincoat. "Try to relax."

Maybe she could bolt down the hall, down the stairs, and get outside before they could catch her. She'd hail a cab to the airport and take the first plane to anywhere. Fat chance.

The two agents walked her out, with Norman Green bringing up the rear. By the time they got to the black sedan, Kara was sweating. She tried to concentrate and think through her lines but she could feel the perspiration beading her nose and making her blouse damp. Better to leave on her raincoat throughout the conversation lest he see the evidence of her betrayal.

When they reached Zach's building, Kara took the elevator to the twenty-fifth floor. The receptionist checked Kara's name on a list and Zach's administrative assistant came out to meet her.

"He told me to send you in the minute you arrived," the woman said without any words of welcome or introduction. "May I get you a cup of coffee, tea, a glass of water?"

Kara declined.

Zach's corner office was spacious. A walnut desk devoid of paper dominated the center of the room. Behind it were windows on two sides. The views of New York Harbor were splendid, although Kara's nervousness made it hard for her to appreciate them. She could see the Brooklyn Bridge crossing the East River. A barge chugged north. The greenish-blue patina of the Statue of Liberty glinted in the morning sun as a tour ferry sailed by. The new Freedom Tower soared straight up, a reminder that bad things happened but good could prevail. Kara turned away.

"It's beautiful. How do you concentrate with such a grand vista calling you?"

Zach moved close to her. "You're the only sight I find distracting." He put his arm around her waist. "I'm glad to see you." He pulled her to him, kissed her cheek, and nuzzled her neck. The soft hairs of his beard stroked her skin. There was no hint of the trouble he was in or of the unkempt man who had visited her the day before.

"How are you? You seem stressed." He motioned toward the couch and wing chairs in the right corner of his office. "Let's get comfortable. Shall I ask Dottie to get you some tea, water?"

"Nothing, thanks." She tried to slow her rapid breathing. With her coat still on, she sat down where he indicated and placed her tote by her side.

"Give me your coat."

"I can't stay long." She raised both hands palms up. "My students . . ." She let him fill in the blanks.

Zach sat in one of the wing chairs, leaned back, and crossed his legs, his argyle socks peeking out below the cuffs of his slate-gray suit. "I haven't heard a word from the FBI or SEC."

Kara stayed quiet.

"Have you?"

"No," she said, shaking her head for emphasis.

"Maybe we should go on the offense," Zach said. "Call their bluff." He peered at her, as if he were trying to read her mind.

We was encouraging—he believed she was there to help. "I'm happy they aren't bothering you." She tried not to shift around and to keep her gaze steady. "That's probably a good sign."

"Perhaps." Now he sounded suspicious, or was she over-analyzing every word and gesture?

"Anyway, what happened? I mean, you did say this was going to be your home run. Was it?"

For the first time since she'd entered his office, his attitude became enthusiastic. "We did get lucky."

Kara plunged in, her tone light and flirtatious: "Lucky? You're too smart for luck, Zach."

He laughed. "Let's say fortunate—a combination of strategy and luck."

"So?"

He eyed her but didn't respond.

How could she make him talk? "Zach, I've been thinking: I know you said you need my help if the authorities come snooping around, and frankly, I think they will. After all, they've been following me." She didn't wait for a reaction. If she stopped now, her courage would fail her. "So, let's say I help you. What's in it for me?" The last question just came out; it was not part of the plan.

At first, Zach seemed startled, but then his expression turned amused. Had she gone too far? Agent Boyd had told her to keep it simple.

"This is a surprise. Since when have you ever taken anything from me? I can barely give you cab fare."

"Maybe it's time for me to start looking out for my future."

To her ears, Kara sounded like a B-list actress in a third-rate movie.

There was a definite shift in his demeanor as several seconds ticked by. Finally, he said, "If you help me get out of this, I can provide you with a very comfortable future."

It was happening. She leaned forward, covering his hand with hers. "Life's been tough—you know, financially—and now my friend Flyer tried to kill himself."

"I'm sorry, Kara. Jeez, is he okay?"

"He's in Bellevue. I'm going to need money to help him." Which might well be true.

He squeezed her hand. "Poor baby, I can help you."

"How?"

"We hit the big time with this deal. It was sweet and easy."

In a few more minutes, he would tell her everything. She'd be free. The FBI would have the proof they needed and she could go back to her life. No harm would come to Mrs. E., Flyer, or Danny. Now all she had to do was encourage him to tell her everything, listen, flirt, and applaud his acumen. But the words did not come to her. Instead, all she could think about was what kind of person would do something like this—hurt someone else to save herself? Once again, she thought about her father and the choices he had made. She wasn't like him; she couldn't do it.

In a quick motion, she reached for her tote with one hand and put her fingers to her lips to silence Zach with the other. She ripped the lining of her bag and pulled out the electronic ear, then she did the same with her coat.

Zach stared at her. "What the hell?"

She spotted a wet bar in the corner, walked over, and ran water over both devices. "The FBI said they have a strong case against you. If I were you, I'd be worried."

She put on her ripped coat and slung her tattered tote over her shoulder. Zach moved toward her. "Don't touch me, Zach. I won't help them, but I'm not helping you either."

They really were through—not because she had betrayed him, but because she didn't want him. She'd rather be alone than be with someone like Zach, someone like her father. She deserved better.

Zach's faced twisted with anger. "Don't think they're going to let you off this easy."

Kara moved to the door.

"Wait." He tried for a smile that didn't quite work. "Are they out there, waiting for you?" He gave up on charm. "Shit, Kara, sit down and tell me what the fuck is going on." Much as he had done in his corporate apartment, he moved toward her with aggressive motions.

"Do not come near me," Kara said.

He stopped.

Kara walked into the carpeted corridor and hurried back the way she'd come. In spite of not knowing what would happen next, she felt good. No, not good, but satisfied. She had done the right thing. Somehow, she would protect her family and friends, but not like this. She got on the elevator and rode to the lobby.

They were waiting for her. Special Agent Boyd blocked her path, his eyes the blue-black of a storm, his jaw moving as if he were chewing an enormous wad of gum. "What happened in there?"

Maybe he'd believe her and maybe he wouldn't, but she was done. "He figured it out."

"Bullshit."

"He did. He was searching me the whole time we talked. After he found the device, he ripped it out of my coat lining. Then he searched my bag and found the other one. He poured water on them." She offered the torn lining of her coat as proof.

Several beats went by. Agent Boyd, still blocking her way, stared at her. Kara never flinched.

"We will not forget this," he said. "Ever."

"You do what you have to do." She moved around him.

For the first time in days, Kara wasn't afraid. The powerful feeling she'd had when she'd confronted Agent Boyd in front of her home the night of the murder was back. Terror no longer colored every thought, every action, every decision. She walked away knowing she had made a choice with consequences, though they were not in her control. Her actions were.

CHAPTER THIRTY-FOUR

Alex woke up late. It was almost eight a.m. and she was supposed to be at work by nine. She'd have to hurry. It had been close to three in the morning before she'd fallen asleep and now she felt it. She rubbed her eyes and kneaded her scalp with her fingertips. Last night's events came back to her and she realized Kara was meeting with the FBI and Zach in less than an hour. Alex rolled over and dialed her father's private number at the hospital.

"Daddy, are you awake enough to talk?"

"Sure, kitten." His voice was stronger than it had been since his first heart attack; he sounded glad to hear from her.

"After you're better, could we talk more about what happened with Kara and everything?" She heard him exhale. "I need to understand, because I'm really mad at you." She'd never said that to him before. All the times he had asked her to hold it together, to call Aunt Peggy, to take care of the girls, she had never let herself be angry or let him know how much more she had expected of him. She had never told him he had let her down. Now, she decided to say it. "I always thought you were better than this, that you could be better."

"I know, kitten. I screwed up. Can you forgive your old man?"

"I want to, Daddy, but—"

"I never meant to hurt you."

"I know." She tried to think how to say what needed saying. Coffee would help. "Can you hang on for a sec?"

Alex swung her legs over the side of the bed and padded into the kitchen. She hooked her cell to the waist of her pajama bottoms and inserted the hands-free device into the phone and the buds into her ears. "Daddy?"

"I'm still here."

"Can I tell you something important?" Although she knew she shouldn't burden him with more worries, she also thought it was important for him to know about Kara's troubles. It was time for Kara to become a part of his life.

"Sure," he said. "Anything. I want you to know you can count on me to do better."

Alex told her father about Zach, the SEC's suspicions, and the FBI investigation. "I've been trying to think how I can help her, but I've run out of ideas," she concluded.

There was a long silence on the other end. Alex waited it out as a pot of coffee brewed. The whirring noise the coffee-maker made reminded her of the monitors in his room. She knew he was deathly ill, and that what she was doing was unfair. Still, she waited.

"I don't know either, kitten," he said finally. "Sounds like you're doing all you can."

Alex didn't respond.

"Sweetheart, I want you to know I'm going to beat this thing. I feel better than I have since it happened."

"I know you will." This didn't sound very convincing, but she couldn't hide her disappointment. Why wasn't he more interested in trying to figure some way to help Kara?

"Alex, you're a good person and I love you very much."

"I know you do, Daddy. I love you too." And she did, in spite of all of his failures.

After Alex hung up, the buzzer to her apartment sounded, making her jump. "What the heck?" It couldn't be Sean; it had better not be. She pushed the intercom. "Yes?"

"It's me, Pigeon."

Alex buzzed Pigeon in. At first Alex started to clean up, and then she thought she should get out of her pajamas, but it felt like more effort than she could muster, so instead she just waited for Pigeon to ring her bell.

When Pigeon came in, her bloodshot eyes were pleading with Alex—but for what, she couldn't tell.

Alex hugged her sister tight. "What's going on?" She wanted to be welcoming but she'd depleted her reserves. The mug holding her coffee felt heavy in her hand.

Pigeon stared. "It's so wild to find a new sister." She rubbed her hands on her jeans. "It's disgusting and humiliating."

"*Unsettling* is probably a better word." The only thing humiliating and disgusting was their father's behavior. "Dad screwed up big time. Besides, I like her."

"You like everybody."

Of course it was hard for Pigeon. All her life she'd only ever gotten the last sliver of their parents' attention, and now there was a whole other person.

"What do you know about her?"

Alex pulled Pigeon down onto the love seat in her living area.

"Is she hoping for a payday, you know, after or if—"

"She's not like that."

"What is she like?"

"Her life has been hard—harder than ours for sure." Alex told Pigeon everything she knew about Kara Lawrence.

After Pigeon left, instead of drinking the fresh cup of coffee she'd just made or getting ready for work, Alex crawled back into bed. Justifying Kara to Pigeon, explaining their father's behavior without condemning him, worrying about Vanessa, work, her crazy mother—it was all too much. She pulled the covers up to her chin, rolled on her side, and closed her eyes. A few minutes of rest would help her get her energy and focus back.

The shrill ring of the phone brought Alex fully awake. As she reached for her cell, she glanced at the clock. She'd been asleep for three hours.

"Hello?"

"Alex." It was Pigeon. She sounded panicked. "You have to get over here right away. Daddy's in a bad way."

"That can't be. He was fine a few hours ago."

Pigeon was crying.

Falling back into her old role, Alex tried to comfort her. "It's going to be okay. Is Mom with you?"

"Uh-huh."

"Let me talk to her."

Several seconds ticked by.

"Are you on your way?" Judy asked.

"Do you know how bad it is?"

"You need to get here, quick."

"I'll be there in thirty—" She wasn't even dressed. "Forty-five minutes or less." She thought she heard her mother sob. "Mom, are you okay?"

"How could I be?"

Now it was clear her mother was openly crying. Alex couldn't hold it in any longer. "Oh, Mom. Is this it? What are the doctors saying?"

"I didn't get a chance to tell him how much I still love him," Judy said in a quiet voice. "He's in a coma."

"He told me he's going to make it, and I believe him."

"I prayed, Alex. I don't remember the last time I did that, but as they took him, I prayed to God."

Alex realized she had no idea how to comfort her mother. "I'll be there as fast as I can."

Judy's voice reverted to its more natural tone: "You're coming alone, Alex. You won't bring that awful person with you."

Again, Alex was at a loss. "Is Vanessa there?"

"Of course not."

"I'll see you soon."

For a few seconds after she hung up, Alex just sat there. She took several deep breaths. He could not die. Not like this. Their last conversation was unresolved, there was so much more to say, to experience. This could not be the end. She picked up the notepad and ballpoint pen that she kept on her nightstand for middle-of-the-night ideas and tried to think— making lists often calmed her. Alex felt confident she could find Vanessa, so she wrote down her sister's name and put a check mark next to it. She could always count on Vanessa. No matter what was going on with her, she always pulled it together and helped. Should Alex call Kara? She wrote KARA in block letters. Despite her mother's admonishment, didn't Kara have a right to know? She put a question mark next to Kara's name. Sean would need a call as well, so she wrote him down. Her father's partners—had anyone called them? Mr. Dawes? For a fleeting second, Michael crossed her mind. Wouldn't he care? Tears pooled. Her father was not going to die.

Alex put the pad and pen down, looked up, and caught her reflection in the mirror: her eyes were red and puffy, hair going in every direction, and she was still in her pajamas. She spoke to the woman in the mirror: "Maybe you need to start your list with, *Get up and shower*."

Kara sat on a metal chair next to Flyer's bed. There were straps tied to his wrists and a railing on the bed like he was an imprisoned criminal. The ward was crowded with patients and visitors. The five other men in the room all had family and friends surrounding them. Kara had taken the subway straight from Zach's office to the hospital. She felt weightless. Not the way she did as a child, hovering above the body Big Jim violated, pretending she was with her mother in heaven. This was more about relief than escape. She'd stood up to Zach and the FBI. Whatever happened next, she knew she wouldn't regret her decision.

Yet her elation was short-lived. Tuesday had left the minute Kara arrived, her exit pointed.

Flyer was awake. The sedatives the nurse had given him left him groggy but able to speak.

Kara leaned in close. "I'm sorry, Flyer."

"Not your fault."

"Not yours either."

He closed his eyes.

"I don't know if Tuesday is ever going to forgive me."

Flyer didn't open his eyes and Kara thought that maybe he'd fallen asleep. She touched the top of his hand just below the restraint.

"Not your fault," he said again quietly.

A song by India Arie popped into her mind, "The Heart of the Matter"—*But I think it's about forgiveness, forgiveness; even if, even if, you don't love me anymore . . .*

If Marci Nye were here, Kara knew she would agree with Flyer's verdict and the song's message.

"We were all just kids," Kara said more to herself than to Flyer.

It was the truth. The guilty people were Jim and Nora Smyth—Jim for what he did, and Nora for standing by. In her heart, she knew Liz and her grandmother weren't to blame. Was her father? Not for the rapes; but yes, he was guilty for abandoning her. Could she ever forgive him? *Even if, even if, you don't love me anymore* . . .

A nurse with a cheery voice came by. "How are we doing, Mr. Dresden?" She pulled the privacy curtain around Flyer's bed. "I need to take his vitals, if you could step outside for a few."

"I'll just be in the hall," Kara said to Flyer.

"I'm okay."

"I love you."

Flyer opened his eyes. The whites were yellow and the skin underneath was black. "Tuesday still loves you. She's just scared."

The prognosis was bleak. The attending surgeon, a man with a sunken chest and an egg-shaped head with wisps of gray hair decorating odd spots on his otherwise bald scalp, spoke to the Lawrence family in hushed tones. "He's unable to breathe on his own. We'll just have to wait and see, but I think you should prepare yourself for the worst."

How does one do that?

They gathered in the waiting room—Judy, Aunt Peggy, Vanessa, Pigeon, and Alex—huddled together, everyone's eyes red from crying. Alex forced positive thoughts. She listed in her mind every good thing she could think of about her father: he loved her, he believed in her, and he made her believe in herself; he laughed at all of her jokes no matter how many times she told them; he taught her how to ride a horse, drive a car, ski, play poker, and down a shot of whiskey on her twenty-first birthday.

"Alex?" Pigeon interrupted her list.

"I'm so glad you're here."

Pigeon sat down in the seat next to her.

"When are you going back to California?"

"I'm not."

Alex was surprised.

"I figured something out."

"What's that?"

"I went from you taking care of me to Breeze taking care of me. I need to learn how to take care of myself."

Alex hugged her. "Cool Breeze seems to love you."

"Yeah, but I gotta get *me* straight—you know, before making any commitments."

That got Alex thinking. Was she herself straight? Was she rushing into Michael's arms without knowing enough, being healthy enough?

"Do you think he's sorry?"

"Dad?"

Pigeon bobbed her head.

"For Kara?"

"For everything."

Was he sorry? Alex felt and then saw Vanessa's emotionless stare. With effort, Alex tried to gauge her sister's sobriety, but she couldn't tell. What was going to happen to Vanessa?

"There's a lot for him to regret."

The sisters stayed quiet as Pigeon rested her head on Alex's shoulder. A fluorescent light above flickered on and off with an insistent buzz.

A footfall followed by a small cough. Alex raised her head. The attending physician, his eyes cool and knowing, stood before her.

"Is there news?"

Her mother let out a stifled sob.

"Please tell us," Alex said, although she knew—they all knew.

"We did everything we could," he said. "I'm sorry for your loss."

CHAPTER THIRTY-FIVE

For the third time, Kara read the obituary in the *New York Times:*

> *Worth Jackson Lawrence, prominent New York lawyer and friend to powerful political figures in New York and Washington, DC, died Tuesday of massive heart failure. He was fifty-eight years old.*
>
> *Mr. Lawrence spent his entire professional career in the Fifth Avenue law firm of Hobbs, Austin, and Lawrence, a respected international practice established in 1945 by his father, the late Jackson Lawrence.*
>
> *Colleagues described Worth Lawrence as a confidant of senators, governors, and presidents, an adroit deal maker and generous philanthropist, who made well-placed connections in each political party and enemies in none.*
>
> *"He was a man who wielded power with compassion and finesse," said long-time associate, Martin Dawes.*
>
> *Mr. Lawrence is survived by his wife, the former Judith Colonie, and his three daughters, Alexandra, Vanessa, and Monica. His remains will be interned at the Sleepy Hollow Cemetery in Sleepy Hollow, NY.*

In spite of the sunlight filling her sitting room, Kara felt cold. She pulled her shawl around her shoulders and reread the obituary. He was dead. She thought about Alex and the pain she must be feeling. She thought about Pigeon, the sister she had barely met. They must be devastated. Would a life-time of memories comfort them? Kara had met him once in her adult life, and now she'd never get to know him, ask her questions, find a path to a relationship. For a few seconds, she let her mind wander back to the day at Rock Creek Park, the day she only remembered as a photograph. Then, just like all the other times Kara fantasized, reality jumped the line. *Survived by three daughters*, not four. Even in death, no one wanted to claim her. His death didn't end the possibility of a relationship, reality did.

"What are you going to do?" Danny stood in the doorway, his arms hanging at his sides, his expression filled with empa-thy. "I'll take you to the funeral if you want to go."

"He left me, Danny. He left me to be raped and beaten." Her voice faltered. Tears came so quickly now. She reached for a tissue and stemmed the flow.

Danny stepped into the room, walked over, and squatted beside her. "Do what feels right for you." The sound of his radio voice blended with the strands of Dave Grusin's piano easing from the speakers in the corner. "What did Alex say when she called?"

The message was on Kara's cell. Alex had begged her to come to funeral.

"What you'd expect. I feel bad for her, this has to be hard."

"Maybe go for her sake?"

Kara stayed quiet for several seconds. Danny lowered his frame to the floor. Grusin's piano filled the room.

"I went to see my therapist." She liked the way Danny lis-tened; his whole body appeared to pay attention and he didn't seem to mind the long pauses. "I think I'll make a few more appointments—you know, to get through all of this."

"When my Dad died, I spent some time with my pastor. Talking can help."

"Mrs. E. has her own answer," Kara chuckled. "She said I'm an old soul, a soul who has been around for thousands of years. Everyone in my life, even you, has always been with me."

"I thought she was Catholic."

"Very Buddhist sounding, right? Anyway, I asked her why. I mean, do we all just keep coming back over and over again, living the same pain, making the same mistakes for eternity?"

"Ouch."

"Exactly. She said when you get it right, it's not only about being a good person, it's also about learning the lessons you need to learn, living out those lessons. Once that happens, you've lived your last life and you find peace."

"If that's true, then I'm counting on this life being my last one."

"Me too," Kara said, this time with a genuine smile. "I'm going to figure out those lessons and get stuff right this time around."

They stayed quiet. Once again, Danny seemed fine with the stillness. Yesterday's visit with Marci Nye centered on Kara's father and Alex, but they also talked about Danny. *Take it slow and see how things unfold*, Dr. Nye had advised. *Trust yourself.*

"Speaking of lessons," Danny said, "how's Flyer?"

Kara's face brightened. "Better. Well, maybe not *better*, but coming along." Tuesday and Kara were with him when Alex called. Even though Tuesday was still chilly around Kara, they worked together to make sure Flyer had company during every second of visiting hours. That's why Kara hadn't answered her phone. "His color was better and I like his doc. She asked me a lot of questions about our past and seemed to understand." Grusin's album ended. The only remaining sounds were muffled traffic from three stories down.

Danny asked, "What's happening with the FBI?"

It was funny, but she had barely given them a thought since she walked away from Zach's building. "All's quiet," she said.

"That's good, I guess."

"Thank you for being here." Danny and Mrs. E. had taken turns staying with her whenever she wasn't with Flyer, letting her cry when she needed to, watching funny movies, and listening when she went on talking jags. Kara reached out her hand and touched his. "I don't know how I would have made it through all of this without you and Mrs. E."

"You're welcome."

For a few seconds, he just stared at her. Then he unfolded himself from the floor, stood, took Kara's hand, and gently pulled her up from the chair. He stepped closer and wrapped his long arms around her. She rested her head on his shoulder, closed her eyes, and tried not to think about tomorrow.

CHAPTER THIRTY-SIX

Somehow, it didn't seem right to Alex that the sun was shining or that daffodils, bent over like old men, had poked their heads through the thawing ground. This morning, Alex saw a robin building a nest under the overhang of her apartment building. Spring had finally come and her daddy was dead.

She let the minister's words of comfort ease the ache. With her left arm around Pigeon's shoulders, her own eyes cried dry, Alex let his words about the better place her father had gone to seep into her consciousness. Worth Lawrence was with God. Still, she felt so sad.

Filled to overflowing, the church was decorated with white lilies tied with white ribbons. Reverend Strong's father had married Worth and Judy. The original Reverend Strong, now close to eighty, sat with her mother while his son led the congregation in prayer. Ten women and ten men, all dressed in white robes, made up the choir, their soaring voices calling for the celebration of a soul now with Jesus and at peace.

When the hymn ended, Reverend Strong said, "We'll now hear from Worth's family. His eldest daughter, Alexandra, will speak on their behalf."

Vanessa had loaned Alex a black sheath with three-quarter sleeves and a lace scarf for her head. Judy contributed a strand of pearls and a pair of pearl studs. Even Alex's shoes were new, thanks to a girlfriend who'd gone shopping for her. Now, standing in front of everyone, her feet cramped in pointy-toed black pumps, Alex longed for her cowboy boots. It was funny, but for the first time since she quit, the thing she didn't crave was a cigarette.

Alex walked to the podium with a crumpled page from her notepad clamped in her damp fist. Over the past few days she must have rewritten what she would say a half-dozen times. The usually efficient Vanessa had collapsed, sleeping on and off on Alex's couch. Despite keeping a watchful eye, Alex couldn't tell if Vanessa was clean and sober or not. When Alex suggested her sister might be more comfortable at her own apartment, Vanessa had turned her back, pulled the covers up over her head, and appeared to go back to sleep. Pigeon tried to help, but Alex had trouble letting go and trusting that Pigeon would get things right. Judy and Aunt Peggy stayed stashed away at the house. Neither offered a suggestion or asked a question. Therefore, once again, it fell to Alex to manage it all, from funeral arrangements to flowers to notices— every detail. Their father's longtime administrative assistant was helpful. The family had no idea how many people Worth knew, how many people cared, but his assistant did.

Alex looked out at the standing-room-only crowd, the high and low, so to speak. Sean, his handlebar mustache carefully groomed, sat several pews back next to Gracie, their receptionist. Michael had come. Of course Martin Dawes was there, as well as almost every member of the firm of Hobbs, Austin, and Lawrence. Alex recognized several local politicians, the mayor, state assemblymen and -women, and one of New York's two senators. Someone from the State Department had given her condolences. The senator read a message from the president. There were several Bedford neighbors who Alex also recognized, and a bevy of Alex's friends—some from high school, and others from Smith. Sonja came. (Kara and her question about Alex's black friends jumped to mind.) To look at this crowd, you'd see that Worth Lawrence knew people of every stripe. Even a few of Alex and Sean's current and former clients had shown up. The biggest surprise was Jonas Frankel. Through all the misery, Alex had pulled together his package and hand-delivered it. Now, here he was.

Who were the rest of these people who had come to mourn her father? There was a woman in the fifth pew weeping audibly, her narrow shoulders shaking. A whole row of men in dark suits and white shirts sat shoulder to shoulder, grim-faced, like capos at a crime-family funeral. In the very last row, a large woman in a bright floral dress and floppy straw hat, as if this was an Easter Sunday service, blew her nose. Each of them was a stranger, a stranger who must have known her father and had come from some corner of the country, perhaps of the world, to say goodbye. There were whole chapters of her father's life, and actors in it, about which Alex knew nothing.

She cleared her throat and began: "My father would be so appreciative that all of you joined us today. On behalf of my mother, his beloved sister Peggy, and his other daughters, Monica and Vanessa, we thank you for coming, and for caring. We are also thankful he didn't suffer at the end. In fact, he was feeling better, optimistic, right before slipping into the coma from which he never returned. His thoughts at the time of his death were of his family and friends. His last deeds were to right wrongs from his past. I can carry with me forever his final words to me: *I love you, kitten.*"

Alex drew a calming breath before continuing. "Worth Lawrence was a good man—not a perfect man, but a decent human being. He did the best he could, and sometimes he did extraordinarily wonderful things." She paused again. Her mother and sisters sat together in front, white ribbons marking the pews occupied by family members—Kara should be there with them. Alex had begged her to come, to be a part of the family and sit with them. Just that morning, Alex had reached her on her cell and repeated her request. Kara had refused. *I am sorry for your loss, Alex,* she'd said. *You've been good to me, and I appreciate all you've done. Thank you for finding me.* Alex could hear the *but* that was about to come. *He was not my father. This is a terrible day for you and your family. I will always be your friend, but we are not family.*

Tears threatened, so Alex wrapped up her remarks: "I know he would want this to be a dignified affair, so I'll save my tears for a more private time. Please join us for the burial and later at the house for refreshments. Come share your happy memories with us. I know it will help us move through this difficult time, and I hope it will also ease your personal loss. God bless you all, and thank you."

Reverend Strong returned to the podium to conclude the service with a prayer. The choir sang "Amazing Grace," and then it was over. More than five hundred mourners piled into cars and headed for the cemetery for the brief burial ceremony.

By the time they left the historic Sleepy Hollow Cemetery and got to the house, things were a little easier. Family, friends, dignitaries, and Worth's colleagues crowded into the great room of the colonial house Alex's parents had raised a family in, its vaulted ceiling reverberating with voices no longer hushed or sad. It was warm enough to sit outside on the wraparound veranda. Alex had hired a catering service and valet car parkers. Housekeepers picked up dirty glasses and plates and kept the bathrooms fresh.

Alex greeted and thanked guests, listened to stories, and

solved problems as they arose. Several hours into the gathering, just as things were winding down, she joined her siblings. Hours earlier, she had shed the offending shoes and put on more comfortable flats. Now, she sat on the couch, her feet tucked under her.

Aunt Peggy was in the middle of one of her stories: "There we were, huddled in Judy's bedroom, scared to death," she said, patting her neck with a damp hanky, tortoise-shell glasses sliding down her nose. "All we could hear were the splashes from the pool." She paused for dramatic effect. "Someone or something was swimming at two in the morning."

Vanessa, her blond hair swept up, wearing a tailored black suit and patent-leather pumps, nodded ever so slightly as if she didn't want to encourage Peggy but couldn't help herself. Her eyes were bloodshot, but from what, Alex wasn't sure— maybe she'd been crying.

"We were going to call the police," Peggy went on, "but suppose it was Worth coming home unexpectedly."

"A common occurrence," Vanessa said without humor.

"Or a neighbor kid. We decided to creep downstairs, flashlights in hand. Practical Nessie," Aunt Peggy said, pointing to Vanessa, "had Worth's five iron in her hand and, of course, our Alex was holding the wireless phone, ready to call the police if needed."

"What was I doing?" Pigeon asked.

"You held onto Alex's robe as tight as you could."

Alex did recall this night—not just from a million retellings of the story, but the actual memory. There had been a full moon, and the cicadas were making a racket from the surrounding trees.

Peggy had the audience in her hands. "Shining the flashlight, we peered toward the direction of the splashes."

A second cousin on her mother's side asked, "So what was it?"

Peggy laughed. "Pigeon's raccoons, swimming away, thank you very much. Doing the backstroke as if they were at a raccoon resort."

Pigeon said, "They were my friends. You scared them away."

"You made us scramble eggs and fry bacon for them," Vanessa said, this time without her usual disdain.

Peggy was still laughing. "Only our Pigeon would make friends with a family of raccoons." She pulled off her glasses and polished them on the hem of her suit skirt.

Vanessa made a derisive sound. "One more night in the Lawrence household minus the wayward Worth."

"Shame on you," Aunt Peggy chided.

Alex uncurled and got up. No drama today, she couldn't bear it.

"May I go with you?" Without waiting for a reply, Michael jumped up from his spot on the couch. He reached for her hand and she took it.

"I thought she'd come," Alex said. They navigated the people-clusters saying their final goodbyes. She and Michael went out the front door onto the veranda.

"I spoke with Liz, who sends her condolences, by the way. She hasn't heard from Kara."

"I think she's hurt, you know, about Liz suspecting and not rescuing her sooner."

"Liz appreciates that. She's called her and left messages."

"Want to take a walk?"

The two strolled down the winding driveway, past the rocks from which the builders had carved out the Lawrence property, and onto the road. The crunch of their heels on the asphalt, pebbles, and twigs mingled with birdcalls and the thrash of deer in the woods. Alex stopped.

"Isn't that Danny's car?"

"Kara's friend?"

A battered Toyota had sailed past.

"Do you know what's happening with the FBI and Kara?"

Alex stared at the empty road. She could have sworn it was Danny's car.

"Alex?"

She faced Michael. "They're not going to prosecute her."

"Really?"

They had come to the end of the street on which Alex had lived her whole life until she left for college. The intersection, marked by four-way stop signs, was devoid of traffic. She looked again for the Toyota, hoping Kara had changed her mind. Across the street, on both corners, wooded lots hid five-bedroom, six-bathroom mansions. To their left, a ten-acre horse farm. On their right, an open lot sprouting a field of wildflowers. No sign of the Toyota.

"Where are you?" Michael asked.

"Sorry, I keep hoping."

"You have to let that one go, Alex."

A young male deer loped across the lot to their right, his budding antlers announcing his age and sex.

"I didn't say it in church today, but the last good thing my father did before he died was square things with the SEC for Kara. I wanted to tell her when . . . *if* she came today."

"How did he pull that off?"

"He had a knack for eleventh-hour miracles. It seems he contacted our family lawyer, Martin Dawes, and had him call in some of Worth's favors from the powerful and connected. The FBI is not going to bother her anymore."

"Wow, that's great."

"He knew a lot of people and a lot of them owed him, liked him, and made gobs of money because of him. I'd told my dad about Kara's mess, and at the time he didn't seem to care. I guess, in the end—*before* the end—he decided he did."

"What happens to Zach Lowe?"

"Don't know. Martin thinks Kara was gravy. The FBI had lots of evidence. Zach will probably lose his license, maybe get some jail time."

They moved to the shoulder of the road as a Mercedes SUV barreled past.

"Maybe it is better Kara didn't come. I could tell her when things are less emotional."

"You could write her."

"I don't think so." She'd put together a photo album of family pictures for Kara including grandparents, second cousins, and great aunts, plus lots of pictures of Vanessa, Pigeon, and Alex. Her plan was to give Kara the album and the FBI news today. "In person feels better. Plus, I don't want her to worry about the FBI. Maybe I should text her about that now?" She wasn't asking Michael for advice. Mostly, she was thinking aloud. Alex dug out her phone from her pocket and typed.

"You could still take the album to her later. Give her some space now."

Alex finished her message and hit *Send*. "I'll definitely find a way to give it to her, no matter what." She was determined for many reasons, but the main one was to let Kara know that as his final act, their father had gotten it right.

Kara and Danny sat in his car several driveways down from the Lawrence home, Danny at the wheel, Kara beside him, the engine running.

Earlier, Mrs. E., Danny, and Kara had sat down to a comfort-food feast: macaroni and cheese, fried chicken, greens slow-cooked with ham hocks, and chocolate cake with vanilla-cream icing. Kara had pushed the food around her plate.

"Regret is bad enough." Mrs. E. heaped another serving on Danny's plate. "But holding onto anger, guilt, and blame eats you up."

Kara stirred her greens. "Flyer's doing better. He could be released on Monday."

"Good," Danny said, his voice muffled by his last mouthful. "I have to agree with Mrs. E. Learned the hard way, forgiveness sets you free." He mopped up the juices with one of Mrs. E.'s buttermilk biscuits.

"Including forgiving yourself," Mrs. E. said.

Danny spoke in a quiet voice: "I bought a ticket to see my mom."

The night before, for the first time in weeks, Kara had slept for nine hours with no nightmares. She woke up feeling strong. Didn't Kara want Tuesday and Flyer to forgive her? Shouldn't Kara forgive as well? "I'll do it, I'll go."

"Give me a few minutes." Danny hopped up. "I need to change." He bounded up the stairs.

"Eat something, girl. You're wasting away."

She tried, but the food stuck in her throat.

On the way to the wake they had stopped so Kara could buy a bouquet of flowers—pink, white, and purple tulips, the ultimate harbinger of spring. She wanted to tell Alex thank you, meet the third sister, and get to know Pigeon. Now that they had arrived, however, she was no longer sure. Why hadn't Alex told everyone who Kara was, acknowledged her existence in the obituary, introduced her to Pigeon as a sister?

Kara closed her eyes. She imagined Alex in the house, mingling with family and friends who Kara didn't know; who didn't know her.

"What do you think?" Danny asked.

They only thing Kara knew for sure was that she had made the right decision about the FBI and Zach—he was out of her life. She'd managed that without turning him in—not to protect Zach, but to be the kind of person she wanted to be. Whatever happened, she'd deal with it when it came.

"I'll go in with you, if you like." Danny was wearing a navy suit she'd never seen, with a blue shirt and purple tie.

She could forgive her father from afar; visit his grave some other time. She knew how to find Alex. There were too many people now, and there was too much to explain. "Not today. Let's go home."

The car zipped past the Lawrence driveway, through the narrow streets, to the highway. Radio music soothed her. Her phone vibrated. She glanced down—it was a text message from Alex.

The End

Confront the dark parts of yourself, and work to banish them with illumination and forgiveness. Your willingness to wrestle with your demons will cause your angels to sing.
—August Wilson

Acknowledgments

With gratitude, I thank Open Lens for giving me this opportunity, especially Marie Brown, along with Regina Brooks and Marva Allen. Thank you Johnny Temple, publisher of Akashic Books, for taking a chance on me.

Thank you to my early readers for their patience, care, insights, and support: Marianne Haggerty, Robert Osborne Jr., Willa Hograth, Dorin Hart, Heidi McCrory, Annette Marfording, Annona Joseph, Beth Herman, and my Gotham Writers teachers and fellow students.

Thank you to my husband Bob for his extraordinary help, support, and encouragement, and to my family, Bob Jr., Suzy, J.P., and Alicia, for their love and support.

I am most appreciative of two great teachers—Jacob Miller and Russell Rowland. They taught, inspired, and encouraged me.

Finally, thank you to Dr. Marci Korwin for helping me walk through the fire and come out of the tunnel of pain into the healing light.